A SACRED MAGIC

A Wild Hunt Novel, Book 9

YASMINE GALENORN

A Nightqueen Enterprises LLC Publication

Published by Yasmine Galenorn

PO Box 2037, Kirkland WA 98083-2037

A SACRED MAGIC

A Wild Hunt Novel

First Electronic Printing: 2019 Nightqueen Enterprises LLC

First Print Edition: 2019 Nightqueen Enterprises

Cover Art & Design: Ravven

Art Copyright: Yasmine Galenorn

Editor: Elizabeth Flynn

A Nightqueen Enterprises LLC Publication

Published in the United States of America

ACKNOWLEDGMENTS

Welcome back into the world of the Wild Hunt. We're at book nine, and with this book, we return to Ember. This time her adventures take her deep into the heart of Annwn. I love this world, and am so grateful you do too. It's become a living, breathing entity in my thoughts and imagination.

Thanks to my usual crew: Samwise, my husband, Andria and Jennifer—without their help, I'd be swamped. To the women who have helped me find my way in indie, you're all great and thank you to everyone. To my wonderful cover artist, Ravven, for the beautiful work she's done.

Also, my love to my furbles, who keep me happy. My most reverent devotion to Mielikki, Tapio, Ukko, Rauni, and Brighid, my spiritual guardians and guides. My love and reverence to Herne, and Cernunnos, and to the Fae, who still rule the wild places of this world. And a nod to the Wild Hunt, which runs deep in my magick, as well as in my fiction.

If you wish to reach me, you can find me through my website at Galenorn.com and be sure to sign up for my newsletter to keep updated on all my latest releases! If you liked this book, I'd be grateful if you'd leave a review—it helps more than you can think.

Brightest Blessings,
~The Painted Panther~
~Yasmine Galenorn~

WELCOME TO A SACRED MAGIC

Life isn't easy when you bear the mark of the Silver Stag.

Ember's about to face the showdown of her life...

Things are coming to a head with the Tuathan Brotherhood, and Ember finds herself right on the front lines. The goddess Brighid calls in her favor, sending Ember on a journey through the world of Annwn. Her quest? To find an ancient weapon that can turn the tide in the war against Nuanda and the Tuathan Brotherhood.

But as Ember journeys to the Well of Tears, she must face not only the demons that inhabit the mystical forest, but the demons that haunt her blood heritage. Can she recover Brighid's Flame in order to end the Tuathan Brotherhood? If she succeeds, Ember must face an enemy unlike any other she's ever battled. But if she fails, the Brotherhood will permanently destroy the delicate balance of power between the Fae Courts and the rest of the world.

Reading Order for the Wild Hunt Series (for Timeline, click here).

CHAPTER ONE

"*D*amn it!" I dodged the dagger as it whistled past me, the blade coming dangerously close to slicing my nose off. How many blades were these goblins carrying? *Too damn many*, I thought, as another came spiraling toward me. I was near a cedar tree, so I took a chance and darted behind it, pressing flat against the trunk. As I rested, panting, I took stock of the situation.

We were still facing six goblins, and the sub-Fae didn't seem to be tiring. They were armed with a fuckton of daggers, and who knew what else. And they didn't seem to care if they lost their blades, because they were sending them after us at a daunting speed. The scary part was how accurate they were. Viktor's bicep had already been a target, and he'd had to yank the blade out from where it had lodged in the muscle. Yutani had barely avoided being skewered in the jugular. Instead, the goblin had managed to graze his throat, which wasn't good, but it was better than a severed artery. Herne and I were uninjured so far, but I wasn't laying odds that our luck would hold out.

1

As I caught my breath, I tried to figure out how best to work my way around to the back of the group. I glanced around, trying to think of a plan.

We were on the outskirts of the Carlsford Café & Cattle Ranch—an urban ranch owned by Jet and Maxine Collins. They also ran a diner and a storefront, where they sold beef, milk, and butter. The ranch was located near Crystal Lake, off Crystal Lake Road. The Collinses had retained the services of the Wild Hunt a couple of weeks before to chase down a group of sub-Fae who were scaring their cattle and stealing vegetables from the expansive garden they kept for their café. A couple of calves had also gone missing. The cows had been bewitched and were drying up, which was hurting the calves, as well as milk sales. Neither Jet nor Maxine were sure why the goblins were picking on them, but they wanted the creatures gone, as soon as we could hunt them down and dispatch them.

We had already tried twice to eradicate the goblins, with no results. Kipa and Herne had even managed to chase down one of the creatures and destroy him, but that hadn't stopped the vermin. Goblins were like rodents. Let one loose into an area, and it was an open invitation to a dozen brothers and sisters. They took advantage of every opportunity that came their way. Not to mention, goblins —along with other sub-Fae—were supposed to stay outside of the city limits, but they never paid any attention to the rules.

I took a deep breath, a cloud of vapor coalescing in front of my mouth. We were just coming out of a two-week snowstorm, and while the snow had partially melted and we were back to rain again, there were clumps of dirty, frozen ice and compacted snow scattered around, especially in the shaded woodlands. At least it was melting, though the rain was creating a slushy mess.

Wiping my forehead, I brushed away stray beads of the water that drizzled down from the skies. Late January was a dreary time of year in the Seattle area, and February, even worse.

Letting out an exasperated sigh, I adjusted my grip on my handheld crossbow. At least we had managed to take down three of the goblins so far, but there were six left and they were determined to have their fun. Sub-Fae could be incredibly stupid.

You'd think they would back off when they realized we were stronger than they were, but it finally dawned on me that the sub-Fae just didn't care. They didn't reason things out logically. They were rabid little buggers—or not so little, as the case may be—and they were determined. And they were all too good with weaponry.

Both Yutani and Viktor had brushed off their wounds and were fighting on, but I hoped that we could wrap this up and get back to the agency soon. Viktor was massive, with muscles on his muscles, given he was a half-ogre, but the goblins sometimes used poison. And *that* could down even a half-ogre like Viktor. And Yutani, well, he was lithe, if wiry, and I was worried about the amount of blood he might be losing.

I cautiously peeked around the edge of the tree. There, directly in my line of sight, skulked one of the goblins. He was focused on Yutani, trying to track him. The creature might be small, but he was tough. What he and his ilk wanted with the vegetables was a mystery. Goblins were mostly carnivorous, and they loved human flesh most of all. But *beggars can't be choosers*, as the old saying went, and anything that either was—or had been—alive was considered fair game.

I tried to pinpoint the remaining Nobs, as we called them, but they were good at cloaking their presence. Squinting, I tried to pick out anything that might remotely be considered a part of goblin anatomy. Nobs had scattered patches of hair on their heads—rough like steel wool—and their faces were lined and wrinkled, even when they were babies. With wide-set, beady eyes, and sharp yellow teeth, they were ugly suckers and they always made me queasy because they stank to high heaven. But there weren't any others in sight, not that I could see.

I slowly brought my pistol grip crossbow up, aiming as I did my best to move as smoothly as possible. *No sudden jerks, no sudden moves.* I squinted, staring through the night vision scope attached to my bow, and let out my breath, squeezing the trigger as I steeled myself for the recoil. It wasn't bad, but I didn't want anything throwing off my aim.

The arrow sailed through the air and I held my breath, listening, trying to figure out whether or not I hit the goblin. There was a moment's silence, but then I saw the shaft sticking out of the goblin's heart. He went down with a shriek.

I couldn't take a chance on running over to see if he was dissolving into the earth, but I crossed my fingers that my one arrow was all it would take.

Some of the sub-Fae didn't last long once they were killed. In fact, some of them—goblins being a good example—decayed with an alarming rapidity, bubbling into primordial ooze within minutes. They vanished as though they'd never existed, leaving the ground around them enriched thanks to the goo that had been their body.

I waited for another moment, but saw no movement. My aim had been true. The goblin was dead. Pulling back, I glanced around to see where the others were.

Herne was flat on top of a tree branch about twenty yards away. He was eyeing something in the distance and, as I watched, he paused, then brought up his crossbow, aiming carefully. The arrow silently flew through the air, and a few seconds later another shriek echoed through the forest. Herne glanced down, catching sight of me, and blew me a kiss, then gave me a thumbs-up. He was in his element, deep in the forest, on the hunt.

I caught his kiss and blew one back, then slipped around the trunk of the cedar, creeping through the underbrush, trying to make certain I wasn't making myself a target.

Viktor was standing near Yutani, and when he saw me, he motioned for me to join them.

I darted over, leaping over stone and root, landing softly on a patch of decaying leaves and moss. It occurred to me that I was so much more nimble than I had been less than a year ago. There were several reasons for this, but most of all, the shift came when I went through the Cruharách, transitioning into full adulthood. Both blood-lines had come to the surface and they both brought their skills into play. While I was still cautious, I was slowly beginning to accept my new abilities. The ramifications of what I *could* become continued to haunt me, but there was no going back. I could never again return to the Ember I had been, and I wasn't sure I'd want to.

I reached Viktor's side, and he nodded to Yutani. The coyote shifter was grimacing as he leaned against a tree. The collar of his leather jacket had been ripped through by the blade—which meant it had been incredibly sharp, and I could smell the blood on him.

"You need to stay out of sight," I said, keeping my voice low. "You don't need to play hero over a group of goblins. I killed one, and Herne took one out, so there are only four left." I turned to Viktor. "What about you? You're hurt, too."

"Not so bad. It sliced into me, but then bounced off. I'm good to go." He paused, looking up into the trees. "Look," he whispered, pointing.

I glanced up. Herne was slithering through the tree-tops. He glanced down and saw us. Pointing to me, he crooked his finger.

I gave him a nod. "Okay, Viktor, keep an eye on us and take your cue from what we do. Yutani, stay out of sight. Don't play hero. I'm going up." I eyed the fir. It stood at least eighty feet high, and while the branches on the lower trunk were a little sparse, there were enough beyond about the ten-foot mark to use for climbing. "Viktor, can you give me a boost?"

"Sure thing." He held out his hands, fingers inter-locked. I stepped on his hands and he boosted me up. The half-ogre was six-five, and when he lifted me up, I was able to grab hold of one of the lower branches and swing my way up into the tree.

As I did my best to climb toward Herne, I stayed near the trunk, trying to avoid making too much noise. A few moments later and I was sitting on the branch below his. He swung his legs around, so he was facing me.

"If we climb another fifteen feet, we should have an ideal place to aim at the others. We'll have to be quick, though, before they scatter." Herne turned to look at me, a feral spark lighting his eyes. He was Lord of the Forest, and he belonged to the woodland as much as any of the trees or wildlife. Herne the Hunter was not only a demigod, but he was my boss and my lover. And he was gorgeous. His shoulder-length wheat-colored hair was gathered back in a plaited weave, bound by a leather thong, and he was wearing a camo-sweatshirt, black jeans, and a black leather jacket. He was covered in pitch and dirt, and he stared at me with a wild, intense stare.

"Can you climb farther?"

I nodded. "I can. Lead the way."

As he began to shimmy up the tree trunk, I grabbed hold of the next branch and swung my way up on it, following him as he ascended the tree. As we reached another large crotch in the tree, Herne gestured and I looked in the direction he was pointing. I could barely make out the movement of a couple creatures in the snow below. I looked at Herne.

"Goblins," he mouthed, raising his bow. He could see in the dark a lot better than I could, but when I slid on a pair of night-vision goggles, I could see them. There were three of them, and one a little farther away. I took my cue from Herne, watching which one he was going after, and then raised my bow to focus on one of the others. We'd have to be quick to get the others, but Herne could move like lightning and he seldom if ever missed with a bow.

He took aim, and I waited. I'd shoot the moment his arrow went winging toward the enemy. And when the arrow was halfway to the goblins, I would loose my own.

Herne's struck true without fail, piercing the heart of the goblin. Mine missed by a fraction, but still tore into the goblin's arm. By that time, Herne had nocked another arrow and let it fly, and the third goblin was down. I scrambled down out of the tree as Viktor raced forward toward the fray. He was ahead of me and by the time I got there, he had killed off the goblin I'd injured. With Herne's two kills, that left one more.

"Where the hell did it go?" I glanced around, hoping to catch a glimpse of the last goblin. And then, before I realized what he was doing, Herne raced toward me, grabbing me and sending me flying to the ground. I landed in a pile of snow and immediately rolled to the side, hunching low as I realized what must have happened.

I tried to catch sight of the goblin, who had sent a dagger winging my way. The blade had lodged in the tree that I'd been next to, and Herne had managed to keep me from getting skewered. But before I could find him, Herne sent an arrow winging in the direction the blade had come from, and there was another shriek.

"He's toast?" I asked, standing up.

"Buttered and ready for breakfast," Herne said. "That takes care of all of them."

Viktor and Yutani joined us, both looking tired and ragged. Yutani had managed to stanch the flow of blood drizzling out of his neck, though he looked queasy.

"How can we be sure they're all gone? That we've found the entire gang?" I chewed on my inner cheek, hoping that we hadn't missed any. We had been out here at the ranch several times over the past two weeks, and each time only managed to catch glimpses of the goblins before they got away.

"The owner told me he caught sight of nine goblins this afternoon. With the one that Kipa and I caught the other day, that would make ten in the raiding party. That's a standard size for Nobs. There's no way to know for sure, except to wait and see if any other incidents happen on the ranch. But I'm fairly certain we took care of them." Herne wrapped his arm around me, hugging me to him. "I'm going to call this a wrap. Good work, guys. Let's head up to the café and tell Jet and Maxine the good news."

It was a long walk back to the café, but we'd left our cars there, so we had to make the trek anyway. By the time we reached the diner, it was ten P.M. Shivering, I pushed through the doors, grateful for the warmth that enveloped me. The café was open until eleven, and I tapped Herne on the arm.

"I'm going to order something to go. We need to stop at urgent care for Yutani and Viktor, but I'm hungry."

"Make it quick," Herne said. "I don't want to wait too long before we get their wounds attended to. Goblins are notorious for using poison, and I don't want to take any chances."

Jet came over, smiling as he saw us. He and his wife were human, but they were friendly with most of the SubCult, and their diner was frequented by shifters and Fae alike.

"You guys look roughed up. Can I take that as a good sign?" He folded his towel and threw it over his shoulder, straightening his apron.

"We dispatched nine goblins tonight. I'm pretty sure you shouldn't have any more trouble, although if you do, just give me a call and we'll come out and take a look again. But I think your problem's taken care of." Herne shook the man's hand, giving him a friendly nod.

"How much do I owe you?" Jet asked, pulling out his checkbook.

"We'll bill you. Give it a couple days, and then if you haven't had any more trouble from the goblins, let us know and Angel will send you out an invoice. I want to make sure we've done the job right." Herne went above and beyond for some clients, especially those who were quick to pay, and easy to work for.

Jet smiled. "That's why I come to you when I have problems, Herne."

"Do you have anything quick to fix that we can get to go?" I asked. "We have to get these two over to urgent care, but I'm starving." My stomach rumbled, punctuating my remark. I rolled my eyes, blushing.

"If you can give me ten minutes, I'll have burgers, fries, and doughnuts all around. Shakes, too. Will that work?"

Herne nodded, glancing toward Yutani, who just shrugged. "That would be great."

"What flavor of shakes?" Jet asked, pulling out his pad. "And what do you want on your burgers?"

"I want chocolate," I said. "Ketchup and cheese, no onions, mayo, or mustard."

Herne and the others put in their orders and we settled into one of the back booths to wait. Less than ten minutes later, Jet carried over four large bags.

"Here you go. Burgers, fries, doughnuts, and shakes. They're on the house. I'll call you in a day or two and let you know if it looks like the goblins are back. I have no idea why they picked us to bother, but it was putting a dent in our business, that's for sure."

"Goblins don't care who they go after. If you have something they want, and they think they can get it, you're going to be a target. Luck—or ill-luck—of the draw," Herne said.

We waved good-bye and tired, grubby, and hungry, we headed toward Herne's Expedition.

When we returned to the office, we stopped in at the urgent care clinic that took up the entire first floor of the building. It was open till one A.M., a good thing considering how many streeps—the street people—were living on the streets.

While Yutani and Viktor got themselves taken care of, Herne and I took the elevator to the fourth floor, to the Wild Hunt Agency, which Herne owned and ran. Talia and Angel had gone home for the night, but Charlie looked up as we entered, a startled expression on his face.

"You surprised me. I didn't expect to see you this late. You take care of the goblins?" Charlie was a vampire, and he was in school, learning accounting so he could take over the books for us when he graduated. In the meantime, he came in at night and helped with data entry and anything else we might need him for, especially when we were overwhelmed with work. And lately, *overwhelmed* was an understatement.

"I think so," Herne said. He turned to me. "I'll meet you in the break room. I need to take a leak first."

"Okay." I gave Charlie a tired wave and headed to the break room, where I slumped into one of the chairs. It'd been one hell of a night, and all I wanted to do was eat my food, take a shower, and fall into bed. I pulled out my burger, gratified to see not just one, but *two* cheeseburgers in the sack. The fries were large, and the shake was also large. Jet and Maxine didn't skimp when it came to portions, or gratitude.

Herne entered the room as I took a bite of my food. The yeast scent of the buns and the smell of grilled ground beef were making me ravenous. He dropped into the chair next to me, reaching out to take my free hand. He brought it to his lips and kissed my fingers.

"You were almost a shish kebab," he said, leaning back and stretching out his legs.

"Thank you, by the way. You saved my life, yet again." I set down my burger and took a long sip of the shake. The frozen chocolate slid down my throat and I closed my eyes, grateful that we were done for the night.

"Hey, it's what we do. We watch each other's backs. All of us." But he had a worried look on his face.

"What are you thinking about? Yutani? I'm sure he'll be okay. Viktor, too. They were hurt but their injuries weren't terrible."

"No. I know they'll be okay, even if the blades were poisoned. The urgent care clinic downstairs is good at what they do. No, I'm just…mulling over something else, to be honest." He glanced up at me, the blue of his eyes mirroring the first light of dawn.

I leaned over and gave him a kiss on the cheek. "So, what is it?"

"The growing unrest because of the Tuathan Brotherhood. The Fae aren't going to sit around and accept the role of scapegoat much longer. When the United Coalition shut them out, it stirred up very deep, very bad blood. And the hate groups against the Fae are getting worse. I've heard of no less than four vigilante groups starting up in the past few days. Pretty soon, things are going to blow sky high. *Boom!* Powder keg time. And I'm not sure what to do about it. We aren't making much progress."

I stared at my cheeseburger, trying to think of something to say that would make him feel better, but came up with zilch. Herne was right. The situation was volatile—a true powder keg. If we didn't find an answer soon there would be rioting in the streets, and a lot of innocent people would end up hurt, caught in the crossfire. Collateral damage wasn't just a theoretical term.

Hell, I had my own scars to prove that. I was still scarred from some of the lacerations I had received in the blast that had taken out the Associated Shifters Credit Union. I had been in the way of a glass door that had shattered, turning me into a pincushion for hundreds of glass shards.

"I know," I said. "I know."

We sat there for a moment, staring at each other, and finally I picked up my cheeseburger again. There was nothing we could do at this moment to solve the crisis, and that was another fact we knew.

CHAPTER TWO

The next morning, I woke to the smell of bacon and waffles wafting up from downstairs. I groaned as I sat up. I might have been in better shape than I'd ever been, but stints like last night's goblin chase still left me stiff and aching.

I rolled out of bed with a yawn and glanced out the window. Rain was pouring down from gloomy skies. Typical winter weather. At least we'd left the snow behind, according to the meteorologists. I was ready for spring weather, even though we still had several months to go before the trees leafed out and flowers showed their heads.

I had taken a shower the night before, but a hot soak under running water sounded too good to pass up, so I hopped in my shower and lathered up with black rasp-berry–scented bath wash. The water pelted my back, hot and stinging, easing some of the stiffness out of my muscles. After a few minutes, the ache began to unknot and fade, and by the time I finished, I was feeling more flexible. I wrapped my robe around me, bundled my hair up in a towel, and slid my feet in a pair of fuzzy slippers. Then, feeling ready to face the morning, I headed downstairs.

Angel was in the kitchen, and breakfast was on the table. Mr. Rumblebutt looked up from his dish, purring as he dug into the new food we had picked up for him. Cats normally didn't like much change in diet, but now and then, Mr. Rumblebutt decided he needed to change it up, and I'd have to search out a new food that he'd willingly eat. This time, it was ocean fish fillet dinner, with a very stinky gravy. But he loved it.

"Morning, *chica*," Angel said. "You catch the goblins?"

"Yeah," I said, fitting the filter into my espresso machine. I needed a buttload of caffeine today, and so pulled five shots into a tall mug, adding hot milk and chocolate syrup to make a power-packed mocha. "We got them, finally. But not before they managed to skewer both Viktor and Yutani—neither got hurt badly," I hastened to add before Angel could worry. "I almost ended up shish kababbed, but Herne saw the blade coming and knocked me out of the way."

"I'd say I wished I was there, but not so much," Angel said, grinning. "Eat. Build up your strength." She handed me the bacon. "I've taken my fill. You can have the rest."

Suddenly feeling happy, surrounded by good food and my best friend in the whole world, I accepted the bacon, sliding all six pieces on my plate. I added a waffle off the stack, and slathered it in butter and syrup. As I forked a bite of the crisp, airy cake into my mouth, I glanced at Angel again. She was practically glowing. Her rich brown skin had a dewy radiance to it, and she was wearing a salmon-colored top and white jeans that set off her coloring. Her hair was neatly swept into a bun on the top of her head, and she had big turquoise hoop earrings on and a necklace to match. I maintained that Angel could have been a model if she wanted—she was tall enough and beautiful enough, but she'd chosen a vastly different route for her life.

"You look…luminous. Have a good evening?" I asked after swallowing the waffle.

"Rafé and I had a wonderful evening. It was the first time since we were over on the peninsula and we've been together that he hasn't fallen into a depression. I'm hoping he's coming out of it, now that he has the casts off."

Rafé, one of the Dark Fae, was Angel's boyfriend. He had helped us out on a case, and ended up with a broken leg, a broken arm, several fractured ribs, and a whole lot of bumps and bruises. He'd also been tortured, and that had definitely left an impact on the actor/waiter.

"I hope so. I hate that he went through what he did. We still don't know who tipped them off to the fact that Rafé was a spy, but when we find out…" I paused, once again feeling my mood settle into a quiet melancholy. I glanced at the clock. "We have to be at the agency by noon for a meeting. I should get dressed and dry my hair."

"We have time," Angel said, a note of concern in her voice. "I'm sorry. You seemed in such a good mood and now you have that look again."

I shook my head. "This whole mess with the Tuathan Brotherhood is just a nightmare. I don't know what we're going to do. But *whatever* we do, it had better be soon. Herne and I were discussing the subject last night. We're worried that Seattle's turning into a powder keg, ready to explode if we don't put a stop to the Brotherhood and clear the Fae from suspicion."

Angel caught my gaze, nodding slowly. "I hear you. But finish your breakfast. We have time enough for you to eat. I'm going to put a load of clothes in the laundry. Do you have anything that needs washing?"

I laughed. "I have two weeks of laundry. I just haven't had the energy to keep up with it lately. I'll wash a load of clothes tonight, though, so don't worry about it." I chugged down the rest of the mocha, feeling the caffeine stream into my bloodstream. "Oh, this is what I needed. Caffeine will get me going," I said, shaking my head as I went back to finishing breakfast.

I FOUND A PAIR OF JEANS THAT WERE CLEAN AND, SINCE WE weren't planning on slogging through the woods after goblins today, I chose a cobalt blue overbust corset to wear with them, and a cropped lace shrug over the top of that. I was a curvy woman—with well-padded hips and boobs, but I was also strong and fit. And getting more so every week. Herne had taken over as my physical trainer, and he put me through my paces, in more ways than one. Some of those exercises were a lot more fun than others, I thought with a grin.

As I combed through my hair, it occurred to me that I needed a trim. My hair was almost down to my waist, jet black with a strong curl to it, and the ends were showing a little damage. I plugged in my blow dryer and dried it into coiling waves, then put on my makeup. I used a plum eye shadow and black liner to set off my eyes—which were a brilliant green—and a pale peach lipstick.

As I glanced down at the tattoo on my arm, I caught my breath. Even now, almost nine months after I had joined the Wild Hunt, the dagger emblazoned on my left forearm was a vivid reminder that I belonged to one of the most elite organizations in the world. Every member of the Wild Hunt bore the same tattoo, and it not only marked us as members, but protected us in certain situations.

I slipped on a pair of black leather ankle boots with chains that fastened across the side zipper. They had chunky three-inch heels and a rubber nonstick sole, and I could run in them, as long as I wasn't out in the woods with a lot of rocks and roots around.

Angel was waiting for me downstairs. She handed me my purse. "Want to ride in together?"

I nodded. "I thought this evening, we could maybe take in a movie? Herne's going to be busy, though I'm not sure what you have planned with Rafé."

"He's meeting with his family. They want to talk to him, which is one event I'd rather skip."

She grimaced. Rafé was estranged from most of his family. He was the black sheep of the clan, or at least, *one* of them. His brother Ulstair had been an outcast too, before he was killed. Ulstair had been engaged to our friend Raven, one of the Ante-Fae. In addition to being a bone witch, she was one hell of a firecracker, and a blast to hang out with.

"Yeah, I don't blame you." I shrugged. "The Fae don't mess around when they oust somebody from the fold. I know." I was a tralaeth—half Light Fae and half Dark Fae, and in the eyes of both Fae communities, I was one of the unmentionables.

"Movie it is, then," Angel said as we locked the door behind us and headed to her car. "What were you thinking of seeing?"

"*Atomic Brenda.*" I snorted. "I know it's a cheesy franchise, but you have to admit, it's fun."

Angel laughed. "I'm up for that. Come on, let's get this show on the road."

I grinned, but as I settled in the passenger side of the car, a crow began to screech overhead. I glanced up at it, a shiver passing over me. There was a warning in the shriek, but I didn't know what it was about, and right now, I didn't really feel like finding out.

THE AGENCY WAS LOCATED ON THE FOURTH FLOOR OF A five-story brick walkup in downtown Seattle, on First Avenue. The city had made an attempt to gentrify the area, but all it did was leave downtown Seattle looking a lot like a faded Southern plantation—with only the hints of the strength and beauty the city had once had, hidden beneath a ragtag assortment of old buildings and crumbling brick.

A tall concrete staircase led to the main door and all around were brothels, dive-bars, and fast food joints. Trees lined the street, turning the older, risqué part of town into a shaded pedestrian zone during the summer, where the streeps hung out. Most of the streeps were young, either runaways or kicked out of their homes for one reason or another, a few were older and homeless, and some were—as all cities had—mentally ill with no one to care for them. Over the months, Angel and I had come to know a number of the streeps by name, and once a week, Angel had taken to bringing a huge box of cookies she made and she'd hand them out at lunch, on the staircase. Her mother had owned a diner that also acted as a soup kitchen once a week, and this was Angel's way of continuing her mother's work in the only way she knew how.

During the winter, there were still panhandlers, but mostly they stayed out of sight. I wondered where they went to during the cold weather, but they were like squirrels in the park, hibernating through the cold weather. While there were numerous shelters around the area, Lizzy, one of the sex workers across the street at the Spank-O-Rama, a fetish boutique brothel, had told me that when she was on the streets, it had been safer to sleep in back alleys than to go to the mission houses. I believed her, given the lack of funding for the city-run shelters. And then there were the flophouses in the dismal areas of the city, where slumlords rented beds to transients in shifts, where violence was a way of life and it was dangerous to even drive down the streets at night.

Seattle was a multicultural city, with the Fae, shifters, human, and other Cryptos intermingling, and until recently there had been scattered issues between the different groups, but nothing major. That is, until the Fomorians had come to town.

Mortal enemies of the Fae, they had first tried to poison both the Light and the Dark Courts. When that hadn't worked, they managed to finagle themselves a place on the United Coalition—the group that ran the country's government. The UC was a union of the Shifter Alliance, the Fae Courts, the Human League, the Vampire Nation, and now the Cryptozoid Association. It was the best compromise that the government could manage. Even though things were fucked up right now and the Fae Courts had been suspended from the governing council, I held tight to the hope that we could put Humpty Dumpty back together again.

Angel managed to find a place in the parking garage and we dashed down the street to our building. As we hurried up the steps, we passed Barclay as he exited the urgent care clinic and came through the front doors. Barclay was one of the streeps, a shifter. A real lone wolf type, he was friendly enough when he managed to find enough Carnie-Party, a hybrid form of cannabis that was used for cooking, and ten times stronger than most forms of pot. It was legal, though it came with a strong warning because, unlike regular marijuana, it was addictive.

He glanced at Angel and me as we passed him on the steps.

"Hey." He slowed, an uncertain look on his face. He had been kicked out of his pack because his addiction had led to him losing his little brother out in the woods. Even though the boy had been found safe, the Keystone Pack had booted Barclay's ass right out. He had come over from the peninsula and settled in downtown Seattle.

"Hey Barclay," I said, as Angel raised her hand in greeting. "How goes it?"

"Kind of rough," he whispered, glancing away. Barclay had a hard time meeting anyone's gaze. He was still ashamed of being shunned by his people, and from what we knew, he was genuinely trying to kick the habit. But

Carnie-Party was a hard one. It evened out the bumps in the road, smoothing the daily ups and downs. A lot of streeps used it as a makeshift anti-depressant because it was a whole lot cheaper than therapy.

I paused. "What's wrong?"

He shifted nervously from foot to foot. "I dunno…the weather, I guess. I don't like it when it's cold. And the house where I'm staying has a weird feel to it, lately. I think it's haunted."

I paused, thinking. "You hang out in the Worchester district, don't you?"

He nodded. "Yeah. In an old Victorian flop. I'm not sleeping well. I get nervous just walking into the place any more. But there's not much I can do about it. I don't have the money to go anyplace else, and most of the flops are full right now."

I held up my hand, then opened my purse and went through it until I found one of Raven's business cards. "One moment. Here's my friend's business card. I don't know if she can help you, but she cleanses haunted houses and reads the bones and tarot cards. You might ask her if she'd be willing to help. She does some pro bono work."

He glanced at the card I'd handed to him. It was purple, with a filigreed scrollwork around the edges. He stared at it for a moment. "Raven BoneTalker? All right. Maybe I'll give her a call."

"Good. She might have some advice she can give you over the phone, but I can't promise. But do give her a call." I waved at him and he ducked his head in a grateful gesture, then turned and hastened down to the sidewalk.

As Angel and I entered the building, she poked me in the side. "You know as well as I do that Raven's not going to clean out a flophouse just so the owner can make more money off the poor in this city."

I shrugged. "Maybe. Maybe not. She wouldn't be doing it for the landlord, but for the people who have to stay there. You have to admit, he's not going to find help anywhere else." I punched the button for the elevator, glancing around the lobby. There were a couple people waiting near the entrance to the urgent care clinic, but nobody else I recognized.

The elevator arrived and we stepped into the lift, standing back as the door shut and the creaky compartment slowly began to ascend.

"I swear, one of these days this elevator's going to go crashing down and I just hope we're not in it at the time. You'd think the landlord would get his ass in gear and fix the thing." Angel frowned at the ceiling, where we could see a crack in the metal overhead.

"I know," I said. "Herne keeps bitching at him, but the guy is off in his own world. One of these days, I expect to see Viktor and Yutani taking care of it themselves."

As the elevator shuddered to a halt, it opened. We were facing the waiting room of the Wild Hunt Agency— the elevator opened directly into it—and given that the elevator actually stopped and opened, that meant that somebody had gotten here early and unlocked everything. When the office was shut up and locked up, the elevator went past without stopping.

I glanced around, trying to figure out who was here. As Angel headed over to her desk to turn on her computer, Herne came out of his office, which was in back of the U-shaped desk Angel worked at. He was carrying a thick file folder and his tablet, and he was looking over his email.

He glanced up as he noticed us. "Hey girls, glad you're here. We're just waiting on Talia. Yutani and Viktor are in the break room."

He held out his arm and I slipped into it, giving him a kiss as we headed toward the break room. It was to the right of the waiting room and Herne's office, at the end of the hall. To the left of the break room was a hallway that led to my office and Talia and Yutani's office, as well as the bathroom and the storage room.

As we entered the break room, Viktor glanced up. He was playing a game on his tablet. Yutani was studying something on his laptop. The coffee was brewing and it looked as though somebody had brought a cheesecake. The chocolate-covered New York–style cheesecake was hefty and all thoughts of the waffles and bacon I had consumed went out the window when I saw it. I was a junk food aficionada and though Angel did her best to keep me on track with eating healthier, when it came to sweets and caffeine, I had no control.

"Yum, that looks amazing. Who brought it?" I made a beeline for the paper plates and the plastic forks.

"I did," Herne said. "We've all been working so hard that I thought we could use a little comfort food. Especially since my mother's coming to visit today."

I paused, glancing over at him. "You didn't tell me Morgana's going to be here."

"That's because it doesn't matter one way or another. You'd have to be here anyway."

I loved Herne's mother—in fact, I was pledged to her service. But the goddess had been on my back the past few weeks about a task she expected me to do and I'd been putting it off. I really didn't want to have her push me on it today, but it was too late to duck out now. Besides, if I skipped the meeting, she'd just find some other way to hound me.

Angel and Talia entered the room together.

"I locked the elevator now that we're all here," Angel said. She eyed the cheesecake and then looked at me as I parceled out a good-sized piece. "*Really?* We just ate."

"Get off my back, woman. It's cheesecake." I grinned at her.

Viktor stifled a laugh. "How you two live together, I don't know. You're always fussing over each other like a couple of hens."

"Dork," Angel said, swatting him.

"Damn it!" Viktor let out a loud groan and Angel jumped.

"What did I do?"

"You hit my stab wound," Viktor said, grimacing.

Angel winced. "Oh, hell. I'm sorry—I really am! I never even thought. I didn't know, Viktor—"

"No, I know you didn't. It's okay. I know you didn't mean to. But please, no more rubbing salt in the wound, so to speak." The half-ogre settled back, peeling off his jacket to expose the bandaged wound. Angel rubbed her head, looking pained.

"We're all a little on edge," Herne said. "So everybody just take a deep breath. Angel, Viktor knows you didn't mean to hurt him. Viktor, take a couple aspirin or whatever else you need to." He glanced over at Talia. "Good to see you."

"I got a late start. My dishwasher decided to overflow

and vomit suds all over the floor. I had to clean them up or the dogs would have tried to eat them and that would be akin to giving them a dose of Ex-Lax. Not the best idea." She snorted. "Anyway, we're all here now, so let's get this meeting started. I assume you took care of the goblins last night? Or at least tried, by the looks of Viktor's arm."

"And my throat," Yutani said, stripping off his jacket. His bandage covered the entire right side of his neck.

"That was a close call," Talia said.

"Understatement of the year," Yutani shot back.

"Okay, we're here. We just need to wait for Morgana. But to bring Talia and Angel up to speed, yes, we took care of the Carlsford Café and Cattle Ranch. I'm almost positive we managed to kill all the goblins, though I guess we'll find out in a day or so. Angel, make a note to reach out to them on Monday. If they're still pest-free, send them the invoice for the remainder of the fee." Herne glanced at his tablet.

"Check." Angel jotted down a note to herself.

"Meanwhile, Yutani, how are you coming on Nalcops's laptop?" Herne turned to the sloe-eyed coyote shifter.

Yutani pushed his hair back. "I'm working on it." He paused, then held up a hair tie. "Can someone pull my hair back in a ponytail? My neck's a little sore and I don't want to pull the wound as it's scabbing over."

Angel hustled out of her chair, moving to help him. She pulled his long, straight hair back and bound it with the hair tie, then returned to her chair.

"I know there are hidden files on this computer. I can feel it, but so far, I haven't been able to find them. Give me some time, though, and I'll crack through." Yutani was our resident IT genius, though Talia could give him a run for his money in the research department. But when we needed a computer hacked, it was Yutani we went to.

Nalcops had been a doctor working for the Tuathan Brotherhood, until we took him down. We had stolen his laptop, and Yutani was searching for any clues as to where the leader of the movement might be. Until we found out *who* Nuanda was, and then found out exactly *where* he was hiding, we were fighting an uphill battle.

At that moment, the door to the break room opened and Morgana walked through. The goddess turned to me and, without missing a beat, said, "So when the hell are you going to get your ass over to TirNaNog and Navane and retrieve those items I asked you to find?"

So much for goodwill and cheesecake, I thought, as I let out a sigh and prepared for the inquisition I knew was coming.

CHAPTER THREE

*A*s far as goddesses went, Morgana was one of the more approachable ones. The daughter of The Merlin, who belonged to the Force Majeure, she had chosen to ascend to deityhood rather than become a part of the elite team of magic-born like her father. She was also part Fae. When Cernunnos, the Lord of the Forest, had married her, he brought her into the fold of the gods. Together, they were Herne's parents. My mother had been pledged to Morgana, and my father had worked with Cernunnos, and so it was natural for me to follow in their footsteps. What I hadn't expected was to fall in love with their son.

"Ember, I asked you a question." Morgana stared at me, crossing her arms as she stood at the end of the table.

"Don't we even get a hello?" Herne stepped in, trying to deflect her attention. "Good morning, Mother." He usually called her by her given name, keeping the familial term for when he was trying to get on her good side, or wheedle something out of her.

Morgana gave him a long look, then laughed. She was beautiful when she laughed, and terrifyingly beautiful when she was angry, and beneath her perfume, there was always the wild scent of the sea. With raven hair down to her ass, she usually appeared at around five-seven when she was in a good mood. When she decided to be imposing, she rose up to over seven feet tall. Today she was wearing a linen pantsuit—her usual garb when she visited our realm—and her eyes were glowing silver, with dark flecks in them. She was carrying a designer briefcase, and her hair had been pulled back into a tight chignon, with lacquered combs smoothing it back on both sides.

"All right, I'll play nice, my son. But I'm here on serious business, so don't expect me to be a pushover today." She shook her head, leaning over to kiss him on the cheek. It felt odd, watching their interplay. The fact that Herne was a god was always in the back of my mind, but I usually swept it aside during our day-to-day activities. But now, watching him interact with his mother, the power radiated off both of them in waves.

She gave me a dubious look. "Ember, we really do need to talk about this. But first, someone bring me some coffee and I'll have a slice of that cheesecake."

Angel hastened to pour her some coffee while Talia cut her a slice of the cake and slid it across the table. I curtsied to Morgana—it only seemed polite to acknowledge my patron goddess—and then sat down on the opposite side of the table. There wasn't going to be any getting out of a conversation I really didn't want to have, it seemed.

When we were all gathered around the table and

coffee and cake were at hand, Morgana let out a long sigh and sat back, staring at us.

"First, Lord Cernunnos sends his regards. And while I hesitate to ask, because somehow I think you would have told us if the answer was affirmative, have there been any more breakthroughs on the Tuathan Brotherhood?" She opened her briefcase—it wasn't just for show, it seemed—and withdrew a sheaf of papers.

Herne pressed his lips together, shaking his head. "Only a few minor things."

Yutani cleared his throat. "I'm working on Nalcops's laptop. I know there are hidden files on it, but finding where they are is a massive chore. I don't think he was the one who set up the computer because it shows all the marks of someone with real computer know-how. But I'm a damned good hacker. I'll find them. It's just a matter of *when*."

"Sooner is better than later," Morgana said. "Though I realize this isn't necessarily something you can control. But do your best, Coyote's son. We need any information we can find." She glanced at me. "And now to the core of my visit. Ember, I told you last month that you needed to make a trip to TirNaNog and to Navane. There are two artifacts that your family possesses—one on each side. They rightfully belong to you, and it's time you went in search of them."

My families—either of them—weren't likely to just hand them over. I was pariah in the Fae Courts, and not only had my parents been killed for their forbidden love, but it had been their own families who had killed them. They would have taken me out, too, if I'd come home from school early that day. As it was, I'd arrived home to

30

find my mother and father on the floor, soaked in blood, stabbed to death in a grisly murder scene. Recently, I had confirmed that my paternal grandfather and my maternal grandmother had been at the heart of the double murder, and that knowledge had strengthened my resolve to never darken their lives. When Morgana had first told me that she expected me to show up on their doorsteps, I had rebelled. I was still rebelling.

"Can you please explain to me why these things matter? An old bow, and a crown? Why do I need to have them?" Deep inside, I knew I wouldn't change her mind, but I was going to do my best.

"They play a part in your future. They're interwoven in the tapestry of your life. I'm not certain how—if we knew the future and all was preordained, what point would there be to living? But I *do* know that you will need them. And if you don't get them back now, it may shift the direction of things to come."

She caught my gaze, holding it, and I found myself falling into a great silvery sea that stretched farther than any ocean could. She was a goddess of the Great Sea, goddess of the Fae, and I owed her my allegiance. The crow necklace around my neck was the mark that I belonged to her. She had given it to me, and I wore it day and night. More than anyone, more than even Angel, I owed Morgana my devotion.

I swallowed hard as the feeling of *belonging* swept over me. Morgana wasn't out to make life difficult for me, regardless of what it sometimes felt like.

I swallowed, then nodded. "All right. I'll go. I'm taking Raven with me—she's volunteered. I know Angel wouldn't be welcome in the great cities."

TirNaNog and Navane were the great Fae cities. Both Dark Fae and Light Fae had bought up vast quantities of land out near Woodinville, and they had established sovereign cities based on their massive counterparts in Annwn, the world of the gods. They were considered sovereign nations, belonging only to themselves, and whatever went on within the cities was a matter for the Fae, and the Fae alone.

The Dark and Light Fae were enemies. They had been at each other's throats since the beginning of time, and they probably would be till the very end. The queens— Saílle and Névé, respectively—were currently under a temporary truce as long as the threat to the Fae nations remained. They both decried the Tuathan Brotherhood, and they were as anxious for us to find and destroy the hate group as everyone else, given it had ruined their reputations within the United Coalition.

"Raven? Your Ante-Fae friend? That should be interesting," Morgana said, a droll tone to her voice. "I'd like to be a fly on the wall when you show up with her in tow. You're determined to give them the finger, aren't you?"

I coughed. "I wouldn't put it that way, but…"

"But nothing," Talia said with a grin. "You'll do whatever you can to piss off Saílle and Névé, and you know it."

I determined that it was an excellent time to take a big bite of cheesecake so I couldn't answer. Morgana waited a moment, then cleared her throat.

"Well, I want you out there in the next few days. No more procrastinating. Take Raven if you like, but just get your ass in gear and do as I ask." She smiled as she spoke, but her eyes were glittering and cold, and I knew she meant it.

"Yes, my Lady, I will." I spoke softly, meeting her gaze with acquiescence. There came a time in every battle—whether it be of will, wit, or body—to lay down the flag and give in. And this was that moment.

Morgana laughed, holding out her coffee cup. "Now that we've got that taken care of, how about another cup of coffee? And tell me what the agency's been up to lately."

As Herne poured her more coffee, Viktor and Yutani began telling her about the goblins out at the Carlsford Café and Ranch. I moved to the window overlooking the alley in back of our building. Rain was sleeting down and the day looked dreary and worn. I glanced up to find Talia beside me.

"You know, sometimes wearing the yoke of the gods can be difficult," I whispered, keeping my voice low.

She nodded. "I imagine. But I also think that it must feel nice, to have someone watching over you. I've never had that." Talia was a harpy who had lost her powers. When she met Herne, long, long ago, he had taken pity on her and brought her before Morgana, who had offered her a permanent glamour so that she could fit into society better. Talia had chosen the guise of a woman in her mid-sixties, gray hair but fit and strong, and she had gone to work for Herne after that. They had been friends forever, it seemed.

"When you put it like that, I suppose, yes." I glanced over my shoulder at the others. "But in a way, Herne looks after everybody here. And Cernunnos and Morgana, even if it may not seem like it. We're quite the odd little family, aren't we?"

Smiling, Talia agreed.

So, a little more about who I am. I'm Ember Kearney, and as I said, I'm half Dark Fae and half Light Fae, and never the twain shall meet, according to the Fae Courts. I just turned thirty-one years old a couple weeks ago, and I've passed the Cruharach—the Fae coming of age ritual—so now my body's aging mechanisms are drastically slowing down. That's why most Fae you meet, unless they're incredibly old, look somewhere in their thirties.

My parents were murdered when I was fifteen, and I went to live with Angel, my BFF since I was eight. Mama J.—her mother—owned a diner that subbed as a soup kitchen, and she was an incredible tarot reader. Angel inherited both her mother's cooking and empathic skills, and our friendship has stayed the course since we first met in grade school. She had pushed me in the mud. I dragged her into the muck with me, and we both ended up in the principal's office. That cemented our friendship.

Life went on. I became a freelance bounty hunter, chasing down goblins and other sub-Fae who were creating a hazard for people. Then, last year, everything changed.

Angel's little brother vanished. I found him, alive, thank the gods, but the situation ended up with Herne recruiting Angel and me into the Wild Hunt. The Wild Hunt Agency officially keeps war from breaking out between the Fae Courts, and we're a law unto our own. We work on the fringe of society, though the police and government know about us. We do our best to keep the squabbles that break out between the Light and the Dark from affecting humans and shifters and other potential targets. But a few months ago, the Tuathan Brotherhood raised its ugly head. They claim to be Fae, out to take back what's rightfully theirs. The Fae Courts both disavow knowledge of them. Lives have been lost and we're all at a stalemate. Right now, things are only promising to get worse before they get better.

AFTER MORGANA LEFT, I CALLED RAVEN. SHE ANSWERED on the second ring.

"Hello?" She sounded breathless, and I had a sneaking suspicion I had caught her fresh out of bed. She and Kipa were all hot and heavy. Kipa, or Kuippana, was sort of a distant cousin of Herne's, from Finland. He was Lord of the Wolves, and wildly chaotic, but he tried to help out when he could.

"Did I catch you at a bad time?" I laughed. "Kipa's there, isn't he?"

"Oh good gods, Kipa's not always here." She paused. "Yeah, he's here. What do you need?"

I cleared my throat. "So, I'm down to the wire. I need to go to TirNaNog and Navane, like I told you, and I have to go tomorrow. You said you could go with me. Still up for it?"

"Hell, yes. I'm looking forward to it, too."

I paused, thinking over the wisdom of taking Raven. She was full-tilt, impulse driven, and a little bit on the crazy side, but that was one of the reasons I liked her. We hadn't known each other a long time, but we already had a backlog of adventures to talk about—some of them our own fault, others not so much.

"I'll pick you up at your house tomorrow morning at ten. Can you be ready to go?"

"Sure thing. I'll be ready." She let out a peal of laughter and I heard her whispering, "Stop that, I'm on the phone."

"Listen, you're clearly occupied so I'm going to go, but I'll see you tomorrow." Before she could protest, I laughed and said good-bye, then tossed my phone on the table. "Raven and Kipa are at it again."

Herne glanced at me, his eyes flickering. "They're made for each other." For once, he didn't try to run down Kipa. Herne and Kipa had some male-testosterone thing going, and while I knew they had a lot of baggage between them, it could be annoying. It had also nearly gotten Raven and me killed at one point.

"Ah-ah…," I said, waving my finger at him.

"What? I didn't say anything bad," he said with a grunt. "All right, so the meeting's over. You can go for the day if you want."

"I think I'll stay for a bit and work on the laptop," Yutani said. "I feel like I'm getting close to finding those files."

"I'm out of here. I need to stop at the farmers market, then go grocery shopping, and I have a friend coming over for dinner," Talia said, waving at us as she slipped her jacket on and headed for the door. "See you Monday."

Viktor headed out too. He had a date with his girl-friend, Sheila.

I glanced at Herne. "You sure you're busy tonight? Angel and I are going to see a movie, but I thought after-ward, we might get together." We hadn't made plans, but I wasn't averse to spending the evening with him. We could take a cue from Raven and Kipa, I thought. The past couple weeks the physical side of our relationship had been a little quiet, mostly due to all the extra hours we were putting in.

He gave me a regretful look, dropping the file folder on the table. As he held out his arms, I slid into them and he wrapped them around me, kissing my head.

"I'm sorry, love. I've got business. I have to put in calls to Mielikki's Arrow and Odin's Chase, to find out if they're facing the same problem with the Tuathan Brotherhood. They were having a few issues for a while, but we haven't heard from them in some time. Then I promised my father I'd touch base with some of the portal keepers and make certain all the entrances to Annwn are working smoothly. You could come with me, but it's really not going to be much fun." He tilted my chin up, staring deep into my eyes and slowly pressed his lips against mine.

I melted into his arms, wanting more. I wanted to slide my hands under his shirt, against his chest. I wanted to feel him slide his body against mine.

As I broke away, I looked up into his eyes and put my hands on his shoulders. On my left ring finger was a ring made of antler. Herne had made it out of a sliver of his own tines, carved it into a polished circle and given it to me as a promise ring on the solstice.

I held up my hand. "Go do what you need to do. This ring promises me you'll be here when you can. We'll have time soon."

"I love you," he said, never taking his gaze off me. "I love you, and I want you. Tomorrow night? Your place?"

"My place," I said, and he kissed me again. I lost myself in the feel of his lips against mine, the scent of deep woods and fern surrounding me. I could smell the rain dripping off cedars, moss growing on the trunks of trees, the cool scent of morning fog rolling along the ground. Herne was the embodiment of all of these things.

A moment later, he reluctantly pulled away. "I'd better get moving. What are you going to do tonight?"

"Movie with Angel. We're going to see *Atomic Brenda*. Are you sure you don't want to come with us? I'll even buy the popcorn."

Herne laughed. "I think that I can safely say I'll pass. But truly, love, I do have to work, or I'd go with you even if I didn't want to see the movie. Is Rafé going?"

I shook my head, glancing around to see if Angel was still in the room, but I could see her down the hall, near her desk. "No. Apparently he's expected at some family gathering. Which *won't* be a barrel of laughs. Rafé's family cares as much about him as my grandparents did me, I think. Although, maybe since Ulstair was killed, they've come around. The loss of one child would, I would hope, make them value their remaining children more."

"You'd hope so, but it doesn't always follow. Especially among the Fae."

I wrinkled my nose. "You don't have to tell me that. All right, I'll see you tomorrow night. Text me when you're planning to come over. By then, hopefully I'll still be alive and have the bow and the crown to show your mother next time we meet."

"At least you'll be able to tell her that you tried, if nothing else. Morgana is demanding, but if she knows you're trying, she tends to go easier on you. Or at least, that was my experience when I was growing up. She and Father were exacting, but they were also just. I never really felt like they were unfair."

He gave me another kiss, then grabbed his files and headed for his office. But he barely made it a couple feet before Yutani let out a yell and came flying out of his office.

"Yes!" He thrust his fist into the air. "I found it!"

"What? What did you find?" Herne said, turning.

"I found the wormhole. I found out the location on the laptop where the files are hidden. I don't know what's in them yet, but I should be able to recover them. And when I do, we may just find the break we've been looking for. Nalcops wouldn't have hidden them if they weren't vital to the Brotherhood." Yutani sobered, shaking his head. "Whoever set up his system is brilliant, and I think—a technomage."

"Uh oh. That could be bad news," Herne said. "Techno-mages are also brilliant at creating computer viruses. You'd better hurry, because I've seen cases where files self-corrupted when they were discovered. Sort of like an electronic suicide command."

"This tape will self-destruct in five minutes," I quipped, then sobered as they both frowned. "I know, *don't be so flippant.*" I turned to Yutani. "How long till we know what's there?"

He shrugged. "I don't know, to be honest. I know how to get to them, but Herne's right. I'll have to be cautious so I don't trigger a virus that might erase those files. So it might take an hour, it might take a week. I'll know more once I get my hands dirty. But I wanted to let you know. It's time we caught a break, and at least this gives us a glimmer of hope."

Herne clapped him on his shoulder, gently. "Good going. Thanks, bro, and do what you have to in order to preserve as much information as you can. Every single thing we can discover is a step in the right direction."

And with that, we disbanded for the day. Yutani went back into his computer cave, Herne headed into his office, and Angel and I took off for dinner and a movie. Yutani was right, I thought as we got in the car and pulled away from the building. We needed a break, badly. And maybe, just maybe, this would give us one.

CHAPTER FOUR

*a*fter the movie, Angel and I decided to make a stop at Medinos, one of the local SubCult clubs. We were still wound up from the movie—*Atomic Brenda* was a kick-ass super ninja action heroine and the movie was fun, cheesy, and left us in a really good mood.

"No goblin blasters, though," Angel warned. "I can't drag you up the stairs by myself."

Last time I'd succumbed to the lure of goblin blasters, I'd gotten shit-faced drunk and made an ass of myself. I blushed, shaking my head. "Nope. No goblin blasters. If you want a drink, I'll drive."

She snorted. "No, I'm good. I'll stick to a burger and fries. You go ahead and have whatever you want."

We settled into the booth, and the waitress hurried over. Angel ordered her burger and fries, and I ordered grilled cheese, tomato soup, and for a change—a micro-brew. I didn't drink much beer, I didn't have the taste for it, but now and then it just hit the spot. I wasn't planning on getting drunk, I just wanted a little buzz to take the edge off of the day. Considering what I was going to be facing tomorrow, I felt I needed it.

"Do you think Yutani can actually find out something that will help us?" Angel asked. She winced as a loud burst of music hit us. Glancing around, she added, "I'm going to ask if they can turn it down a little. There are barely any people in the club right now, and nobody's dancing."

I nodded, waiting as she walked up to the bartender. A moment later he turned the music down to a more reasonable level and she returned to the booth. As she slid back in, the waitress brought my beer and Angel's hot cocoa. When she left, I took a long drink of the beer and slid it back on the coaster.

"I don't know. I hope he can. If there are hidden files, and it seems he's hit on at least several, then they're hidden for a reason. That gives me hope."

"It seems like we've been fighting the Tuathan Brotherhood forever, but it's only been a couple months, hasn't it? Since October?"

I nodded. "Yeah, only two months. Almost three. And that's three months too many. I'm so tired of dealing with them. If something isn't done soon, relations between the Fae Courts and the rest of the United Coalition are going to break down even further. I wanted to believe the Fomorians were behind this, but it's looking more and more like it's not them. Did you hear that Elatha actually has offered to help find out who did this? Of course, he probably hopes that the Fae Courts are behind it. That would turn the tide against them even more."

Angel played with her cocoa, stirring the whipped cream into the steaming drink. "What do *you* think about the Fomorians? Do you hate them as much as the rest of the Fae do?"

"Given they've tried to wipe my people out since the beginning of time, I don't hold a whole lot of love for them." I paused for a moment to gather my thoughts, then continued. "But I also know that groups are made up of individuals, and not every individual conforms to the stereotype. I wouldn't kill a Fomorian just for who they were. I'm not that bigoted. But I most definitely would be on guard around them, given they tend to have a *The only good Fae is a dead Fae* attitude." I hesitated again, then added, "You remember the KKK? Before they were outlawed and went underground?"

The KKK was a hate group targeting nonwhites—mostly Blacks. They had been outlawed years ago, but they had just taken their organization underground, because hate—especially hate without reason—didn't just vanish because of a law. But at least it became harder for the KKK to meet, and harder still for them to take action against their targets, given the swell of feeling had turned against them.

"Right."

"Well, the Fomorians don't work like the KKK do. They aren't as clumsy. Most of their actions are done with the intent to undermine without claiming responsibility."

"How so?" Angel asked.

"Remember last summer? The iron disease that could have wiped out my people? We know they were responsible for infecting the food at the Fae Day festival. But there's no way we can prove it. They did a good job of covering their tracks. They're not sitting on the council right now, demanding the genocide of the Fae race. But given the history between our two races, and given what we know of them, you know that they're working in the background, hoping to achieve their goals. I'm not sure which enemy I'm more leery of, the one who's vocal about their bigotry and hatred, or the one who is friendly on the surface and scheming underneath. Neither can be trusted, but which one is the more dangerous?"

Angel nodded. "There are plenty of subtle bigotries that I face every day, that my family faces. That *any* person of color faces. We understand all about privilege, and the lack thereof. It's better now, but it's still rife within some organizations. I don't know if we can ever be rid of it. I hope so, but to be honest, I'm not sure it's possible to wipe it out."

"Why?" I asked, even though I agreed with her.

"Because people are people, and when somebody takes it in their head to hate somebody else, logic doesn't usually win out."

"You can say that again," I said, somberly staring at the table.

Our waitress arrived then, bringing our food. As we ate, we turned the conversation to happier subjects, because sometimes, you had to get away from reality, even for just a little while.

THE NEXT MORNING, I WOKE WITH THE LINGERING FEELING that something was off. Then I remembered what I was scheduled to do, and I groaned. Pushing myself to a sitting position, I stared forlornly out the window. It was raining again, but that was common enough for this time of year. Most of the snow was gone, melting as the rain splashed down. I blinked, and yawned. Luckily, I had limited myself to one beer the night before, so I woke clearheaded.

I glanced at the clock. It was eight A.M., and I needed to get showered and dressed and over to Raven's by ten. With yet another groan, I pushed myself out of bed and headed for my shower.

As I studied my closet, I realized I had no clue what to wear. It had to be something appropriate, since I could only push my luck so far with either court. Saílle and Névé both knew that I was due in their cities today, and I would be provided with an escort once I reached the gates. Otherwise, I could easily be run out of the city by angry Fae who didn't take to having a tralaeth walking the streets.

I opted for a new pair of black jeans and a silver corset that zipped up the front. I fastened a black leather belt around my waist, and was going to wear a black leather jacket.

I brushed my hair into a high ponytail and applied my makeup carefully, accentuating the blue and silver colors of my eye shadow with a navy eyeliner. Then I added a slick of pale pink lip gloss and sat back, staring at myself. I had gone out of my way to make sure that the necklace Morgana had given me was visible, hoping it would provide some sort of protection. I thought twice about the leather jacket and tossed it onto my bed. Instead, I found a black denim jacket with slouch sleeves that I was able to push up to my elbows. That way, the tattoo on my arm showed, marking me as a protected member of the Wild Hunt.

"That's better," I said to myself, finally slipping on a pair of chunky-heeled ankle boots and zipping them up. I slung my black leather bag over my shoulder, and headed downstairs.

Angel was waiting in the kitchen, breakfast ready. I glanced at the table, seeing a bowl of oatmeal waiting for me, along with three fried eggs, four sausage links, two pieces of toast, and a tall travel latte mug.

"I thought you might want to fortify yourself with a lumberjack breakfast." She gave me an encouraging grin.

I smiled gratefully at her. "Thank you so much. I'm really not looking forward to today, and it helps to have you on my side."

"Always! We aren't BFFs for nothing." She carried over another dish, a smaller amount of oatmeal, along with a plate with sausage and eggs on it. "I'll eat breakfast with you, then I'm heading out on a shopping trip. My favorite jeans ripped out in the crotch. And while I'm at it, I thought I'd replace the waffle iron because it's about ready to give out. And we need more coffee and groceries."

I pulled out my wallet, handing her a hundred bucks. "Here, this will help defray the costs. If it costs more than that, let me know and I'll stop at the ATM on the way home."

"Thanks." She took the money and tucked it into her purse. Angel did most of the grocery shopping because she was the one who cooked most. I usually took care of the dishes. On Saturdays, we did chores together, though yesterday we had let them slide.

I glanced around the kitchen. "If I'm home early

enough today, I'll try to get to the floors. I think it's my week for them."

"Yeah, they are getting a little muddy, especially by the door. It's been a wet season out there." She glanced out the window behind the table.

Our kitchen was huge, an eat-in kitchen. We had a table that could seat upward of eight to ten guests. I had bought the house a few months before, and Angel moved in as my roommate. It had been a murder house, but we cleansed it, and everything negative seemed to be gone. As long as I didn't think about being forced to kill my grand-father in the kitchen, I was fine. It'd been his fault, and I tried not to let myself entertain ideas that the house was cursed from the murder–suicide that had happened here earlier.

"You're picking up Raven at ten?" Angel stabbed a sausage with her fork.

I nodded. "Yeah. I'm grateful she's going with me. I doubt if many of the Fae will fuck with one of the Ante-Fae. They may not like having her in the city, but I don't think there's anything they can do about it. And I doubt if Saílle or Névé will tell her to get out. They're both leery when it comes to dealing with me, given I work with the Wild Hunt."

"While you're in TirNaNog, can you check and see if they have any of that beautiful lacy Elven woven material that looks like embroidery on tulle? I'm looking for some in a bright green."

I blinked, cocking my head to the right. "I didn't know you wanted any of that. I'll see if I have time." I glanced at the clock. It was eight forty-five. "I better hurry and finish my breakfast, then get on the road. Who knows what the traffic is going to be like over to the Eastside."

And with that, I dug into my oatmeal, focusing on fueling up for the day.

TRAFFIC WASN'T BAD AS I DROVE OVER THE 520 FLOATING bridge, at least eastbound. Westbound, it was backed up like crazy, because there was a Seahawks game in the early afternoon, and fans were hurrying to get to their seats. I wasn't much of a sports person, although I loved watching snowboarding and the X Games, and the Olympics. In fact, Viktor and I had discovered a mutual love for the Winter X Games, so we watched together now.

The rain had lightened up, but the waves were still frothy in Lake Washington, churning like crazy on one side of the bridge while they were calm on the other. I wasn't sure why the lake had that effect, at least where the 520 and the I-90 bridges cut through the water, but it was odd, to say the least. It wasn't unusual for the water on one side of the lake to be perfectly calm, while on the other side the waves would be frothing up and splashing across the roadway.

I turned off 520 onto Lake Washington Boulevard, heading north. Then I followed the road until it became Lake Street, in the heart of Kirkland. Lake Street T'd into Central Way, and I turned left, making another quick turn right onto Market Street, still headed northbound.

Market Street took me into Juanita, a suburb of Kirkland, and I followed Northeast Juanita Drive, winding

around the edge of the lake. Juanita Drive eventually
entered the UnderLake Park district, and just beyond that,
I turned into Raven's suburb.

She lived at the end of a cul-de-sac, which ended at the
trailhead into UnderLake Park. Raven was on the left, and
the house on the right of the trailhead had been owned by
a couple of nasty neighbors, but now it looked tidier, and
neater. I wondered who had moved in.

I eased into her driveway, next to her Toyota sedan. As
I jumped out of my car and strode up the walk, I saw that
Raj was out in his doghouse. Raj was Raven's gargoyle,
and he was a funny little piece of work. Well, not so little,
given he was the size of a good-size rottweiler. His wings
had been clipped when he was a baby by a nasty demon,
but Raven had ensured that he didn't remember the pain.
She had won him off the demon in a game of poker, and
she and Raj had become fast friends. I had the feeling
there was more than met the eye to Raj, but I never
pushed for information. Raven would let me know if she
wanted me to know anything about him.

"Hey Raj," I said, giving him a hearty pat on the back as
he lumbered out of the doghouse to look at me. He sat
down, eyes bright and expectant. I groaned. Angel always
brought him a treat when we came over, and I had forgot-
ten. "I'm sorry, Raj. I forgot this time. But it's good to see
you." He let out a grunt, then rubbed against me and
turned back to his doghouse.

I was about to ring the bell when Raven opened the
door.

"I heard you out here. Hey Raj, you need to come
inside while I'm gone. Come on," she said, kneeling to
unfasten his collar from the leash that held him near the

doghouse. Apparently, he had the habit of wandering off if he was left off his leash. And curiosity didn't just kill cats, as Raven was fond of telling me.

"How are you this morning?" I asked, giving her the once-over.

Raven was wearing a black satin skirt over what looked to be a black tulle petticoat, along with a purple corset with PVC accents. She had on a pair of lace-up knee boots with thick rubber platform soles, and a crop top jacket. She was curvy, like me, though she was plumper than I was, and she had long dark brown hair with purple streaks running through it. She had a large number of tattoos all over her body, though most of them were generally covered up because she liked to wear tights and long sleeves. I could see some of her ink poking out from beneath the corset, around her breasts. Her eyes sparkled as she flashed me an infectious grin.

"About as good as it gets. Jazzed up on enough caffeine to fuel an army. And, I have to say, I'm looking forward to seeing TirNaNog and Navane. I've never been in either one, so this is the perfect time to assuage my nosiness."

I laughed. "I'm glad my discomfort gives you some joy. Seriously, I am not looking forward to this, but Morgana insisted and I can't get out of it." I stared down at my hands for a moment. "You do realize I'm going to be visiting the woman who was instrumental in my mother's and father's deaths?"

Raven sobered immediately. "Fucking hell. If there's anything we can do to make her life miserable, just say the word and I'm there."

"Thanks for having my back. I guess we should get going." As much as I didn't want to do this, now that it was staring me in the face, I just wanted to get it over with.

"Let me lock up and make sure Raj has his snacks. I'll be out in a moment. Did you want to take your car or mine?"

"Let's take mine. I'll buy you dinner afterward as a thank-you."

She finished locking up, then came dashing out and jumped into the car, fastening her seat belt. "Well, let's get this show on the road. We'll get you through this, Ember. I promise."

THE GREAT CITY OF TIRNANOG WAS PAST WOODINVILLE, having taken over a good section of the northern Eastside. The easiest way to get there was to take Highway 522, and about twenty minutes later, we saw the great wall surrounding TirNaNog off to our left. I took the exit leading to the front gates, hoping to hell that Saílle had let them know I was coming.

Both TirNaNog and Navane were surrounded by massive gates. They had been built of marble, quarried in from all over the world, and they surrounded the outstretched cities, creating citadels set off from the rest of the surrounding area.

TirNaNog was the city of the Dark Fae, and Queen Saílle ruled over it with a cool, ruthless command. In some aspects, I liked her better than Névé, because Saílle was direct, and blunt. She didn't sugarcoat anything, and she never pretended to like anybody just for appearances. I had met her several times, and while she would never look on me as true Fae, because of my half-blood heritage, I had the feeling she gave me a grudging amount of respect for being independent enough to not give a flying fig about her.

Massive parking lots surrounded the city. Apparently, once inside the gates, you were expected to use city transport—be it bus, taxi, or the sidewalk. There were shuttles for mobility-impaired pedestrians, but the Fae were as snobbish about disabilities as they were about anybody else. It still amazed me that my mother and father had been such nice people, but then again, they had run away from their families and their cultures to be together. And they had paid with their lives.

I parked as close as I could to the eastern gates, and looked at Raven. Then, slinging my purse over my shoulder, I stepped out of the car and took a deep breath. The air felt clearer here. Why, I wasn't sure, but there was a magical tinge to it, an electric current that made everything feel more alive.

Raven joined me, and we stared up at the gates that were in front of us. There were guards in front of the gates, dressed in deep indigo and dark plum and silver. These were the colors of TirNaNog, the Dark Fae Court. I gnawed on my lip, then gave Raven a quick look.

"Well, I guess I'm about as ready as I'll ever be. I'm nervous, I don't mind telling you that." I shivered, thinking that, if they had their way, a good number of the people inhabiting this city would like to see me dead.

"I'm here. And trust me, I can bring down hell on their heads if need be. I can make them remember why the Ante-Fae are stronger than they can ever hope to be.

Come on, let's get this over with. Who do you have to see?"

"My great-uncle lives here. Farthing's brother. I have no idea what to expect. If he's anything like my grandfather was, he's treacherous and I won't be able to trust a word he says."

"All right. Take a deep breath, steady yourself, and let's go see what we can find out."

With Raven at my back, I headed toward the gates of TirNaNog, a city I had once sworn I would never set foot in.

CHAPTER FIVE

he guards at the gate looked like they'd been cloned, they looked so much alike. There were nine booths that stretched in back of the massive gates leading into the walled city. The gates were opened, and there were long lines at several of the booths.

"What's this?" Raven asked.

"If you live in TirNaNog or Navane, you have to carry passports proving residence. If you aren't a citizen of the Fae Courts, you have to wear a visitor's pass at all times when you're within the borders of either city." I had taken time to learn about the rules. I didn't want to unwittingly do something that could get my ass hauled up on charges.

"So, what do we do?"

"We get in line and I'll give them my name. There should be a guard waiting for me, if everything goes right. With a little luck, they won't hassle us about who we are. Or *what* we are, rather." I straightened my shoulders as we approached the nearest entrance booth. There were only four people in line in front of us, and they were passing through quickly.

By the time we reached the window, I had steeled myself for an argument. Regardless of the fact that Saílle had agreed to my visit, I didn't trust that we would be allowed in without a problem. I'd learned over the years just how fucked up the Fae Courts could be.

To my surprise, when we reached the guard sitting in the booth, which reminded me all too much of a ferry toll booth, he merely asked, "Name and reason for visit?"

"Ember Kearney. I should be on the list of approved visitors and I was told there would be a guide waiting for me. This is my friend, Raven BoneTalker. I'm here to see my great-uncle." I cleared my throat and showed the man my license. He glanced at it, then glanced at me. If he was shocked, he didn't show it. He merely pulled out another list and scanned it for a moment.

"Here you are. All right, hold on. It looks like the guide assigned to escort you is sick. You'll have to go in on your own. I have a visitor's badge for you, but I'll have to make one for your companion." He jotted down Raven's name off her license and turned his back on us.

Damn it. Without a guide along, there was a lot more chance of trouble. But I was in no place to bargain. I had my suspicions that the guide had conveniently woken up with a cold, but I said nothing.

The whir of a printer sounded and the guard turned back to us, two badges in hand. Mine had a green border around my name, Raven's a yellow border. Both were sheathed in plastic cases and hung on long strings.

"Wear these at all times while you're in the city. The green on yours means you're under protection of the queen. If anybody messes with you, call a guard and they'll put a stop to it." He didn't sound enthusiastic, but I didn't really care.

He handed us the badges. "Please drop these off at any registered badge recycling unit when you leave TirNaNog today. Have a good day." It was all rote, as though he'd said the words a thousand times before, which he probably had. But we took the badges and hung them around our necks, then headed through the gates, into the Dark Fae city.

MY FIRST IMPRESSION OF TIRNANOG WAS THAT WE'D simultaneously traveled back in time, and yet forward to the future. The buildings were built of smooth stone and marble, giving them a decidedly crisp, clean look. They were minimalist, sleek with the windows smooth and flush against the façades. And yet, the streets were paved with cobblestones, and the street lamps were clear glass—or I thought they were glass—tubes, with flickering flames in various colors wicking up and down inside the tubes. They reminded me of Lightning Flits from Annwn—shards of lightning captured by the gods to use for light. The flames were blue and pink, green and yellow, and they sparkled. Magic, perhaps. Or some sort of gas enclosed within the sealed tubes.

It seemed odd to see so few cars. The only approved methods of transit were taxis, buses, shuttles, and walking. We were at the eastern gates and the city stretched out to the west, north, and south. I had the address where my great-uncle lived, so I hailed a passing cab. The driver pulled over, but when I opened the passenger door, he took one look at me and shook his head.

"No tralaeths in my cabs," he said with a sneer.

I gritted my teeth. "I have the queen's permission to be here." I held up my badge.

He looked at the border around my badge and grimaced. For a moment I thought that he wasn't going to let us in, but he finally let out a sound of disgust and thumbed the backseat. "In, but neither of you sit in the front."

I glanced at Raven, whose eyes were so dark I thought she was about ready to unleash a fireball on the guy, but we slid into the back without incident.

"3215 Brambleberry Street, please."

The taxi driver muttered, then said, "Payment first. Ten dollars. Cash."

I knew the ride wasn't that expensive, but I said nothing, just handed him a ten-dollar bill. Then, without another word, we were off, heading toward the southern side of town, toward my great-uncle whom I really didn't want to see.

THE CITY OF TIRNANOG REMINDED ME OF A HYBRID BABY —a Victorian techno-city that didn't quite know what it wanted to be. We passed an open farmers market and several large bazaars. It was odd. I was Fae, through and through, but I felt divorced from the bustle around me. These might be my people in theory, but I was more comfortable around the streeps and the streetwalkers on

First Avenue than I was here in this gorgeous, oddly exotic, city.

I glanced at Raven, longing to talk, but not wanting to give the taxi driver any gossip fodder. After about ten minutes we pulled up in front of a tall building. It looked like an apartment building, or condo complex.

"Out." The driver motioned to the door.

I chewed on my inner lip, debating whether to bother asking, and finally decided that it was worth the try. "Will you wait here for us? I'll pay you for the time."

He rolled his eyes. "How much you willing to pay?"

"Fifty dollars and then another twenty for the ride back to the gates."

He chewed his lip for a moment. "Make it a hundred total—with the ten you already gave me—and I'll wait."

"Give me your word," I said, eyeing him shrewdly. Even if he did give me his word, it wouldn't guarantee anything, but at least it was better than nothing. Or at least, I tried to convince myself of that.

"All right. You have my word. I'll wait up to forty-five minutes. If you're going to be longer than that, you fork out another fifty before the hour's fully up. And get your ass out here to pay it—I'm not going to come find you in that maze."

"Fifty now and forty when we get back," I said, holding up a fifty-dollar bill.

"Eh…I should have my head examined. Scram, and hurry it up." He begrudgingly took the fifty-dollar bill and pulled out a book, settling back in the seat.

Raven and I hustled over to the building. "I wish you'd let me tell him who I am."

"He's probably already figured out that you're one of

the Ante-Fae. And if I let you tell him who you are, he'd most likely drive off out of fear and leave us without transportation. I don't feel like using the city bus. It's bad enough having one person sneering at us. I don't want to face an entire busload of passengers."

It wasn't that my feelings were hurt—I was more angry than injured. It was that I didn't want any wannabe vigilantes to decide that a tralaeth was worth going after. The last thing Raven and I needed was to find ourselves on the wrong end of a fight with a fanatic.

"Fine. But this isn't turning out to be nearly as much fun as I thought it might be." She shrugged, looped her arm through mine, and we headed up the stairs toward the main doors. "What unit does your great-uncle live in?"

"Two-fourteen. Second floor."

We climbed the two flights of stairs that led to the main lobby of the building. I glanced around. No ramps, no nothing. If this building was handicapped friendly, there was no sign of it. Of course, since it was on sovereign Fae land, nothing in the city had to conform to general building codes in the rest of the state. While I knew that Saílle and Névé tended to run tight ships with their cities, there were enough differences between the world of the Fae and the rest of us that it was noticeable.

We pushed through the glass doors into the main lobby, and found ourselves in what felt very much like a hotel. The lobby was wide, with a reception desk, a sitting area, doors leading to what I suspected were a gym and other amenities, a stairwell, an elevator, and a café. Whatever they were cooking in there smelled good and my stomach rumbled, loud and clear, demanding something to eat.

"We're not stopping for lunch," Raven muttered, glancing at me.

"All right. Let's just get this over with and then drive on to Navane." I rubbed my head, grumbling. "I don't want to do this, Raven. I really don't," I said in a low voice as we approached the elevators.

The car was quiet, spacious, and again, reminded me of some conference-hotel. It all felt oddly generic, and yet not quite familiar. The wallpaper in the elevator was a dark blue, with pale blue and lilac patterns that made me think of spatter paintings. The metal surrounding us in the car was bronze.

The second floor was set out in a square surrounding the elevators, the hall running in a complete circle. The hallways were carpeted in deep blue, and the walls were painted an antique ivory. Art studded the walls, but it was less generic than I was used to—pictures of white horses racing over rolling plains, and scenic landscapes that looked just off enough to feel alien.

"Here we are," Raven said, pointing down the hall.

To the left of the hallway was a door with "214" emblazoned in bronze on it. I caught my breath, steeling myself. Finally, I knocked first once, then again. Another knock and we could hear shuffling coming from behind the door. *Somebody* was home, and I hoped it was my great-uncle. The last thing I wanted was to have to explain to some unwary family member as to why I had shown up on their doorstep.

The door swept open and there, in front of me, stood a man who looked like the spitting image of my grandfather. His hair was shorter, just past his shoulder blades, but it was the same rich brown sprinkled with silver, and he had the same green eyes that mirrored my own. He looked somewhat younger than Farthing had, but that was relative, given my grandfather hadn't looked much older than me. But he had felt *old*—ancient, to be exact— and his brother had the same feel to him.

"Are you Sharne?" I had barely known my grandfather had a brother. None of Farthing's family had contacted me when he had been killed, and I suspected that Saílle hadn't told them *how* he had been dispatched. Otherwise, I was pretty sure that I could have expected a blood debt hanging over my head.

"I am." He looked me in the eye, then inhaled sharply. "Ember?"

"Yes, I'm Ember." I waited to see what he would do.

After a moment, he stepped to the side and ushered us in. "To what do I owe this visit? I'm sure we haven't scheduled some family reunion or other oddity." His tone had that same regal, aristocratic note that my grandfather's voice had held, but he was watching me curiously, as though he were waiting for me to perform a trick.

Raven and I followed him into the apartment, which was clean to the point of sterility. It felt oddly out of place, so minimalist that I wondered if he ever did anything here other than sleep or stand out on the balcony, against the far wall. There were two doors, and while one could have led to a hall, I had the feeling that this was just a very small, ultra clean, apartment.

"If you're looking for anything material from your grandfather, you're too late. The queen had his place thoroughly dismantled and most of his belongings were confiscated."

"I don't want anything of his. No, I'm coming here

because Morgana ordered me to. I'm pledged in her service and I follow her command. Otherwise, nothing on this wide, wild planet could drag me here." I paused, then added, "You do know my grandfather tried to murder me?"

Sharne paused, then motioned to the sofa. It was immaculately white and I was afraid to sit on it, but Raven marched over, sat down, and patted the seat next to her. I followed more slowly.

"You are one of the Ante-Fae, I surmise?" Sharne said, turning to Raven. He held out his hand, gracefully.

"Raven BoneTalker, and yes, I am." She stared at his fingers for a moment. "You haven't yet taken your great-niece's hand, so you don't get mine."

He blinked, then cleared his throat and extended his hand to me. "Ember, welcome to my house." His tone was civil, and he sounded sincere.

I blinked. I had expected surliness, or disgust, but never anything like genteel civility. I slowly—very slowly —accepted the handshake. His grip was firm, but not annoyingly tight. He also didn't grimace when he touched me. After he had shaken my hand, he turned back to Raven and she graciously held out her fingers. He gave her a gentle shake of the hand and then joined us, sitting down.

"What can I do for you?" He seemed so straightforward that I felt my guard slip a little, but then I quickly walled myself back off. I didn't know what to think about him, he seemed so like my grandfather, and yet so unlike him.

"Morgana says you have something that belongs to me, by right of birth. It's a bow." I cleared my throat. "I'm not sure which bow she was talking about, but she said you would know." I glanced around the room. It seemed ridiculous that Sharne would have any need for a bow, not in the city, and not with a home that reminded me of something out of a house and garden magazine.

He pulled back, a look of surprise washing over his face. "The bow," he said, his voice low. "So that's why I was given it."

"What bow, and what do you mean? I know very little about family matters, given the circumstances." I didn't bother to hide my irritation. Once again, the memory of my parents, dead on the floor, filled my thoughts and I could still remember the silence of the house, the sound of my own screams, the smell of the blood that was coagulating around them, and the panic when I realized exactly what I was seeing.

Something must have shown on my face, for Sharne hung his head. "I know, and I'm sorry about that. My brother and his wife were...they did not handle change well, but the world will change and there's no getting around that fact."

"Yes, well, tell that to Saílle and Névé. They could shift the tide if they chose to. Instead, they flog on the hatred and..." I paused to stop the sudden rush of words coming out of my mouth. "What I wish is neither here nor there. I'm simply here to gather the things Morgana told me I needed to ask for."

Sharne gave me a long nod, then stood. "Please wait. I'll be right back." He exited through one of the doors and we heard a few thumping noises.

I turned to Raven. "This isn't going the way I expected it to."

"You thought he would turn you out, or argue with you?"

"I halfway thought he'd try to finish what my grandfather started. I don't trust any of these people, Raven. They don't like my kind and generally want us either gone or dead, whichever is more convenient for them. I can't figure out what his angle is." I didn't feel guilty for suspecting him of having some ulterior motive. My grandfather had been nursing a doozy of one.

"I hear you. But see where it goes. If things get too awkward, we can always leave and you can blame me if Morgana comp—" she stopped as Sharne entered the room again. He was carrying a bow. It was a pistol grip crossbow, made out of what looked like yew wood, polished to a high sheen. The bow was shimmering with a faint nimbus and I blinked as he held it out to me.

"I think she's talking about this. It belonged to your great-great-grandmother. She was killed in a raiding party long ago. Her daughter inherited it—your grandfather's mother—and she passed it on to him. Your grandfather was supposed to pass it on to your father but he refused to. This, along with a couple other personal items, were all I was given when Queen Saílle confiscated his property."

I hesitantly reached for the bow, feeling the cool wood slide into my hand with almost a soft hush. It felt right, like it belonged to me. I held it up, looking down the scope. The bow was level and brilliantly made. The scope almost seemed magical—I could see so clearly through it. I held it for another moment, and then—as I was about ready to ask Sharne what he wanted for it—something whispered so loudly it startled me.

Finally, a huntress worthy of my make.

"Say what?" I blinked, pulling back. "Who said that?" I looked around. Raven hadn't said anything, and the voice hadn't been Sharne's.

"What are you talking about? I didn't hear anything." Sharne glanced around the room. "I don't see anybody here."

"No ghosts around," Raven said, looking equally as confused. She paused, then snapped her fingers. "If you heard something, my bets are on that bow. It reeks of magic."

"The bow?" I looked down at the bow, confused. "But neither of you heard anything, right?"

Sharne cleared his throat. "I think your friend is correct. There are family stories that the bow can make itself known to some members of the family. I believe Grandmother used to tell us that during some of the raiding parties, the bow helped her chase down her quarry by giving her directions on where to shoot. I think everybody thought she was just being...*poetic?*" He smiled, then, and his face suddenly blossomed out. For a brief moment, I saw my father's face, smiling and laughing. The sight sucker-punched me in the gut and a rush of loss swept over me. I burst into tears.

"Ember? Are you okay?" Raven was at my side immediately. She took the bow out of my hands and gently set it down, then pulled me onto the sofa again, wrapping her arms around me. "What did you do to her?" she asked, whirling to look at Sharne.

He blinked, and through my tears, I saw what looked like sincere consternation. "I don't know—Ember, what did I say?"

I stammered, trying to calm myself. "You... It wasn't..." I fell silent, furiously trying to wipe the tears out of my eyes. I looked at Raven. "He looked like my father for a moment," I mouthed.

She caught her breath and glanced at Sharne, who was looking more and more confused.

"It wasn't what you *said*," I told him, managing to find my voice. "Just, for a brief moment, you looked like my father." I prayed that he wouldn't throw my father's choices in my face, that for once someone in my family would behave in a decent manner. And for once, my prayers were answered.

"I'm so sorry. I can't imagine what you're going through." Sharne hung his head. "While my brother was alive, I kept out of things. He was the eldest and I had no real standing in the family. They wouldn't listen to me. Now, I'm one of the few left of our generation. I have no children. This branch of the family will die out with me, except for you."

"Maybe it's better if it just disappears," I said hoarsely.

"No, hear me out. I want to apologize—for your grandfather. For what my brother and the others in the family did to you and your parents. I know that my apology can never mend the wounds, but I just need you to know that I had nothing to do with the plans. I spoke out against them, but I was overruled. I was a coward. If I'd been courageous enough, I would have warned your parents. But I was worried about my brother disowning me. I wish now that I had just gone ahead and done it. I have no excuses. I'm just so very sorry."

I stared at him, trying to process what he was saying.

My entire world was spinning. This shouldn't be happening—it made no sense to me.

Sharne hurried to the kitchen and brought me back a glass of water. I sat there, sipping it, trying to sort out my feelings. I had thought I was over my parents' deaths—at least, as far as anybody could ever be over trauma like that. But seeing Sharne's smile had sent me right back to my childhood, to the two people who loved me like no one else ever could. It reeled me back to a time when I felt carefree and happy. Regardless of the way others treated me, my parents and Angel had been there. Sharne had known they were going to die, but he'd done nothing to stop it. But where did the spiral of blame end?

Sharne hadn't killed them. Sharne had—according to his account—tried to talk them out of it. Maybe it was time to let some of the anger go. Maybe it was time to let Farthing slip into the past. I still had to face my grand-mother, who had helped Farthing with his murderous plan, but Sharne said he hadn't been part of the conspir-acy, and I believed him. In the core of my heart, I knew he was telling the truth.

Slowly, I set down the glass and leaned forward. Sucking in a deep breath, I let it out slowly and said, "Sharne, I can never forgive my grandfather for what he did, but you... I believe you. And I forgive you for not warning my parents."

And with that, I felt like I could move forward toward the future.

CHAPTER SIX

*A*fter that, the atmosphere in the apartment felt lighter, and I felt much more relaxed. Sharne handed me the bow again.

"This is yours. It was supposed to be your father's, and so it belongs to you. I would have sent it to you, but Farthing kept it. One way or another, it's now back where it belongs. You say you think it spoke to you?" He seemed genuinely curious.

"Yes, I do." I slowly turned the bow over in my hands. "It's beautiful. Who made it, do you know?" The workmanship was incredible. It was obviously hand carved. Every mark on the bow had been made with decision. I couldn't find a single flaw, even though I knew it was extremely old.

"I don't know," he said. "The bow's at least a thousand years old. My mother inherited it, and she passed it on to Farthing, since he was the eldest. As I said, it should have gone to Breck, but Farthing refused to give it to him. And he wasn't about to pass it to me. For one thing, I have no children so the line ends with me. And for another, he didn't approve of my liberal ways." Sharne gave a little shrug.

I paused, then held out the bow. Morgana may have wanted me to have it, but I felt like I had to offer it to Sharne. "Do you want it? It seems like it should go to you."

He stared at the bow, then softly shook his head. "The bow's not mine to claim, and I have no use for it. I'm a black sheep in more than one way. I don't have the hunting instinct of our forebears. I just…don't. You know what I do?"

"What?" I placed the bow on my lap, one hand on the grip. I was relieved he had said no. I felt a kinship with the bow, and had offered it out of what seemed right, not what I wanted.

"I'm a tailor. I make clothes. I've always had a love for fashion and cloth. But that wasn't respected in our family."

I suddenly remembered what Angel had asked. "You wouldn't happen to have any of that embroidered lace the Fae Courts are so famous for? In green? My roommate and best friend would love to have some."

He laughed then, and his eyes seemed to dance with joy. "Yes, I do. Let me get you some. It's the least I can do." Before I could say anything, he jumped up and disappeared through the door again. When he returned, he handed me a bag. In it was about three yards of the most exquisite lace I'd ever seen. "I wove that myself. Do you like it?"

"It's beautiful," I said, in awe. "Thank you. Are you sure you don't want me to pay you for this?"

Sharne shook his head. "No, it's a gift—a peace offering, from me to you." After a pause, he added, "Do you know what your grandfather did?"

I shook my head. "No, I don't."

"Farthing was a favorite in the Court, and he was also an agent for Saílle when he was actively working. He retired many years ago, but he still managed to ferret out dirt on members of her Court that she suspected of being disloyal. And he would turn them over for punishment."

My heart sank. *Of course* Farthing would do that— what else could he do? It was his nature, and no wonder Saílle had done what she could to cover up his death. I wondered if Sharne knew how he died. And if he'd been fed a line, should I illuminate him?

"Do you know what happened to Farthing at the end? Did they tell you?" I forced my voice to remain neutral.

He held my gaze for a moment. "The official line is that Farthing died of a heart attack. That he was out visiting someone and died in their house." He paused, then added, "If you have a differing version, best leave it outside the walls of TirNaNog. Never question Saílle. Never contradict her. I gather her agents are widespread in the city, and they don't discriminate between friend or foe when it comes to turning in dissidents."

I caught my breath. "Do her agents work outside of TirNaNog? Do you know?"

"That I can only speculate on, but I would say it's best to be cautious around *any* member of the Dark Fae. I'm certain Névé must have a similar setup, so I'd go so far as to say, be cautious around any member of either Fae Court. You never know where your enemies are going to be hiding." Once again, he held my gaze, his eyes flickering with a warning light.

It suddenly occurred to me that, even though he claimed to be a tailor, perhaps Sharne himself was an agent. A sudden wave of paranoia washed through me. Finally, I pushed the fear down and sat back, staring at the bow.

"Now that I have what I've come for, I should let you get on with your day." I stood, motioning to Raven. "Thank you, though, for your kindness. And for…talking to me."

Once again, Sharne seemed to be what he claimed he was: a simple tailor who looked relieved that he'd done the right thing. "You are welcome in my home at any time, my great-niece. And perhaps I'll one day chance a visit to you, with your permission."

I wasn't sure how far I trusted him, even though I had decided to forgive him. But I nodded and said, "Yes, do come visit. Text me first, or call—here's my number. Thank you, Sharne. For being honest with me."

And with that, Raven and I returned to the taxi, the bow firmly in hand. Sharne had found the case for it, and as I carried it out to the cab—which was still waiting, miracle of miracles—I wondered how I'd manage with my grandmother. Part of me dreaded the visit, because I wasn't sure I could keep my temper around her. And yet, I kept thinking about how Sharne had seemed so different than Farthing. Maybe my grandmother *wasn't* what she was made out to be. Maybe killing my parents had been her husband's idea. Maybe another miracle would happen and I'd find another relative willing to accept me for who I was.

THE DRIVE TO NAVANE TOOK ANOTHER TWENTY MINUTES.
It was north of TirNaNog, and like the city of the Dark
Fae, Navane, too, hid behind great walls of marble. Actually, there was little to discern the two cities. They seemed
to mirror one another, both with great buildings that
either seemed stuck in history, or reaching out to the
future. The eclectic mix disconcerted me. Granted, a lot
of cities mirrored that aspect, but the fusion seemed more
pointed in the Fae cities.

The colors of Navane, however, were shades of green,
orange, yellow, and gold, and the energy felt a little less
chaotic and more structured. But beneath the superficiali-
ties, the cities could almost be interchangeable. Yet both
Light and Dark would swear up and down that they were
the original, and their sister-city had ripped them off.

I parked, once again, in the parking lot next to the
eastern gates. I sat back, staring at the walls of the city.
"This is going to be harder," I said, turning to Raven.

"Because of...?" she asked, looking out the window.
"Damn, those walls are high."

"Yeah, you'd think they were fighting a battle. *Oh wait*,
they *are*. This is going to be harder because my maternal
grandmother—whom we are going to see—oversaw my
mother's death along with Farthing. They colluded to kill
my parents."

Raven shook her head. "The Ante-Fae can be problematic at best, but at least with us, our treachery is out in the
open most of the time. And while some parents and children don't get along, it's usually for all of the normal
reasons—the child doesn't live up to the parents' stan-
dards, or they don't agree on everything. I mean, look at
my mother. Phasmoria left me when I was twelve. She's

not geared toward children, but she never tried to have me killed, she still checks in on me, and we get along fine, most of the time."

"Well, in the world of the Fae, it's different. Status means so much to my people, and even if your status isn't your fault, you pay the price. Half Fae of any kind are shunned, and those few like me—half Light and half Dark—we're outright pariah. The only way I can walk through these gates, or the gates of TirNaNog, is because the queens left word to let me in. And if Morgana hadn't pushed the point, even that wouldn't have happened." I leaned back, hands still on the wheel. "Granted, things worked out far better than I expected with Sharne, but I'm not banking on that happening twice."

Raven picked up her purse. "Come on. Let's get this over with and then go have a drink. At least you got the bow."

"At least I have the bow, and damned if I don't want to get to know it a bit better. That thing talked to me, Raven. I'd love to find out more about its history."

We headed toward the gates. This time, the guards were much more snide, and once again, no guide was waiting for me, but they let us through when they found my name on the list. Once again, I finally managed to hail a taxi, only it cost me double what it had in TirNaNog.

"I'm beginning to think that the Light Fae are more snobbish than the Dark," Raven said.

"I'm think you're right," I whispered back. This time, the cab refused to wait, so we'd have to find another way back to the gates. But as we headed up the steps toward the house—it was a large house in a row of large houses—I paused. There was a sign on the door.

"What the hell?" I scanned the notice.

Under Order of the Militia of Navane, this building has been locked and sealed until an official investigation has been completed, and the Court has given permission for the building to be opened. Looters and vandals will be executed without trial.

I stared at the paper. "What the hell? What's going on?" I stared at the paper, wondering if I should try knocking. Or maybe I could manage to pick the locks. But the part about looters being executed gave me pause. I wasn't really *that* anxious to find out whether they were bluffing.

"You want to try to break in?" Raven asked, glancing nervously at the door.

"Not so much, no." I glanced around. There was nobody hanging around on the sidewalk. I thought about heading next door to ask what was going on, but I was pretty sure that any neighbors would probably take one look at me and slam the door. "What the… Hold on. I'm calling Morgana. Or rather, Herne." I pulled out my phone and sat down on the porch steps. Raven sat beside me. I dialed Herne and two rings later, he answered.

"Ember, what's up? How's it going?"

"I got the bow, and a surprise to boot, with it. But dude… I'm sitting here on the steps of my grandmother's house—the porch steps. There's a notice plastered across the door warning that the house is sealed until an investigation can be done, and that looters and vandals will be executed without trial. Do you know what's going on?

Can you call Névé for me and see what's happening? I'd go ask at the neighbors, but I'm not sure that would do any good, considering the circumstances."

Herne paused, then said, "I'm on it. Stay there, and I'll call you back as soon as I can." He hung up.

I turned to Raven. "He's calling Névé."

"Good." She paused, then asked, "How well do you know Kipa?"

"Eh, somewhat. I don't dare get too chummy with him or Herne would go ballistic. You do know about their past, right? That Kipa stole Herne's fiancée many years back?"

She blinked, then sighed. "Yeah, I thought it was something like that. I was wondering, though…I told you the neighbors moved out, right?"

"Yes, and good riddance to human trash."

Raven's neighbors had been part of the Human Liberation Army, a hate-based group. They had moved abruptly a couple weeks back, and Raven was gearing up to throw a celebratory dinner party because of it.

"It turned out that Kipa bought them out. He offered them enough money so that they couldn't refuse, and then offered them more if they would move that day. They took the cash and ran. Now, Meadow and Trefoil live there."

"Who are Meadow and Trefoil?"

"Irish brother and sister. They're part of LOCK. Apparently they're demon hunters."

I stood as I saw a woman walking down the street, holding onto a leash. On the other end of the leash was a gorgeous Bengal tiger and it paused in front of the house, staring at us. I stared at the tiger, then at the woman, who was watching us, open mouthed. A moment later, she shook her head and headed out again.

"Cripes, what the fuck?" Raven asked. "You don't walk a tiger on a leash—that's absolutely insulting."

"Some of the Fae are full of themselves. Not all of them. I may have a lot of disdain for my own people, but there are some very good, very caring members of the Fae community. But good gods, keeping a tiger as a pet? That's just wrong."

As though she heard us, the woman paused by the end of the lot and turned back, returning to the sidewalk and heading up the walk toward us.

"Oh shit, she's gonna feed us to the beast," Raven whispered, standing as the woman drew near.

"I heard what you said about me. I thought maybe you'd like to know a little more about me, and my tiger here." She was glaring at us, looking like she was about ready to jump down our throats.

"Um…sure. What would you like to tell us?" I wasn't one to pretend I hadn't said something, or to try to get out of it when I had insulted them, but I couldn't help but wonder just what she'd have to say about her tiger and why it was okay for her to own one as a pet.

"This tiger's my son. He's a tiger shifter by nature, and he's been trapped in this form for the past ten years." She spat out the words as though by rote. "He was cursed by a witch on a trip to Annwn ten years ago and we've never found anybody to break the hex. So, I walk him because he needs exercise. And I take care of him because he's so soft hearted he'd never survive out in the wild. And yes, damn it, I own a tiger—because he's my *son* and I won't just cast him out in the wild to die. So you want to say anything else about how irresponsible I am? Come on. I'm right here. Take your best shot."

I groaned, sinking back onto the step. I felt like a first-class heel. "I am so sorry. I just assumed..." I paused, realizing what I was saying. I had just assumed she was an asshole like a lot of people assumed things about me.

"Yes, you *just assumed*." She paused, then hung her head. "You *assumed* that I was a careless, rich idiot. Like *I* would have assumed that you were less than nothing a decade ago, because you're a tralaeth. But I've learned a lot about assumptions over the years. I hope you will, too. And I hope you won't assume that everybody in this city will look at you and smirk." She turned to go.

"Wait," Raven called out before I could. "What's your name?"

The woman turned around. "Honesty. My name's Honesty, daughter of Verebas. I doubt you know who that is, but my mother's name carries a lot of weight in this city. Mine no longer does."

I scooted over on the steps, motioning for Raven to make room. "Would you like to sit down? It's not raining, at least." I was grateful for that much. If we had to wait on the steps, at least we weren't getting soaked.

"What are you doing here?" Honesty glanced up at the house, frowning. "Nobody's supposed to bother a crime scene."

I blinked. "Crime scene?"

"Yes, didn't you hear? The woman who lived here was murdered last night."

Once again, I felt like I had been slugged. Just then, my phone rang. It was Herne. "Can you excuse me for a moment? I have to take this." I walked down into the yard, a few yards away from Raven and Honesty. They were chatting, Raven keeping her talking so that I could have privacy.

"Herne? I just found out something—"

"Your grandmother was murdered, Ember. I'm sorry to have to tell you over the phone, but Névé didn't have the time to call you this morning and warn you off."

"I know," I broke in. "I just found out. But that's all I know. What happened? What about the crown?" I knew that sounded callous but the facts were that the visit probably wouldn't have gone well at all.

"Nobody knows who's to blame. Névé said that if they find the crown in her effects, they'll make sure you get it. But it looks as though someone broke into the house, overpowered two of the servants—they were killed, too— and then stabbed your grandmother. She died instantly, the medical examiners told Névé. There's no way she could have remained alive with…the savagery of those wounds," Herne finished slowly. "Again, I'm sorry."

"No, that's all right," I said, feeling hoarse. "We'll leave, then. I don't want to attract any more undue attention. When I get back to the office, I'd like to speak to Névé and find out everything I can. I'll call you when I get home." I turned to Raven and Honesty, who were having what looked like an intense conversation.

"I think we'd better leave," I told Raven. "She's right. My grandmother was murdered, along with two of her servants."

Raven eyed me carefully. "Are you all right?"

"*Grandmother*?" Honesty asked, staring at me like I was the one walking a tiger. "Lady *Tealique* was your grandmother?"

I shrugged, staring up at the silent house. "Doesn't matter. We never met. She helped kill my mother and father. I just... I had some unfinished business with her."

Honesty stood, giving me a nervous look. "Unfinished business of what kind?" She was edging her way down the steps and I realized how that could sound.

"I didn't kill her. Don't worry yourself over that. But...there have been times I prayed for her death. I'll admit that freely. No, I had something I needed to ask her. But, you know, I doubt she would have answered." I turned to Raven. "Let's go. It's going to start raining again, and I want to get the hell out of here and go home."

Raven nodded, silently crossing to stand beside me.

Honesty paused. She twisted her lip, as though she wanted to say something, then finally summoned up what I imagined was a buttload of courage, considering the situation.

"I'm sorry about your parents. I'm sorry about your grandmother. She was a decent neighbor, though she seldom had anything to say to anyone. She kept to herself a great deal."

I held her gaze for a moment. "Do you mind giving me your phone number? I may have some questions, later on, about her. If you..." I paused. "Never mind, I have no right to ask and you don't owe me anything."

"That's not a problem," Honesty said, pulling out a card from her pocket. "Here's my business card. My number's on the back. Feel free to call me. Nice to meet you, and you, too, Raven." She gave us a half wave and, taking up the leash on the tiger—her son—again, she headed down the sidewalk and out onto the street.

I turned to Raven. "I'm not at all sure what to think," I said. "This has been one of the oddest days of my life."

"I can imagine," Raven said. "Let's hail a cab and get the fuck out of this town. It gives me the creeps." She looped her arm through my elbow and we walked away from the house. We ended up walking half a mile before a taxi would stop for us, and we kept silent the entire way back to the gates of Navane. When we reached my car, Raven took my keys from me as I pulled them out.

"You've had enough shocks for today. I'll drive. I still think we should stop somewhere and get a drink and eat dinner." She motioned for me to get in the passenger seat.

I slid in and fastened my seat belt. "I don't feel up to going out to a restaurant, but Angel and I have a good selection of wine at home. So if you want to come over, you can crash in the guest room and we can get shit-faced drunk."

"Let me call Kipa and ask him if he can feed Raj," she said. A moment later she was talking to the Lord of the Wolves. "Babe, can you feed Raj for me? I'm staying at Ember's tonight. She's had a bit of a shock today and I— never mind what. I'll tell you later. We're going to drink wine and watch stupid TV and basically get shit-faced... Right... Do *not* give him more than two cans. He'll get fat if you keep spoiling him—oh, all right. Whatever." She paused, then snorted. "Yeah, I can guess just *how* you'll be thinking of me." She hung up and started the car.

"We're good to go. Let's go to your house and drink and watch TV and eat pizza and cookies, and forget about what an incredibly weird day this has been." And with that, Raven eased my car out onto the road and we headed back to Seattle.

CHAPTER SEVEN

*T*he next morning, I could barely pry my eyes open. I groaned, trying to sit up, and realized that I was sprawled on the floor in the living room, still in my clothes. But I wasn't the only one. Raven was snoring, pretzeled in the overstuffed armchair, and Angel was stretched out on the sofa, a thin line of spittle trickling down her chin. There was a smell of stale...*something*...in the air. It smelled like stale booze, I thought. As I rolled up to a sitting position, I squinted as a beam of light splashed through the window, striking me. The morning had broken with clear sky and the sunlight instantly gave me a headache.

Grunting, I managed to push myself up to where I was propped against the side of the sofa. Mr. Rumblebutt came meandering into the living room and he paused, staring at me with a scathing look as he let out an earsplitting meow.

I glanced at the clock. It was eleven A.M., well past his breakfast time. At that moment, my phone rang. It was on the coffee table. I crawled over to it, surprised that neither Angel nor Raven had woken up yet. As I slid the phone off the table, glancing at the caller ID, I saw that it was Herne and everything came flooding back to me.

Crap! It was Monday, and Angel and I were late for work. I quickly brought the phone to my ear.

"Hello?" My throat felt like I had chewed on gravel all evening, and my voice reflected it.

"Where the hell are you and Angel? I was just about ready to come looking for you." Herne sounded pissed.

"I'm sitting on my living room floor. Angel and Raven and I apparently decided to have a party last night. I just woke up, and they're still asleep." The room started to spin, and I closed my eyes and leaned my head back. I wanted nothing more than to sleep it off.

"Morgana will be here at one P.M. She expects to see you here. Therefore, I expect you here by twelve-thirty. I don't care if you have to take a cab here. Do you understand? No excuses." He paused, then said, "I love you. Now, get your ass down here."

As he hung up, I tossed my phone back on the table, missing it. It landed on the floor. As I leaned forward to pick it up, my head swam again. I managed to stagger to my feet, and leaned over Angel, shaking her shoulder.

"Hey, we're late for work and Herne just called. He's pissed out of his mind. Wake up."

Her eyes fluttered open, and she groaned as well. "What do you want? Let me sleep."

"No can do. Herne is waiting for us, and we're three hours late for work as it is. Morgana is going to be there by one, and we have to be there, too."

Angel sat up like she'd been shot. "Oh fuck. I can't believe we did that."

She pointed to the coffee table, and I followed her finger. There, sitting on the end of it, were four empty champagne bottles. But it wasn't just any ordinary champagne. No, it was Mountain Kingdom champagne, and we had bought it from Ginty's waystation bar. It was made by the dwarves, and they had constitutions like a rock.

"No wonder we're so plastered. I'm going to make myself a quint shot mocha, and then I'll take a quick shower. I suppose we should eat something." I paused, expecting the thought of food to make me feel sick. But it didn't. My head was spinning and I felt like I had sand for brains, but my stomach felt relatively okay. It must be the brand of champagne, I thought.

"I'm going to stumble upstairs for a shower. Can you put on the teakettle for me? Actually, never mind. Make me a double shot mocha if you would. I don't think tea's going to do the trick this morning." Angel slowly made her way toward the hall. "You might want to try and wake Raven up as well."

I hurried into the kitchen, every step jarring my brains, and turned on the espresso machine. Dropping four slices of bread in the toaster, I made my way back to the living room.

"Raven, hey Raven?" I said, shaking her arm. "Wake up. It's time to go home, Raven. Come on."

Raven muttered, then sprang up, her eyes wide.

"What?" She looked around, then shook her head. "Oh, we did it, didn't we?"

I nodded. "Apparently we knocked back four bottles of dwarven champagne. I think that was about two bottles too many. Angel and I have to get ready to go into work. We're three hours late and Herne is having a fit. I'm about to make mocha all around. Do you want some, and how many shots?"

Raven nodded. "I'll take a quint shot. And do you have anything to soak up the bubbles that are still rolling around in my stomach? Bread would be good."

"I'm making toast for all of us. Come on in the kitchen when you're ready. Angel's taking a shower, and you can freshen up in the hall bath if you'd like. I'll take my shower after she's done." I headed back to the kitchen where the espresso machine was ready, and the first round of toast was done.

As I spread butter on the toast and bit into one of the slices, I threw four more slices in the toaster and began to pull Raven's and my shots of espresso. Ten minutes later, I had fed Mr. Rumblebutt, and Raven and I were sitting at the kitchen table, mochas and toast in hand, while Angel's mocha was awaiting her return.

"Well, we know how to party," Raven said with a laugh.

"I'm afraid to see what would happen if we decided to *really* cut loose," I said with a grin.

"We already did that and my walls had the ectoplasmic stains to prove it," Raven said, shaking her head.

My headache was beginning to lift thanks to the caffeine, and the toast was settling the shockwaves that were still running through my system. "Do you want anything else to eat?"

"Eggs would be good, if you have any. Why don't you take your mocha and go up and shower, and I'll make us some eggs and bacon. I'm a competent cook."

Raven was more than a competent cook. While she

wasn't as good as Angel, she had her own mad skills in the kitchen, much better than my own.

"Thanks. I think I'll take you up on that." I picked up my cold cup—iced mocha seemed a better choice than hot this morning—and headed up the stairs, meeting Angel as I turned on the landing.

"Raven is making eggs and bacon for breakfast. Your mocha's on the table. I'm going to go take my shower now."

Angel looked almost human, although her eyes were still bloodshot and she looked like she hadn't had a good night sleep in a week.

"Thanks. I'll meet you downstairs. What time is it?"

"Eleven-thirty. We have time for breakfast and then we can leave and get down to the agency before Morgana gets there. I warn you, though, Herne sounded like he was in a snit about us being late. He's probably mad that we didn't call. I think he was worried."

By the time I was clean, dressed, and ready, Raven had called an LUD, and Angel and I were both more coherent, and a lot more grounded. Carrying the bow that I had got from my great-uncle, I slung my purse over my shoulder and grabbed my keys. We said good-bye to Raven as she waited for her ride, and Angel and I headed off to work.

LUCKILY, TRAFFIC WAS LIGHT AND WE ARRIVED AT THE office at quarter after twelve. Talia was sitting at the desk, answering phones for Angel. She looked up as the elevator doors opened, a grin on her face. She stood, taking Angel's key from her desk and going over and locking the elevator behind us.

"Break room. *Now.* Boy, are you two in trouble," she said with a snort.

"Yeah, I got that feeling from Herne's tone. I can't believe we did that." I straightened my shoulders, and glanced at Angel. "Are you ready to face the music?"

"About as ready as I'll ever be. Let's go."

With Talia in the lead, we headed back to the break room. Herne, Yutani, and Viktor were already gathered around the table, eating lunch. It looked like someone had ordered chef's salads, and the men didn't look too happy. I glanced at Talia questioningly.

"I thought it be a good idea to get some vegetables into these guys. I didn't know if you'd be hungry or not, so there are a couple salads in the fridge if you want them." She carried her salad over to the table and sat down.

I decided I didn't feel like playing rabbit today, so I just stood behind my chair, waiting until Herne looked up at me.

"We're really sorry. I have no excuse except it was a hard day yesterday, and we decided to kick off steam last night. Unfortunately, we chose dwarven champagne to do it with."

Viktor snickered. "How many bottles?"

I glanced at him. "Four. Mountain Kingdom. I had *no* idea it was so strong."

Herne's steely gaze slowly melted, and he burst out in a guffaw of laughter. "The three of you polished off *four* bottles of Mountain Kingdom champagne? No wonder you didn't wake up this morning."

"I woke up on the floor of the living room, Angel was

passed out on the sofa, and Raven was in a chair. Believe me, it wasn't pretty. After we left Navane, I was pretty shaken by the news about my grandmother." I slid into the chair as Angel slid into hers. "Needless to say, I didn't manage to get the crown. And with the notice that anybody breaking into the house would be executed if caught, I didn't like the odds. But I *did* get the bow, and I had a very interesting talk with Sharne." I leaned back in my chair. "I don't think I'd mind talking to him again, to be honest."

"What was he like?" Herne asked, stretching his legs out under the table, his hands clasped on his stomach.

"Apologetic. *Nothing* like Farthing, except in looks. To be truthful, I was kind of shocked. Not only did he willingly give me the bow, he told me a bit of its history. At least what he knew of it." I set the bow gently on the table, feeling incredibly possessive of it. "Something happened when I held Serafina. That's the bow's name." It was practically humming in my hands, and I mused about what it would be like to shoot it, to aim it and test it out.

Viktor whistled. "She's a beauty, all right. How old is the bow?"

"I don't know, and neither did Sharne. He thought it was about a thousand years old. My great-great-grandmother found it somewhere. I'd like to know more about its history, if possible." A sudden premonition swept over me and I glanced at Herne. "What do *you* know about this bow?"

He leaned forward, smiling as he ran a finger down the smooth wood cross-piece, and gently plucked one of the strings. "I see she's still in excellent condition."

"What do you mean, *still?*" I asked.

Herne picked up the bow, holding it in his hands as he turned it around, looking at it from all angles. "I haven't seen her in about a thousand years. I made this bow, Ember. I made it and then promptly lost it in the forest where your great-great-grandmother found it. I was watching from high in one of the trees overhead when she came along."

"You made it? What...*how*...?" A sudden delight sprang over me. Serafina was Herne's bow—and it had been passed down to *me*.

"I had set the bow down to take a leak behind a bush. I heard someone coming, and I didn't feel like being seen, so I scrambled up one of the tall oaks. It was then that I remembered I had left my bow down on the ground, but it was too late. I watched through the leaves as your great-great-grandmother came along. She found the bow. I could have taken it from her, but she seemed so pleased, and I had other bows at home. I decided to just forget about it. I was in a hurry, anyway.

"But I overlooked how powerful the bow was. Your grandmother used Serafina a number of ways that I regret. The bow will need a thorough cleansing before you start practicing with it."

That, I hadn't expected to hear. "But it belongs to *you*."

"No, I left it behind long ago. Serafina seems to like your family. I can feel her purring toward you right now. She has a definite personality, and the minute you claimed her, she chose you as her new owner. She's all yours. Take good care of her for me. My mother will help you cleanse the bow of any energy that shouldn't be there."

He handed me back the bow, and I carefully took her in my hands, cradling her. She fit my grip perfectly. It was as though Serafina had been made specifically for me. I could feel a quiet pulsing from the bow, through the wood, almost like a heartbeat.

Hello, I thought toward the bow, not expecting anything to happen in return. But it was worth a shot.

And then, slowly, a woman's voice answered. *Hello. What would you like me to do?*

I blinked, quickly setting her back on the table. "She spoke to me again. She asked me what I want her to do." I glanced up at Herne. "Is there a spirit trapped in the bow, or is that just the spirit *of* the bow?"

"You're talking to the spirit of the bow. When I was making her, I harvested the wood from a magical forest known as Y'Bain. There's more magic in one leaf of that forest than there is in the entire Olympic National Forest over on the peninsula. And there's a lot of magic in the Olympics."

Angel looked enchanted. "Is there a chance we'll ever get to see the forest? I assume it's in Annwn."

Herne gave her a long look. "If you'd like to see Y'Bain, we can probably make that happen. I hope you like unicorns. And will-o'-the-wisps. The forest is filled with creatures, many of them deadly." He broke out into a wide grin at that point.

Angel's eyes widened. "You really have unicorns over there? Or are you pulling my leg?"

"You have unicorns over *here*. You just haven't seen them yet. But trust me, unicorns are run-of-the-mill compared to some of the creatures found in Y'Bain. I'm serious. If you want to see the forest, at some point we'll show it to you, although I wouldn't be able to enter. The gods aren't welcome within the forest proper." He looked delighted that she had asked.

"She's not going to see unicorns if I don't get to see unicorns. You have to take both of us," I interjected.

Yutani had been finishing his salad, and now he set down his fork. "To be honest, it sounds like a nice trip. Especially with all the crap that's been happening here." He pushed his dish away. "I'll go get the laptop. I assume you're going to want an update." He stood, carrying his dish over to the sink where he rinsed it off, and then stacked it on the side. Then he disappeared out the door.

I glanced at the clock. It was almost one and Morgana was due soon. In fact, Yutani had no sooner exited than Morgana came in. Today she was wearing a flowing indigo gown, and her hair was caught back in massive braids and curls, woven through with seashells and pearls. She was in official dress, I thought.

"Mother," Herne said, hurrying over to greet her. She took his hands and kissed him on the cheek.

" Herne, it's good to see you." Morgana glanced around, nodding to each of us. "Ember, Angel, Talia, and Viktor—you as well." She spied the bow on the table as she sat down beside me. "I see you actually managed to find the bow? Wonderful." She reached for it, picking it up and running her hand over the wood. "I remember when you made this, Herne. It's good to have it back where we can keep an eye on it."

"Serafina chose Ember, Mother. I don't think we're going to have any problems along those lines." Herne beamed. He sounded both proud and relieved.

"Good." Morgana placed the bow back on the table.

"Ember, you need to begin practicing with this right away."

"You'll need to cleanse it first for her, Mother," Herne said. "It's still carrying residue energy from her father's family. And you *know* what her great-great-grandmother was like."

"Of course. And yes, it's carrying trace signatures of their energy. I'll cleanse it and return it later today. So, have you any news for us about the Tuathan Brotherhood?"

Yutani returned at that moment, Nalcops's laptop in hand. He sat down, setting the laptop on the table. "Actually, I think I do. I found a cluster of hidden files. I'm trying to retrieve them. I can't tell you exactly what they are yet, but I hope to be able to by tomorrow. I'm getting close, but I want to ensure that I don't trigger any hidden viruses or trojans that will wipe them out. As we talked about earlier, it's common for a lot of computer geeks trying to keep their work secret to encrypt files with self-destruct methods."

"I see. Well, be cautious, but be as quick as you can. I don't have to tell you how vital the information could be." Morgana gazed into his eyes for a moment, then leaned across the table, her hand outstretched to him. "Take my hand, young coyote."

Yutani placed his fingers in hers, looking worried. "Why? What's wrong?"

Morgana closed her eyes, holding his hand lightly. Then she dropped his hand, sitting back. "Your father comes and goes on his own time, but you need to have a talk with him. His energy is strong within you, and just carrying the energy can cause havoc if you don't know how to handle it. Ever since you discovered that he was your father, his blood has been rising within you. You have a great deal of potential, Yutani, and I'd hate to see you lash out, or go off half-cocked. Because, the truth is, you have a very quick temper." There was a warning note in her voice that was hard to ignore, and Yutani lowered his gaze to the table, averting his eyes.

"It's not my fault he won't come when I call."

"No, it isn't. And neither is it your fault that he's your father. He walks between worlds as easily as you walk down the sidewalk. It's the nature of the Great Coyote to do so, but he owes you the knowledge of how to use the powers his blood bestows. I'll ask Cernunnos to go in search of him, because you need direction, and he is the only one who can give it to you." Morgana sounded serious.

Yutani straightened, and the sullen look banished from his face. "Thank you, Lady. I am so used to being blamed for the things that occur when I'm around, when I no more meant for them to happen than I'd mean for an earthquake to happen. I get used to being on the defense. It's not often that people understand that I walk in chaos, but not through choice."

"People can be cruel, and fear causes many a misunderstanding. Cernunnos will have a talk with the Great Coyote, and strongly suggest that he do his duty by you." Morgana turned to me. "I'll bring the bow back later this afternoon. Once I do, begin practicing with it. You need to learn how she works, especially since Serafina has chosen you for her owner."

At that moment, my phone rang. I pulled it out and glanced at the caller ID. It was Joffrey, a neighbor of ours.

We didn't know him very well, but he was home all day and he loved animals.

"Hold on a second, I'd better answer this." I raised the phone to my ear. "Hello? This is Ember."

"Ember, you have to come home right away. The fire department is here. Your house is on fire. The fire department's here, and so are the police."

I jumped up. "Mr. Rumblebutt is inside! Tell them to rescue my cat!"

"I already did. I think they got him out, but I'm not entirely sure. Come home now, though."

I slammed the phone in my pocket, turning to Angel. "We have to go home, *now*! The house is on fire."

And with that, the meeting was over as Angel and I raced toward my car. The others followed, promising to meet us there. All the way home, all I could think about was Mr. Rumblebutt, and if he was safe.

CHAPTER EIGHT

$\mathcal{B}$y the time Angel and I arrived home, the firemen had managed to put out the fire. I didn't even look at the damage until I had spotted the fireman who was holding a makeshift cat carrier, with Mr. R. inside. The cat looked decidedly grumpy, but unharmed.

"Oh, Mr. Rumblebutt, thank gods you're safe." I crouched by the box, crying as I made sure for myself that he was okay. I anxiously looked him over, but he seemed okay for the moment. There were no singe marks anywhere and he appeared to be breathing all right, though he looked terrified and was yowling up a storm.

"He's okay?" Angel asked.

"Yeah, but I still want to take him to the vet to make certain." When it came to Mr. Rumblebutt, I would rather spend extra money and reassure myself he was fine than find out later that I had overlooked something. He was the only family I really had, besides Angel. I put the cat carrier in my car, and then Angel and I walked over to the fire marshal.

"What happened? I can't imagine what set off the fire. How bad is it?" I gingerly turned to our house, dreading seeing the damage.

Most of it looked intact, but left of the door, at the corners of the north and west walls, was blackened, parts of the siding burned away.

"How about the inside?"

"You can thank your neighbor it's not worse. I'm pretty sure the structural stability is still intact, though I'll check it out, of course. But your neighbor's the real hero. He chased off the arsonist and called the fire department when he noticed something odd going on."

I gasped. "*Arsonist?* You mean somebody deliberately tried to burn down our house?" I glanced at Angel, who looked as shocked as I felt.

"Yes, and we found a can of gasoline near the wall. You didn't leave it there, did you?"

Angel shook her head. "We wouldn't have any reason to leave gasoline outside. In fact, I don't think we have any on hand at all. We live close enough to a service station to walk if we run out of gas." She glanced at me. "Who the hell would do this?"

I shrugged, thinking of all the people that we had crossed over the past months. "I don't know." I turned back to the fire marshal. "You said that our neighbor got a look at the arsonist?"

"Yes. He's agreed to look through the mug books. We haven't had a lot of fire-related crimes lately, so there's no pattern. Unless somebody's just starting up." He paused as a police officer approached. She was Fae, Light by the look of her, and she pulled out her pad and pen.

"You're the owners of the house?" She asked. "I'm Officer Downey. I'd like to ask you a few questions, if you don't mind."

I nodded. "I'm the owner. I'm Ember Kearney, and this is my roommate, Angel Jackson."

She gave me the once-over, and I could tell that she recognized I was tralaeth, but she didn't seem to react to it. Luckily, most of the police were trained to suppress their dislike of certain races or species.

"Both of you were at work? Where do you work, if I may ask?"

"Yes, we were. We work for the Wild Hunt Agency," I said, holding out my arm so she could see my tattoo. Right about then, I noticed Herne pulling up. He had everybody else in his Expedition. "There's my boss right now, Herne the Hunter. They can verify we were at work."

Downey's eyes lit up, and she stared at us for a moment, a new respect sweeping over her face. The fire marshal, who was standing nearby, took note as well.

"I was going to ask for a list of your potential enemies," Downey said, "but somehow I think that's going to be a long one. Is there anybody in particular with whom you've had altercations? Anybody been a problem lately?"

I glanced at Angel, feeling helpless. "There are so many people who are pissed at us. I can't think of any off the top of my head, though. Can you?"

Angel shook her head. "Not at the moment." She paused as Herne and the others walked over to our side.

"Is Mr. Rumblebutt safe?" was the first thing Herne asked, and that made me love him even more.

"He's all right. I want to take him to the vet, though, to make sure he isn't suffering any smoke inhalation. Apparently, someone tried to torch our house. My neighbor chased them away."

At that point, Joffrey hurried over. He had been talking to one of the firemen.

"What happened?" I asked.

The police officer motioned for him to join us. "If you could give us an account of what you saw, it would be very helpful."

"I was out walking my dog. Turvey always goes for a walk at this time of day. Anyway, we were walking past your place and I happened to glance toward your house. I saw a man pouring something on the wall. I recognize the shape as a gasoline can, and shouted at him. I grabbed at my phone to take a picture, and he must have seen me because he dropped the can and struck a match, setting the corner of your house on fire. Then he ran."

"You photographed him? That could help immensely," Officer Downey said.

"I did my best. It's a little blurry because I was trying to juggle Turvey's leash and my phone. But here's the picture." He handed the phone to the policewoman and she stared at it for a moment. Then she turned the screen to me.

"Do you recognize this man? He's a little fuzzy, but it's obvious that he's tall with dark hair and fairly trim."

I glanced at the screen and my blood chilled. There, trying to burn my house down, was Ray Fontaine.

"I know who that is. Blurry or not, I know who it is."

Angel let out a soft gasp. "What the hell? I know he's got baggage, but I never for the world thought he would try to burn down our house."

"You know him? What's his name? And why would he want to torch your house?" Downey asked.

"That's Ray Fontaine. We used to go out, a couple years ago. He stalked me for a while last year. He wasn't able to let go. He came down to my work, he called me incessantly. Finally, I realize that he was hooked on my glamour—I'm part Leannan Sidhe. He's human. I found a way to break the glamour, and I told him what happened because I was hoping he would understand. But he got angry all over again, worse than when I broke up with him. We've had a few altercations over the past few months. But I haven't heard from him for a while, and I thought maybe he just decided to move on."

"Apparently not," the officer said. "What's his address?"

"I'm not sure where he's living right now, but he owns a business called A Touch Of Honey in Redmond. It's a honey shop and bakery." I shivered. Ray hadn't finished the job. I couldn't help but wonder if he was still out there, just waiting for another chance.

"We'll try to get prints off of the gasoline can. But it looks like he might have been wearing gloves. Hopefully, we'll find a way to make the charges stick. Meanwhile, you might want to get a home security system." She gave me a long look. "I can tell what you're thinking," she added. "Don't worry. Just because he was inadvertently glamoured by you, it doesn't excuse arson. Especially since you took the steps to break the glamour."

I let out a sigh of relief. I had been thinking *precisely*

that, and was surprised she had been able to pick up on it. "Thanks. What do I do now?"

"When the fire marshal finishes his investigation, I suggest you get a copy of his report, a copy of our report, and then call your insurance company. Take pictures of all the damage." Downey put away her pad and pen. "Meanwhile, I'll put out an APB for Fontaine, and if he comes back here, I want you to be careful. If he's unstable enough to try to commit arson, he's unstable enough to try to commit murder. At least, in my opinion."

She headed over to talk to the fire marshal and I turned to the others. To my surprise, Herne and his Expedition were nowhere to be seen. I walked over to Talia.

"Where did Herne go?" I had my suspicions, but I didn't want to voice them yet. If he had heard about Ray, I knew where he had gone.

She shrugged. "I don't know. He looked furious, and he told me that he'd be back in a while. He said for us to stick around and help you and Angel out. Then he took off like a bat out of hell."

"Oh, hell." I turned around, frantic, trying to decide what to do. I had no clue where he was, nor did I know where Ray was. I didn't want to set the police on Herne, either. We had a precarious-enough balance with local law enforcement as it was. I motioned to Angel, pulling her aside.

"What is it?"

"I think Herne went after Ray. He heard what the policewoman said. I'm not sure what to do."

Angel glanced around, looking at the firefighters. They were getting ready to leave, while the fire marshal was inspecting the damaged corner of our house. Officer Downey had already left.

"I don't think there's much you *can* do. And you still need to take Mr. Rumblebutt to the vet."

She was right.

"Can you take him to the vet for me? They've got a permanent approval for both you and Ronnie if he needs to be treated. I'd like to stay here for a while, and talk to the fire marshal."

"Sure," she said, with a nod. "Do you want me to take your car or mine?"

"Yours, please. I want mine just in case something happens with Herne."

She transferred Mr. Rumblebutt to her car, which, thankfully, Ray had left alone. Then, giving me a wave, she took off down the road. Yutani and Viktor had been over talking to the fire marshal and now they came back to where I was standing.

"You're going to need a contractor, all right. But the fire marshal says that the fire didn't touch anything inside the house. You can live in it while you have it fixed. The fire is out, and the verdict is—of course—arson." Viktor motioned to Yutani. "Come on, let's take a look at the house."

Before I could tell them about Herne, the fire marshal began walking toward us and they took off to examine the damage.

"Ms. Kearney, the fire's out," the marshal said. "There's a lot of superficial damage, but nothing that looks like it intrinsically damaged the structure of your house. You'll need to contact your insurance company. Start a claim, and they'll ask you for official documents from my office and the police. I'll send them my report as soon as you request it. The house is livable, so you can stay here if you want to. I'd have it repaired as soon as possible, though. Keep a close watch out for the arsonist, since you know who it is." He gave me a sympathetic look. "I'm sorry this happened."

"You and me both," I said.

As soon as he was back in his truck and driving away, I turned to the Talia. "Let's go inside. I need to call Herne. I didn't want to while he was still here."

The scent of smoke hung heavy in the air. I found one of the fans that I kept around for air circulation, and pointed it toward the living room window, opening the window so that I could blow the fumes out.

Talia flipped on my espresso machine. "I assume you want some caffeine?"

I nodded. "I also want sugar. And Ray Fontaine's head on a plate." The shock had worn off and now I was angry. I hoped Herne would find Ray. It would put an end to a whole lot of trouble, and save the taxpayers the cost of a trial. I paused, then asked her, "What do you think I should do about Herne?"

"Leave him alone on this. I've known Herne for centuries. He protects his own, and no matter how independent you might like to think you are, as long as you're dating Herne, he considers you his woman. Not in that icky, possessive way, but you're part of his tribe, part of his pack. He's King Stag of the forest and you're his consort. In the world of Annwn and the world of the gods, that gives him certain rights and as long as you choose to be part of his life, you have to accept that."

"He'll kill Ray. I know it." I stared at the mug she slid in front of me. It was full of frothed milk, chocolate, and caffeine. "It's not like I haven't wanted to kill him myself at times, but I don't know if I could have done it, unless he was trying to kill me."

"If your neighbor hadn't come along, Mr. Rumblebutt would be dead and your house would be gone. Angel's car was out front. Ray had no way of knowing whether the house was empty, unless he watched you both leave this morning. I don't think he *cared* whether you or Angel were inside. Think about it. What better way to get back at you than to kill the ones you love? It's an old tactic used by sadists throughout history."

Slowly, I nodded. I drew the cup toward me and took a long drink. "When I think about it like that, you're right." I pulled out my phone, pausing, thinking of everything that had happened. Then I forced myself to put it back in my pocket. "Sometimes the world can be a hard place, can't it?"

"Oh, Ember. If you only knew *how hard*. This is a rough lesson. And yes, I know your parents were murdered, and I know you found them, and I know your relatives were the ones to blame. But there have been far worse atrocities throughout time, and far more dangerous adversaries."

"I can't argue with you there. Although it's all relative. Some people would be broken forever if they had to go through what I did. To others, finding their parents murdered would hurt, but be just a blip in the road." I paused as my phone rang. Pulling it out, I glanced at the caller ID. It was Angel. "Hey, how's Mr. Rumblebutt?"

"He's fine. They did a thorough checkup and there's nothing wrong. He was due for his shots and regular exam so I went ahead and let them take care of everything."

"Thanks. Are you on the way home?"

"Yeah. Should I stop and pick up something to eat?"

I glanced at the clock. It was well past lunchtime, going on two o'clock. Any fog I might still have from the hangover had vanished along with my fear and worry.

"Yeah. Why don't you stop and pick up a couple pizzas, if you think Mr. Rumblebutt can handle the wait in the car. Actually, never mind. I'll order them from here. Just come home. I'm uneasy enough as it is." I put in a call to our favorite pizza joint and ordered three extra large pizzas with sausage, pepperoni, extra cheese, and pineapple on them.

Yutani and Viktor returned to the kitchen at that point.

"I checked out all your cables and anything that might have been near the fire. Everything looks fine. Have you called your insurance company yet?" Yutani asked.

I shook my head. "No. I've just been trying to wrap my head around this whole mess. I don't know if you heard, but Ray did it. He tried to burn down our house."

A scowl crossed Yutani's face. "Maybe it's time for a hunting party."

I glanced at him, then at Viktor. "I'm pretty sure Herne already is taking care of that."

"So that's where he went," Viktor said. "I wondered what he was so wrapped up about. Well, you can't say Ray doesn't deserve it. I wouldn't want to be in his shoes, though."

"We've caught a lot of criminals in our time, and

stopped a lot of altercations, but I don't think any of us have ever had our houses targeted," Yutani said.

"This is personal, though," Talia said. "Ray's had it out for Ember for a long time. We're just lucky that your neighbor was passing by."

"That reminds me, I owe Joffrey a huge thank-you. I know he's fond of his flower garden. Maybe I'll buy him a gift certificate to one of the local nurseries so he can invest in spring flowers this year."

"That would be a nice touch," Talia said. She turned to Viktor and Yutani. "Either of you want some caffeine? The pizza is on the way. I'm assuming we're not going back to the office today."

"I think you can safely make that assumption. Especially if Herne is out hunting down Ray," Yutani said. "I could go for a triple-shot mocha."

"Double-shot latte for me," Viktor said.

At that point, Angel came through the door, cat carrier in hand. Inside, Mr. Rumblebutt looked properly annoyed. She sat him down on the counter, looking around.

"Should I open the door, or do we need to secure anything before we let him out?"

Viktor shook his head. "Yutani and I took a look around. There aren't any holes in the walls that he could get out through. I'd say it's safe to let him out, if Ember feels okay about it."

I had already opened the carrier by then, pulling Mr. Rumblebutt out and holding him in my arms. He clung to me, looking both indignant and frightened. As I petted him, I finally managed to coax a purr out of him, and I gave him a long snuggle, kissing his head.

I was so incredibly grateful that Joffrey had come along at the point he did. The thought of losing my cat in a fire—or any other way—made me want to cry. How could Ray have been so callous? And Angel could have been home, for all he knew. Her car was in the driveway and he knew that it belonged to her. A well of anger rose up. I wasn't sure what I hoped Herne would do to him, but I wanted Ray to never forget what it meant to cross us.

The doorbell rang, and Angel went to get it. It was the pizzas. By the time she returned I had put Mr. Rumble-butt on the floor and he scurried over to the cat food dish, drowning his anxiety in a pile of kibble. Talia found the paper plates as Angel carried the pizzas over to the table and opened the boxes. While everyone helped themselves, I finally moved to the side and pulled out my phone, calling Herne.

"How are things going?" he asked.

"Mr. Rumblebutt's home and safe. I'm going to call the insurance company in a few minutes." I paused, trying to figure out how to ask what I wanted to know. After a moment, I said, "Where are you?"

"About ready to head through the portal to Annwn. I'm over at Quest Rialto's house."

I blinked. Quest Rialto was one of the portal keepers, and she lived on the Eastside. "Why are you headed to Annwn?"

"Because I'm taking Ray Fontaine to visit Cernunnos. You'll never have to worry about him again."

My heart thudded. "You caught him? And he's still alive?"

"Love, I know you would have mixed feelings if I did

what I *wanted* to do, which was tear his throat open. So I'm taking him to Cernunnos, and Cernunnos will mete out punishment. After all, Ray attacked one of the members of the Wild Hunt, as well as attacking my girlfriend. I forced Ray to write a letter deeding his shop to his next of kin. I'll tell the police exactly what I told you. That they can call off the hunt for him because he's been punished by *divine agency*."

"Divine agency" was the term given to any divinity-appointed agency that had official standing with the government. It allowed us to punish some criminals ourselves, rather than through the courts.

I caught my breath, dizzy with relief. Regardless of how much I hated Ray, I still wasn't sure whether I wanted him dead. This was better. *Much better*. Cernunnos would punish him, but he would keep him alive. And I would never have to worry about Ray again. That much I knew.

"Thank you," I said. "You don't know how relieved that makes me. I love you so much. I hope you realize that. You…*understand* me. Do you know what I mean?"

"Yes, I know what you mean," Herne said. "And I think that you're truly beginning to understand who *I* am. That you accept my choice to hunt the dog down means the world to me. Is there anything you want me to tell Ray before Cernunnos punishes him?"

I thought for a moment. There was a lot that I wished that Ray would understand but I knew he wouldn't. And while I was crestfallen that things had come to this, he had sealed his own fate when he set this in motion. When he chose to try to burn down my house, he had forfeited any protection I might have acceded him.

"No. I'm done with him. Just so long as I never have to see him again, I'm good." There was a lot I wanted to ask. I wanted to ask if Cernunnos would kill Ray, or if he would cast him into his dungeon where a lot of Cernunnos's enemies whiled away the days. But I needed to walk away from it, to leave it all behind. Cernunnos would make sure that Ray never bothered me again, and that was all that mattered.

"I'll see you in a while. I take it everyone is still there?"

"Given you were their ride, yes. We're eating pizza now. I'll save some for you. Come over tonight, please?"

"I'll see you in a couple hours. Tell everyone to wait. I'll be back before quitting time anyway, so I'll be able to drive them back to the office. Ember, never doubt that I love you. Never doubt that I value your safety over my own."

And I knew right then that we had come to a turning point in our relationship. The promise ring on my finger felt very real now.

CHAPTER NINE

After Herne had returned and taken everyone back to the office, Angel and I slumped at the table.

"This has been one hell of a day," I said.

"The end of an era, when you think about it. The end of ever worrying about Ray again." Angel toyed with a piece of pizza crust that was still on her plate. "In a way, he's the last connection to your love life before Herne."

She was right. I'd had bad luck in love until meeting Herne. Two of my lovers died, and their deaths had been connected to me in one way or another. After I realized I was getting serious with Ray, I had called off the relationship, worried for his safety. And now, all of that was done and gone.

"It really does feel like we're living an entirely different life than we were a year ago. You were in a dead-end job, and I was freelancing."

Angel shrugged. "And I still had DJ with me. I miss

him, Ember. I know he's better off where he is, but I miss him."

DJ was Angel's little brother—actually her half-brother. When we had gone to work for the Wild Hunt, DJ had been put into foster care with a shifter family. Though it had originally been for his own safety, the move had turned out to be a good thing all the way around. Unlike Angel, DJ was half–wolf shifter. Living with Cooper's family meant that he was learning how to make his way as a shifter in the world.

DJ was a brilliant boy. He had inherited his father's blood, but thankfully, not his father's attitude. DeWayne didn't know for certain that DJ was his. He didn't even know whether Mama J. had borne a boy or a girl, and we intended to keep it that way. DeWayne was a lazy, money-grubbing leech who had up and run the moment Mama J. told him she was pregnant. He had never contacted her again. When Mama J. had died, Angel had taken over the care of her little brother.

Cooper and his family treated DJ as one of their own, and they took care of him. He was safely tucked away from being a target by any enemies we might have, and he was receiving opportunities that she never could have given him on her own.

"I know you miss him. You'll be able to visit him on spring break, though. That's not too far off—a month and a half. Has he texted you lately?"

Part of Angel's angst also came from the fact that the more DJ assimilated into his new life, the less frequently he contacted her. Oh, he still texted her every morning and every evening, but he didn't seem to need her as much.

"This morning as usual. And yeah, I'm visiting him on spring break. Cooper said the family's going on a camping trip, and I'm welcome to go along. So, as much as I don't like camping, I'm still tagging along so I can see my brother. His birthday's coming up next month. I'm not sure what to buy him, so I'm going to contact Cooper tonight. I don't know what DJ needs or even wants now. I know he's gotten into parkour, and Cooper's enrolled him into a karate program, but other than that..." She drifted off, looking forlorn.

"You *know* this is best for him," I said, taking her hand. "You know that DJ is better off with a shifter family. You can give him all the love in the world, but you *can't* teach him how to handle life as a shifter. And when puberty hits, you know you wouldn't be able to manage the changes. You know how wolf shifters get at that time."

I hated having to reality-check her, but sometimes, it helped to have a friend pointing out the obvious. Sometimes we *all* needed a reminder of the obvious.

She tossed the pizza crust back on her plate and pushed it away.

"I know. And I know he loves me, and I know we'll always be brother and sister. Just, sometimes, it isn't easy. Okay, I'm going to clean up the kitchen, and then I think I'll run over to Rafé's. Now that we know that Ray's been caught, we don't have to worry about him coming back. Did you call the insurance company yet?"

I shook my head. "I decided to save that for tomorrow. I really don't have much energy today, at least not for anything like that. What a mess. I guess tomorrow, we look for contractors to start getting a bid for repairing the house. We can't leave the damage for long."

"At least the fire didn't burn through the walls, and it didn't destroy anything vital. Have you thought about what to do to thank Joffrey?"

"Actually, yes I have." I began to clear the table. "What do you think about getting him a gift certificate to one of the local nurseries? You know how much he loves his gardens, and how he's always admiring the space we have. That way, come spring, he can go hog wild and buy all the plants he wants. You know he's on a fixed income."

Joffrey was disabled. While I wasn't sure what was wrong with him—I didn't want to ask unless he felt comfortable opening up about it—whatever the problem, it kept him homebound most of the time. He was in his mid-forties, and Turvey was his only companion as far as I could tell. The little terrier was a mop dog, cute and overly friendly. Joffrey had his groceries delivered, and we seldom saw him leave the neighborhood. He took a walk every day past our house and up the block, then cut across the street to Discovery Park. We lived opposite the mammoth park, which made it nice when we wanted to go out for a walk.

"That's a wonderful idea," Angel said. "I can drop by there on my way to Rafé's tonight. How much do we want to spend? A couple hundred?"

"Joffrey saved our house *and* Mr. Rumblebutt. Make it five hundred. I can add in the extra if you don't have it."

She smiled then. "Okay, I'll pick it up tonight and a card as well. We can give it to him tomorrow." Angel gathered up the paper plates and the pizza boxes, taking them out to the trash. I washed the table, and rinsed out the mugs. As I turned around, pressing against the counter,

Mr. Rumblebutt came winding around my ankles and I scooped him up into my arms.

"I need you to be safe, buddy. You and Angel are my best friends, and I need *both* of you. You hear me?" I nuzzled his fur, and he began to purr and knead against my chest, making biscuits for all he was worth. As Angel returned from taking out the trash, I let him down and he scampered off. I heard the jingle of one of his toys in the living room. I glanced at Angel, who was sorting through her purse.

"Today is just one more example of why DJ needs to be with Cooper. Mr. Rumblebutt could have been killed. If you had been here, *you* could have been killed. Unfortunately, anybody we love runs a certain risk of danger."

She looked up from sorting through her things. "You're right. I know. I just get lonely for him. But I'd rather have him safe in a place where I know he's being looked after than run the risk of having him with me. When he grows up, he can make the decision to move back here if he wants. All right, I'm ready to go. Are you sure you don't want me to stay until Herne gets back?"

I shook my head. "Ray's been captured. He's in Annwn now. The fire's out, the house is safe. Go ahead and enjoy yourself. Are you coming home before work tomorrow?"

"No, I'll probably stay the night. I'll see you at work in the morning. Call me if you need anything." She gave me a tight hug before she left. "Be safe, sister."

"You too. Love you, Ange." Nobody else used the nickname with her except for me. I waved as she headed out the door.

As I wandered into the living room, feeling slightly at loose ends, I caught sight of a crow outside the slider, sitting on the side patio. It was staring at me intently, and I reached out trying to connect with it. But before I could, a Steller's jay landed on the porch and screeched at the crow, and they both took to the air, screeching at each other with much flapping of wings. Feeling disconcerted, I made sure the door was locked, and then closed the blinds that covered the sliding glass doors. It had been one hell of a day, and I was grateful it was over, but I couldn't help but wonder what would happen next.

WHEN HERNE RETURNED, HE WAS CARRYING A BOUQUET OF roses, and a very large box of chocolates. He handed them to me, stroking my hair back from my face as he kissed me.

"I thought you could use something to cheer you up. I know yesterday and today have both been rough." He stripped off his jacket, hanging it on the back of the chair. As he stretched, the muscles rippled through his shirt, and the sight of him took my breath away. He was wearing black jeans, and a thin, V-neck sweater the color of new spring leaves. He had let his hair down, and it swept down his back, grazing his shoulder blades. It was getting longer, I thought, and it reminded me of a wheat field on a summer's morning. I set the candy and roses down and slid my arms around him.

"Kiss me. I need you." I searched his eyes, hungry for something I couldn't quite identify.

He wrapped his arms around me, his lips meeting mine, and I lost myself in the sensation of his warmth and his musky smell, and the feeling of him holding me tight and safe. He said nothing, but swept me up in his arms and carried me toward the stairs. I draped an arm around his neck, holding on as he carried me into my bedroom. He set me down on the bed and I laid back as he pressed against me, once again his lips meeting mine in an impassioned kiss.

I tugged his sweater out of his jeans, and he sat up, sliding it off and tossing it on the floor. I pulled off my shirt, adding it to the pile and then straddled his lap, my breasts pressing against his chest. He wrapped his arms around my waist and I met his lips with mine again, kissing deep, wanting more.

I was hungry for him, aching as I felt him press hard against his jeans. In a fever, I pushed him back against the bed, still kissing him. I lay against his length and he wrapped his arms around me, rolling me over to slide between my legs. He leaned down and took one of my nipples in his lips, worrying it, sucking hard—so hard it almost hurt. His eyes were glowing as he looked into my eyes. He straightened up, sitting back, his knees pressing against my lower legs.

"Take off your jeans," he said in a throaty voice. "I want you. I want to be inside you."

I caught my breath, scrambling to obey, pulling my legs out from beneath him as I swung over the bed and stood. I kicked off my shoes, then unbuckled my belt, and pushed my jeans and panties down to my ankles where I stepped out of them.

Herne watched me with hungry eyes. Then he, too, stood and unbuckled his belt, sliding it out from the loops in his jeans. He tossed it to the side. I dropped to my knees in front of him, and he gave me a sly smile as I reached up to unzip his pants.

As I lowered his jeans over his massive thighs, he sprang up, hard and waiting for my tongue. I gripped his shaft in my hand, barely able to close my fingers around it, and then licked my lips, bringing them toward the tip of his penis. He reached down, gently running his fingers through my hair as I formed an O with my mouth and then slid his cock between my lips. I ran my tongue along the ridges that veined his shaft. He moaned, dropping his head back as I worked him, feeling him pulse between my lips.

I sucked him hard and long, nibbling on him, gently catching the head with my teeth and ever so gently scraping his length. The drops of pre-cum were salty in my mouth, and I moaned, too full with him to say more.

He withdrew and leaned over. Placing his hands under my arms, he lifted me up.

Herne with the glittering eyes...Herne with the sensual mouth...

He firmly walked me backward, then gently pushed me down on the bed and motioned for me to spread my legs. As he knelt between them, he spread my lower lips with his fingers, circling me with his tongue, first slowly then quicker as I began to pant. He drove all thoughts away from me, leaving only sensation as he laved me with his tongue, and all the cares of the day fell away under his ministrations.

And then it felt as though we were in a field of tall grass, with the smells of apples and cinnamon around us, and I swore I could feel sunlight on my face as my desire quickened.

A moment later, a ripple hit me, spreading in concentric rings throughout my body, widening to pull me under the rising wave. As I climaxed, I let out a loud cry, and burst into tears, not knowing why I was crying.

Herne gave me a moment to center myself, then slid inside me, his girth filling me so full I wanted to cry out again. He took away every ache in my body as he drove himself inside me again and again, thrusting with a single-minded focus.

I wrapped my arms around his chest, pulling him to me, and then he turned over so I was astride him, on top, with him still inside me. I rode him hard, leaning down to press my lips against his chest. I bit him gently, nipping lightly, as I continued to ride him. He let out a loud groan, and I could tell he was near.

"Come for me," I whispered, staring into his eyes, my hands on his shoulders as I held him down. I swiveled my hips as his eyes flashed, little strokes of lightning forking through them.

"Come for me," I said again, quickening my pace. I felt myself building again, and the realization that I could bring a god to climax swept through me like a wave of power and I leaned my head back, laughing with wonder.

At that moment, Herne stiffened, grabbing hold of my waist as he cried out, bellowing like the King Stag he was. He came, and the sight of him coming brought me to orgasm once again. I arched my back, crying out, mingling my voice with his even as our bodies were joined.

As our cries echoed, then faded away, I caught my breath and slumped forward against his chest with him still inside of me. I had never felt so desirable, or loved as this moment.

He wrapped his arms around me, still inside me. Holding me tightly against him, we lay like that as the evening shadows deepened around us. Outside, the rain began to beat a tattoo against the window. But we were safe, inside and warm, and right then, that was all I could hope for.

CHAPTER TEN

The next morning, after we ate breakfast and showered, I fed Mr. Rumblebutt and we headed for the office. We drove separately, because Herne had plans for the evening.

We arrived early, thanks to Herne, so I called the insurance company about my house. I was surprised by how quickly it went. It only took me twenty minutes to open a claim, after waiting for fifteen minutes for them to get around to me. But then it was done, and the claim was open, and now I just had to get the reports from the fire marshal and Officer Downey. Relieved to have that task out of the way, I headed toward the reception room where Angel was just coming out of the elevator, Talia behind her.

"I called the insurance company," I told Angel. "If you could call Officer Downey and the fire marshal today and get the reports from them, I'd appreciate it." I gave her the claim information, so she could tell them where to send the reports.

She was about to answer when we heard a loud shout from back by the offices. As we hurried down the hall, Yutani came racing out of the office he shared with Talia.

"I think I've got it!" He held up Nalcops's laptop. "I think I found the files—and by 'found,' I mean I can gain access to them. There *was* a trap set on them, but I managed to circumnavigate it. Let's meet in the break room in about ten minutes to go over what I found." Without waiting for a response, he turned and headed back to his office.

Talia shook her head, grinning. "Well, score one for Yutani. Ember, tell the boss, please. I'll go start the coffee, and I'll let Viktor know."

I hurried over to Herne's office, knocking briefly before I opened the door. "Yutani's found a way to access the files on Nalcops's laptop. He wants us to meet him in the break room in about ten minutes."

"Really? Wonderful! Let's hope he finds something useful that will help us." Herne stood and tossed the file folder he'd been looking through back on his desk. "I'll be there in a moment."

I nodded, shutting the door behind me. When we were at work, we tried to keep as professional as possible, although that hadn't prevented several trysts in his office after the workday was over, or the occasional kiss. Luckily, nobody minded. And luckily, Herne ran the agency so it was his call.

By the time we were all gathered in the break room, Yutani had set up a projector so that he could project from the laptop onto the screen. That way he wouldn't have to keep passing the laptop around so we could see everything.

"I sent you all copies of these files, and I urge you to keep them in a protected place on your computer. While I keep our IT security system locked down, the Tuathan Brotherhood seems to be extremely savvy when it comes to tech, and I wouldn't put it past them to have a couple of black hat hackers on staff. I'll create a hidden, encrypted folder on your computers, and we'll lock them down with passwords."

I let out a slow whistle under my breath. "This must be pretty sensitive stuff."

Yutani flashed me a dark smile. "Let's just put it this way—I found the break we've been looking for. And the Tuathan Brotherhood sure as hell isn't going to want *anybody* knowing what I've found. This is *make-it or break-it* information, and we'll have to act fast because I'm not certain whether they have any tracking that would show I managed to infiltrate private files."

"Then let's get on with it," Herne said. "If we're on borrowed time, we don't have any to waste."

Yutani fiddled with his laptop and then we saw the picture of a folder come up on the screen. The printing on the front read *The Manifesto of Longlear.*

"What the hell is Longlear?" Viktor asked.

"I haven't had a chance to read the manifesto in its entirety. It's at least one hundred pages long and filled with a lot of incoherent ramblings, just like most terrorists' manifestos. However, what I have read has confirmed this is Nuanda's personal crusade. And I found out his background."

"Longlear," Herne said softly. "I know that name from somewhere. I think I heard it in Annwn."

"Most likely," Yutani said. "Longlear was a shield that

belonged to Lugh the Long Handed. I don't know how Nuanda got hold of it, but he owns it now. Apparently, Lugh is a distant ancestor of Nuanda." He turned Herne. "How much do you know about Lugh the Long Handed?"

"Well, from what little I've had to do with him, I don't exactly trust him. I'm not sure what it is, but there's something that has never set right with me. I've only met him once or twice. I'm not even sure of his lineage, and I don't think my father or mother knows a great deal about him either, even though he's high up in the hierarchy. Why?"

"Because Lugh is the son of Cian, one of the gods of the ancient Tuatha de Dannan. His mother was Ethniu, a daughter of Balor, who was one of the Fomorians. Only, Lugh killed Balor. He turned on his Fomorian heritage. So Lugh is actually a half breed, so to speak. He could be considered part Fae, given Cian was a god of the Tuatha de Dannan, and he's part Fomorian."

I was beginning to get a queasy sensation in my stomach. I had a feeling I knew where this was headed, but I decided to keep quiet and just listen.

"I almost hate to ask, but what is Nuanda's heritage?" Herne asked.

"Funny you should think of that," Yutani said, arching his eyebrows. "Nuanda is the son of a Fomorian giant, and one of the Light Fae."

"Of course," Herne said. "And he's one of Lugh's descendants, so…"

"Exactly. He considers himself to be of divine heritage. Only for Nuanda, his *mother* was Fomorian, and his father was one of the Fae. And the Fae, being Fae, rejected him. The Fomorians rejected him too, though he focuses on the Fae for some reason."

"I know why. The Fae accepted Lugh. But they won't accept Nuanda, so he's out for revenge." I straightened. "But why the hatred against the Fae and not the Fomorians?"

"I'm not certain," Yutani said. "Except that he seems to have overlooked the fact Lugh killed his own grandfather, which kind of sealed the deal for him. He seems to be taking it out on all the Fae by creating an organization that he hopes will bring them to their knees. The Tuathan Brotherhood is both a stab at the Fae who rejected him, and at the Fae in general. By turning them into apparent terrorists, he's attempting to make *everybody* reject them."

"Boy, he's a piece of work, isn't he?" Talia said.

"That's an understatement." Yutani sat back, shaking his head. "And it gets worse. Not only is Nuanda severely unstable, but he's also extremely charismatic. I watched a video of him that I found in the files, and he's an excellent orator. Now that the initial recruitment period is done thanks to drugging and brainwashing Fae, he's managing to appeal to disgruntled Fae, encouraging them to follow him. They don't know his background. Only those closest to him know about his birth. And by wielding Longlear, he's able to give the impression that Lugh implicitly approves of what he's doing."

"Did you find out anything else so far?" Herne asked.

"Unfortunately, yes. Nuanda has picked up a great deal of magic over the years. He can move between the worlds, and his home base is actually in Annwn. We won't find him over here, just his general army. I believe, however, that they'd fall apart without him behind them. Those closest to him know his agenda. But those in the general Tuathan Brotherhood are, for the most part, a ragtag bunch of disgruntled outliers. We all know how disorganized the Fae can be, and without the ruthless stranglehold that Nuanda has on his followers the organization would collapse, at least in my opinion. The Brotherhood is far smaller than we assumed it was. I found a members list. I'd say, all total, there are only a couple hundred members in the entire country. They've focused in this area because of TirNaNog and Navane. Their aim is to destroy the two cities."

As Yutani finished, a silence fell through the break room.

As I tried to process the information, I wasn't sure how I felt. On one hand, I was relieved. This proved that neither Saílle nor Névé were behind this, and neither would be backing Nuanda or his manifesto. In some ways, that was a saving grace. We could prove that the Fae Courts weren't out to disrupt the government. On the other hand, I knew how easy it was for public opinion to hold sway even when the facts weren't there to back those opinions up. Unless we took Nuanda down and did it soon, it wouldn't matter to the hate-the-Fae groups that were springing up. Because hate groups relied on fear mongering and deep-rooted prejudice.

"What's our next step? If we can't find Nuanda here, how can we find him in Annwn?" I asked.

Herne considered the situation for a moment. Finally, he said, "I need to take this information to Cernunnos and Morgana. We have to ask them how to proceed. Given that he possesses a shield from one of the gods means that he's going to be difficult to take down. Even if we were to go to Annwn right now, since he has the shield of Longlear, we probably couldn't kill him. I'm not sure of all of its properties, but you can be sure it's got some sort of protection enchanted into it."

"Also...what does Lugh think of Nuanda? Is he behind this? Is that how Nuanda got hold of the shield?" I tapped my fingers on the table. "We can't overlook that possibility."

"Right. Though, given Lugh is part of the Tuatha de Dannan, I rather doubt it. But you never know what goes on behind the scenes." He turned to Yutani. "Did you find any more information that we might need? Anything else that I should know about before I go talk to my father?"

Yutani shook his head. "That's all I've been able to skim through so far. I just broke into the files around three A.M. I've been up all night trying to hack my way in. I need to transfer the rest of the files and start combing through them. A lot of them look to be statistics and graphs, but if I'm lucky I'll be able to find their list of targets."

"At least we know why they're focusing in this area," Viktor said. "The great cities are here, and of course Nuanda is going to go after them first. And if he focuses his crimes in the Seattle area, it makes it seem even more likely that Saílle and Névé are behind them."

"How soon can you write up a report for me to take to Cernunnos?" Herne asked Yutani.

"Give me twenty minutes. I'll have it printed out for you."

Herne stood, pulling out his phone. "I'm going to call and let them know I'm coming over. I don't know how long it will take, so hold down the fort for me."

"Do you have anything in particular we should do while you're gone?" I asked.

"Not particularly, not unless a new case comes in. I guess... If Yutani opens up new files, help him read through them. Take care of backlogged paperwork. Whatever else comes up on the radar." With a worried look, Herne headed out of the room toward his office.

The rest of us sat there, staring at one another, until Yutani jumped up.

"I'd better get that report ready. I'll be in the office if you need me. I'm going to start in on the other files and find out what I can about the Brotherhood. Maybe I can find out where Nuanda's generals are located."

As he left the room, Angel stood as well. "I'd better get back to my desk."

That left Talia, Viktor, and me. I headed over to the counter where I poured myself another cup of coffee. At least we had the information we had been hunting down for months. We were ahead of the game now, and it was up to us to stay there. I turned around, leaning against the counter.

"Well, what do we do? I've already finished inputting all of my backlogged cases."

Talia frowned before she finally said, "I made a decision about Lazerous."

I blinked. She had been tossing back and forth her options regarding the liche that had stolen her powers. We had found out that he was located nearby, and her sister had encouraged her to attack him.

"What do you want to do? Are you going to try to recover your powers?"

Talia was silent for a moment, then she said, "Honestly? I don't think I want most of them back. You wouldn't like me as a harpy. I wouldn't have the life I do if

I returned to being a harpy—at least if I returned to having my powers. However, I want to destroy Lazerous. I don't want him to do what he did to me to anybody else. I want to take him down. Will you guys help me?"

Taking on a liche seemed like a big order, but we had fought more dangerous opponents.

I let out a deep breath and nodded. "I'll help you. I'll do whatever I can to help."

"Count me in," Viktor said. "I don't like the thought of a liche running around the country here. They're few and far between, and they are inevitably dangerous. Why don't you ask Herne before he goes if we can work on this while he's gone?"

I straightened. "That's a good idea. We can at least get a feel for where he is and do some research to see if he's got any minions or helpers." I paused, then turned to Talia. "Are you going to ask your sister to help us?" I realized I was hoping that she would say no, because the idea of working with a full-blown harpy—especially a chaotic, overenthusiastic one—wasn't my idea of fun.

Talia laughed. "Varia isn't exactly the easiest woman in the world to handle. She would insist that I try to regain my powers. She wouldn't understand my reasoning. So no, I'm not going to contact her until we've ended Lazerous. And even if I do have the chance to get my powers back, I'll just tell her that somebody else got to him before we did and that it destroyed my chances."

I headed toward Herne's office, to ask him for permission to work on Talia's case. I tapped on the door and peeked inside. He was sitting at his desk, staring up at the massive rack of antlers on the wall behind his desk.

Herne's office was large, with pale blue walls and a

white ceiling. There were plants everywhere, draping over bookcases, off of his desk, hanging from the ceiling, and they were all lush and vibrant. The antlers were mounted to the wall behind his desk, and the other walls held cases of weaponry: daggers and crossbows, swords and other hand-to-hand combat weapons.

Herne's desk was handmade out of dark walnut, and it was polished to a rich, warm, sheen. He sat in a leather chair in back of it, and in front of the desk were two leather wingback chairs. Another pair of chairs rested against a wall, with a small end table between them. The daybed was on the other wall, with pillows and a microfiber blanket on it. Herne and I had made good use of it several times.

He waved me in, and I sat down in one of the chairs opposite his desk.

"Did you get hold of Morgana or Cernunnos?"

He nodded. "I'm headed to Annwn as soon as Yutani brings me the report. This is the break we've been waiting for, Ember. You watch—this will be seen as the turning point in our war against the Tuathan Brotherhood. I may be gone all night, so don't expect a call from me. If you tell everyone to be here on time tomorrow, I'd appreciate it. But I may not get back for a while. It may take a day or two. I'll do my best to let you know."

"On that matter, I have a request. Talia wants to go after Lazerous. She doesn't necessarily want her powers back, but she wants to make sure that he can't destroy anybody else. We'd like your permission to help her— Viktor and I."

He leaned his elbows on the desk and furrowed his brow. After a moment, he said, "Do you guys think you can really take Lazerous down? Remember, liches are extremely powerful and deadly creatures. There won't be any wiggle room if you go after him. And don't forget how old he is. He's older than Talia, perhaps by thousands of years. You don't know where he got his start, or how powerful he is by now. He possesses the powers of everyone that he's drained."

I thought about it for a moment, then shrugged. "If something that powerful, that deadly, and that evil is near Seattle, don't you think we should take care of it? Granted, Lazerous has nothing to do with the Fae, but he could have everything to do with harming others. If we go after a band of goblins scaring cows out of their milk, then shouldn't we do something about a liche? And remember Talia's feelings—he drained her of her powers. Maybe she doesn't want them back, but she needs closure. To know this creature who almost killed her is nearby, and that we're okay with him just hanging around, it doesn't make us very good friends."

Herne laughed. "You should have been a lawyer. All right, the Wild Hunt will take on Lazerous. But you damned well be careful. We can't afford to sacrifice anyone at this point. Lazerous is dangerous, and I agree that we need to destroy him. But dealing with the Tuathan Brotherhood is our priority. Do your due diligence on Lazerous but nobody goes running off half-cocked without consulting me first. Do you understand?"

I nodded. "I hear you, loud and clear. And I agree. And maybe all we'll get done over the next couple days is a little research. But at least Talia will know we're doing something."

"All right. But remember what I said. I don't want to

return from Annwn to find you or Viktor or Talia laid up with a broken leg…or worse." He paused, then added, "As soon as Morgana brings her back, I want you to start practicing with Serafina. Get comfortable wielding her. I have a feeling you're going to need her over the next few weeks. Just a feeling."

I smiled. I'd been itching to get my hands on the bow ever since I carted it away from Sharne's apartment. I was about to say so, when Yutani knocked on the door and peeked in.

"I got your report for you."

Herne motioned for him to join us. "Good. That's all I need, so I guess I can head out. Yutani, will you tell Talia and Viktor to meet me in the reception area. You as well."

Yutani nodded, handed Herne the printout, then vanished out the door. Herne walked around his desk to where I was sitting. I stood, trembling. For some reason it felt like this was a bigger good-bye than it should be. Or maybe I was trembling because of the thought of going up against Lazerous. Or perhaps I was on alert because of what we had found out about Nuanda. One way or another, there was a part of me that felt like crying, though I couldn't pinpoint why.

Herne opened his arms and I walked into them as he pulled me tight against him. I rested my head on his shoulder and we stood there, not speaking, not kissing, just holding each other.

"I love you," he whispered, his breath tickling my ear. "Never forget that."

"I love you too," I said. "Come back to me in one piece."

We stood like that for a while, and then I went out into the reception area. Herne followed, wearing his jacket and carrying his messenger bag. Everyone was gathered around Angel's desk. Herne looked at each one of us in turn, then cleared his throat.

"While I'm gone, Ember and Viktor are in charge. Talia, I told Ember that the Wild Hunt will take on Lazerous. While I'm gone, go ahead and start the investigation, but no going after him till I get back. We can't afford for any of us to be hurt at this point. I hope to be back by tomorrow morning, so we'll meet at eight A.M. as usual. If I'm not back, I'll let you know why. Keep out of trouble, and Yutani, if you find anything else of importance before tomorrow morning, text me. I'll set my phone to forward to one of the portal keepers and they'll let me know if any of you have an emergency."

"I'll get on the rest of the files right now," Yutani said. He turned, heading toward his office.

Talia smiled, ducking her head. "Thanks, boss. I'm not so stupid that I'd go charging out there without doing my research."

Herne nodded. "All right then. I'm off. Until I get back, everybody behave." As he headed toward the elevator, he stopped, turned back, and motioned to me. I crossed to him, and he leaned down, giving me a long kiss. Then, silently, he stepped into the elevator and the doors closed behind him.

As I turned back, the tension in the air was thick and I decided we needed to diffuse it.

"Angel, order food for the break room. Don't think health, think comfort. Talia, go ahead and start researching on whatever you can find out about Lazerous. Viktor, check over the armory. Make sure everything is in order and ready for use. I'll be in my office."

As I headed back to my office, I wanted nothing more than to sedate myself with a massive amount of sugar. We had tried for so many weeks to get a handle on the Tuathan Brotherhood, watching them mow down innocent lives again and again. Now we knew who was behind them. We knew *why* Nuanda was driving his agenda forward. The only question was, could we put a stop to him before he managed to turn the entire country against the Fae?

CHAPTER ELEVEN

*a*n hour later, we were eating brunch when Talia, who was reading something on her tablet, let out a shout. "I can't believe it!"

"What?"

"You remember when Varia told us that Lazerous lives about forty miles from here?"

I nodded. "Right. But I don't think she told us exactly where to find him."

"No, she didn't. But I just found a report in *Mage Weekly* that a couple magic-born teens were hiking out in the Mount Rainier area. They were attacked and drained of their powers. One of them survived, the other didn't. The one who made it out alive reported seeing a skeletal figure coming toward them, and that's the last thing she remembered. Her boyfriend pushed her behind him and ended up taking the brunt of the attack. The girl managed to get out of the way, but she was still struck by the energy drain. She played dead, she said, until she was alone. It took her ten hours to make her way down to the road and hail an oncoming car." Talia set down her tablet. "I know it's Lazerous. I can feel it."

"So if he's out near Mount Rainier, then we have to find his lair. And *that's* going to be difficult. Do you know how many places up on that mountain he could be hiding?" Mount Rainier was immense, a huge volcano that loomed over the Pacific Northwest. Part of the Cascade mountain range, Mount Rainier rose 14,000 feet over the landscape, watching in her brooding, pristine glory. We'd never find him if we had to search the entire mountain.

"You're right. But we can talk to the girl and ask her exactly where they were attacked." Talia tapped away at her tablet and after a moment, she looked over at me. "I have her address and phone number. Should I give her a call?"

"How old is she?" If she was a minor, it would probably be better to show up at her door and ask permission from her parents to talk to her.

"Nineteen. It says here that she's a student at Winter Hall Academy. Her address belongs to one of the campus apartments." Talia looked so hopeful that I had to agree.

"All right, since she's of age we can talk to her. Go ahead and give her a call. Be sure and explain who we are. Tell her we look into dangerous situations like this. Don't let on that it was a liche, though, unless she mentions it first. We don't want a panic to erupt through the area. There's enough of that already, thanks to the Tuathan Brotherhood."

"Right. Good point." As Talia made the phone call, I watched her.

The situation with Lazerous mattered more to Talia

than she let on. She was good at remaining unreadable when she wanted to be, but this was too personal, and she couldn't hide her desire to destroy the creature who had effectively crippled her. I didn't blame her. I had felt that way about my grandfather, and he had just *tried* to drain me of one side of my heritage. If he'd accomplished his mission, I wouldn't have just killed him, I would have made him *hurt*.

Viktor returned from taking a plate of food out to Angel, who was watching over the reception desk. We couldn't close up every time we wanted to snack, and it simply wasn't a safe idea to leave the elevator access open when no one was guarding the front desk.

"I'll be right back," I said. "Talia has a lead on Lazerous." I picked up my plate and headed out to join Angel. She was sitting at her desk, flipping through a magazine when I showed up, and she glanced up with a guilty smile.

"Reading on the job, eh?" I laughed, pulling up a chair. I set my plate on the opposite side of her desk. "I know Herne's only been gone a couple hours, but I'm nervous. I keep thinking, what if the Tuathan Brotherhood finds out that we're on to them before we can get to Nuanda?"

"You can drive yourself crazy doing that," Angel said. "You've got to let it go, and let what happens, happen. Besides, I have a good feeling about this. I think we'll be able to find him." She paused to take a bite of her maxifries, then asked, "How's Talia?"

"I think she's okay," I said. "But I can tell you that finding Lazerous matters to her a lot more than she's letting on. We *did* find a lead. She's checking it out now."

"I never even heard of a liche before we met Talia," Angel said. "In fact, half of the monsters that we've encountered, I never even knew existed. It's a scary world out there."

"It sure is," I said. "How are your martial arts classes coming?"

Angel was learning how to fight—both hand-to-hand and with weaponry. She had been attending classes regularly at Herne's request, and she went twice a week. But we hadn't really talked about how she was doing.

Angel gave me a brief shrug. "I think I'm doing okay. My instructor says I'm fine. In fact, he said that I have a natural bent for it, if I could just get over my reluctance to fight back. But I wasn't brought up that way. Mama J.— well—she hated violence of any kind. She raised me to be a pacifist. Oh, she taught me to stand up for myself, but she didn't want me getting into any fistfights, or anything like that. To be honest, at first she trusted that you would keep me on the straight and narrow, but after a while she began to fret that maybe your love for adventure was going to rub off on me and that I'd get hurt."

I had never known that Mama J. was worried about me hanging out with Angel. The thought made me sad. "When was this?"

Angel flashed me an apologetic smile. "After you came to live with us. She was worried that your anger at whoever killed your parents would spill out. That you might join some gang or something like that."

I snorted. "As if any gang in high school would have taken me. She needn't have worried about that, but I will say this: Mama J. didn't know half of what was going on out there. I think she did you a disservice when she stopped you from taking self-defense courses in high school."

"I suppose."

I paused, then asked, "So, I know you still retained some of your pacifistic views until we joined the Wild Hunt. How do you feel now? You've been taking classes for about three weeks. Do they make you feel uncomfortable?"

Angel blushed. "I have to say, I'm actually enjoying them more than I thought I would. They do make me much more able to stand my ground. Granted, I don't know a whole lot yet, I've got a lot of practice and working out to do, but learning to defend myself is one of the most empowering things I've ever done. I'm really grateful to Herne that he was able to find me a place that's both comfortable to work in, and a trainer I trust."

Angel was in no way prepared to join Herne and me at the gym when we worked out, so he had found her a beginners' class for martial arts, and a good trainer who would ease her into her workouts. She was starting with tai chi and karate, and she was working out at the gym twice a week with a physical trainer who could help her at the skill level she was at.

I dug into my fish and chips, grateful that Angel had remembered how much I liked them. She had ordered in tacos, maxi-fries, fish and chips, pastries, fried rice, egg rolls, and pot stickers.

I leaned back in my chair after I finished off a third piece of fish. "Do you ever worry about living up to someone else's expectations?" I asked, slowly raising my gaze to meet hers.

"Well, that's a change in subject. What's going on?"

I bit my lip, not entirely sure of what I wanted to say. "Herne tells me he loves me more than he's ever loved anybody. I'm not sure if I can actually believe that, but it sounds true when he says it. But I'm concerned about meeting up to his expectations. He believes in me so much, how can I live up to that? I'm not even sure *I* believe in myself as much as he does."

Angel reached across the desk and put her hand on mine. Her fingers were warm, and gentle, but I could feel the edges of calluses on her fingertips. She definitely was getting her hands dirty in the gym.

"You can't control what anybody else thinks of you. How many times have you told me that?" she asked. "Herne sees the real you, I guarantee you. He's not blinded by love. The gods don't usually get blinded by anything... unless, I suppose—it's their own greatness. Or maybe another god or goddess."

"Well, I'm certainly not a goddess, that's for sure." I nibbled on another french fry.

After we finished, I carried our plates into the break room and put them in the sink. Then I wandered down the hall to the office that Talia and Yutani shared. I peeked in to see Talia working away on her laptop, and Yutani on Nalcops's.

"Have you made any more headway on those files?" I asked.

Yutani glanced up, nodding. "Page after page of potential targets. I have yet to find a schedule of anticipated dates for them, but I did pull up the members list. I printed it out, and I figure we can give it to the cops. We don't have the wherewithal to track them all down, but I'm certain that if Herne distributes it to law enforcement agencies around the country, they can take care of that. Or maybe to the FBI."

"How many are on the list?" I was hoping he had been right in his assessment that it was only a couple hundred or so.

"Would you believe there are only about two hundred members? Actually one hundred ninety-eight, if you don't round up. And at least ten of those are Nuanda's crack squad that he surrounds himself with. So really, it's not nearly as bad as we feared. At least forty percent of them are located in our area. Which again makes sense when you think that TirNaNog and Navane are here, and those are their primary targets."

Yutani pushed his chair back, crossing one leg over the other as he stared at the screen.

"Honestly, if I divorce myself from what they're doing, I have to admit, I admire Nuanda," he said.

"You what? How can you say that, dude?"

"Look at what he's accomplished. He's managed to capture the nation through fear. He's managed to pit an entire government against one of its own members. And all this with not even two hundred members behind him. He's made it seem like this is a nationwide Fae phenomenon, when really, the membership is incredibly small. He knows how to breed terror. I'm not saying he's a good role model, just that he's good at what he does."

Yutani's dark eyes gleamed. He was an attractive man, and a smart one at that. But I also knew that he was *so far* from vanilla that even if I had been single, I wasn't sure I would have braved a relationship with him. He was always on edge, though that might have been because of his coyote shifter nature. And given he was the son of the Great Coyote, he carried a lot more chaos in his nature than his brethren.

"I hear what you're saying," I said, "but I can't bring myself to find any admiration for Nuanda. I won't underestimate him, don't worry about that. I know he's dangerous, but he's also unstable. But he doesn't give a flying fuck for anybody's life but his own. I wonder, do you think he's more lucky than smart, when you really get down to it?"

"He's unstable, but he's not mentally ill. You and I both know that true evil exists in this world, and I'm pretty sure that Nuanda is an apt embodiment of it. He's smart, and cunning." He paused, then added, "I find it interesting that the gods of the Tuatha de Dannan accepted Lugh into their order, and yet the people who follow him refuse to accept someone with Fomorian blood."

"Nobody ever said the Fae learn by example. Look at me—I'm full Fae. I just happened to be from both sides of the fence. And they don't accept me. They don't even want to admit that people like me *exist*." I shrugged. "I'm only now beginning to admit that the Fae are my people. I don't like to, because of what they did to my parents and the way they've treated me, but I can't deny my blood any longer. That doesn't mean I agree with them."

"Right." Yutani shook his head. "Well, I'd better get back to the files and see what else I can find. I hope to have more information for Cernunnos by the time Herne returns." He glanced over at Talia. "Have you found out anything more about Lazerous?"

Talia swiveled in her chair. "I talked to the girl—her name is Claudia. She gave me an approximate location where they were hiking. Every ounce of her magical powers has been stripped away from her. She might as well be human. That's not a bad thing per se, but for her, it's a traumatic loss. She was in her first quarter of studies at Winter Hall. Now, she'll have to drop out."

Winter Hall Academy was a school for gifted students of the magic-born. The academy accepted pupils from between the ages of sixteen to twenty-four, and only those who were of magic-born blood could attend.

Yutani grimaced. "That had to hurt. And tuition is steep there. I hope they give her a refund, considering what happened."

Talia shook her head. "The opposite, actually. She was chastised for her foolishness. Apparently, the students were warned that the area where she went hiking was dangerous. There have been *five* other attacks out there. Students were told to stay away. It's all been kept very hush-hush. The headmistress doesn't want it getting out that students have been targeted. After all, the school isn't too far away from where the attacks have been taking place."

"Well, crap. Okay, five attacks. We need to talk to the headmistress of Winter Hall as soon as we can. Maybe we can get some useful information from her. But this is shaping up to be something we're going to have to plan our way on. We're not going to be able to charge out there and take care of him in a day or two. My guess is that Lazerous has made a tidy nest for himself and he isn't going to be easy to find, even though we have a specific area in which to start hunting." I jotted down a note to find out who the person in charge was, and give her a call.

"I agree, unfortunately. Luckily, though, given he seems to have found a ready source of energy, he's not likely to leave anytime soon. So we have time. It's just a matter of how many more victims are going to fall prey to him." Talia handed me a piece of paper. "I figured you'd want to know who to talk to, so here's the name of the headmistress. Let me do a little more research on her before you contact her, because you know that she's not going to want this to be brought out into the open, and she may not be that willing to help us."

I carried the paper out to Angel's desk. "Start a file, would you? One for Lazerous. Talia will give you the notes on what she's found out about him. Meanwhile, find the number for the headmistress of Winter Hall Academy. And here's her name."

"Why do you need to talk to her?" Angel pulled out a file folder and began typing in a label for it. She printed out the label and stuck it to the folder, then put an active sticker on the side. One thing that we both liked about Herne's setup, while a lot of our business was conducted electronically, we always kept hard files to back up the information. Herne had confided to us that the Wild Hunt and other agencies like it had been cyber-attacked more than once in an effort to take them down.

"Apparently, there have been a number of attacks up near the academy, similar to the one that Talia found. Winter Hall has been keeping fairly closemouthed about it, probably to protect its reputation, but students have been killed. It's something we need to look into."

"How powerful do you think this liche really is?" Angel asked. "And what kind of powers can he strip away?"

I sat down across the desk from her. "Liches are incredibly powerful. I didn't know much about them before we came to work here but when Talia told me her story, I decided to do a little research. You know that they were powerful sorcerers when they were alive, right?"

"Yes, actually *that* I did know."

"Well, apparently there's an archaic spell, known to very few. We're talking the world's strongest mages and sorcerers, like those belonging to the Force Majeure. It's often used as a curse on another sorcerer, but there are times when one decides to use it on themselves. For example, say a sorcerer knows they're going to die and they have the time to prepare the spell. Well, they can bring themselves back to life. Timing is crucial. If they don't have the spell set up just right by the time they die, it won't work. And their body has to go untouched through the process. That's probably why there are so few liches in existence. But once the sorcerer returns as a liche, they feed off energy."

Angel frowned. "They look like zombies, right?"

"Not exactly. The way I understand it, their skin dries over their corpse during the process, so they're more like mummies without the wrappings. Their bodies are desiccated. Their eyes look like they have flames inside of the sockets. To continue to exist, the liche needs to feed on magical energy. But the energy doesn't just sustain them —they actually absorb it and grow stronger as time goes on."

"If Lazerous stripped Talia of her powers that long ago, that means he's had time to feed on a lot of people between then and now." A horrified look crossed Angel's face. "He must be incredibly strong, Ember."

"Yes, incredibly so. I don't know how often they need to feed, but it's been...I don't know how many hundreds of years since Talia was attacked. I can't imagine how much energy that Lazerous has accumulated during that time." I paused, another thought crossing my mind. "I wonder what the hell his endgame is?"

"What do you mean?"

I paced, crossing to the elevator to stare at the doors. "Does a liche exist simply for the experience of existing? I can't imagine Lazerous attempting to seek power in a structured format, like in government, for example. He'd never be accepted. And he's not powerful enough to take over the country, obviously. But what does he want? What's his end goal? Or is he just obsessed with staying alive and gaining power, like Midas was with gold?"

"I don't know," Angel said, shaking her head. "But I'm pretty sure that we're going to find out before we're done with the case."

At that moment, the elevator doors opened, startling me. Herne stepped out, his messenger bag slung over her shoulder.

"You're back quicker than you thought you would be."

He gave me a quick kiss, then said, "Right. Gather everyone in the break room. I have news. And everybody is involved." As he headed into his office, I turned Angel and raised my eyebrows.

"Well, let's get moving."

But as Angel stood, a queer look crossed her face. "Ember, promise me you'll be careful? I had a sudden premonition that you're in danger. Very great danger. It swept over me like a wave as Herne walked by. I can't sense it now, but it came in on his shoulders."

Angel's premonitions were usually right on track. Suddenly feeling like I had a target on my back, I could only nod as we headed for the break room to find out what Herne had to say.

CHAPTER TWELVE

*H*erne came striding into the break room. "Everything go okay this morning?" He wasn't wasting any time.

I nodded. "We found out more about Lazerous, and I really think we need to take on this case. Talia discovered —" I was about to launch into what we knew, but Herne held up his hand, stopping me in mid-sentence.

"Fine, I trust your judgment. Get the files prepped and the info tucked in there. But we'll have to tackle it later. Right now, we have marching orders from Cernunnos."

The fact that he didn't even want to hear about Lazerous told me that Cernunnos had given him a priority assignment. Which wasn't surprising, given the situation. As we gathered around the table, Herne looked around at the remains of our impromptu food fest. He arched his eyebrows.

"I can see that you had a lot of fun while I was gone." Then, before we could take it the wrong way, he added, "I hope you left something for me."

Talia scrambled to bring him a plate of food, and a cup of coffee. Herne accepted it with a soft *Thank you,* looking more solemn than I had seen him in a long while.

"Well, I had a talk with my mother and father. Also, Brighid was there. First, they thank you, Yutani, for the work you've done. Have you found out anything else?"

Yutani nodded. "Yes, actually. I was going to send the information through one of the portals to you. We have the full membership list. And I have a list of potential targets, although there's no information on *when* they're to be targeted."

Herne's eyes lit up like it was Christmas morning. "That's going to be of tremendous help. All right, we'll take that with us when we head back to Annwn."

"Us?" I asked.

Herne nodded. "Yes, *us.* That's what I was about to tell you. We are *all* headed to Annwn tomorrow morning. Ember, Mother will have Serafina waiting for you."

He gave me such a long look that I started to get nervous. The thought that we were all heading to Annwn was daunting enough. That meant something big was going down.

"Can you tell us anything more about the trip?" I said, trying to coax him without outright asking.

"Make arrangements for Mr. Rumblebutt, Ember, and your dogs, Talia and Viktor, to be taken care of. We may be there for several days to a week. Cancel anything you have going for the rest of this week. Bring whatever clothes you need—it's full-on winter over there. And you need to bring something fit for an audience in front of the gods."

"I'm going, too?" Angel asked.

"Yes, everyone in the agency. So, you'll need to put any active cases on hold. Angel, make whatever calls you need to in order to inform current clients that we'll be out of the office for the rest of the week. We may be back before then, but we want to give ourselves enough wiggle room just in case we aren't."

"Should I print off everything that I found?" Yutani asked. "I'm assuming our tech won't work over there."

"For the most part, you're correct. Print off everything you found and make several copies. But do bring your phones and tablets. We have an interdimensional space in which we can use them. That's how I can contact my mother by phone." He paused for a moment, then added, "I'm sorry to be so vague. But I can't tell you what this is about. Cernunnos explicitly forbade me to talk about it until we get there. We'll leave tomorrow morning at eight A.M. I'll pick you all up. I'll text when I'm on my way. Pack wisely—and bring backpacks, not suitcases. All right, everyone take the afternoon off to get ready. Viktor, we'll want to take some of our best weapons with us."

After Herne dismissed us, it crossed my mind to try and weasel out information from him, but as I approached, he just gave me a shake of the head and pressed his lips together, and I knew that it was useless. He wrapped his arms around me, and kissed me on the forehead.

"I can't tell you, love. Just go home with Angel and get ready." But the look in his eyes was a worried one, and it set me on edge. I returned his kiss, then motioned to Angel.

"Come on. I have to call Ronnie so she can look after Mr. Rumblebutt."

Ronnie Archwood was one of the Light Fae. She was the pet sitter for Talia's dogs, my cat, and Viktor's dog. She was also an outcast from Navane, and we got along fairly well.

"Okay, let me just make copies of everything we have on the Tuathan Brotherhood." She headed back to her desk.

I returned to my office, putting in a call to Ronnie as I entered the room. She answered the phone with a laugh.

"I expected to hear from you. I just got off the phone with Talia. Yes, I can take care of Mr. Rumblebutt for the next few days. However long you need. And I assume Viktor's going to want me to look after Anastasia?"

"I wouldn't be surprised. I know sometimes he leaves her with his girlfriend Sheila, but this is going to be a longer trip. So I'd expect a call from him any minute. I know it's short notice, but can you start tomorrow morning?"

"I'll be over around nine A.M. I'll stop by Talia's to walk her dogs first."

Having taken care of Mr. Rumblebutt, I sorted through my office, trying to figure out what we might need. I printed out everything that Yutani had sent me on the Tuathan Brotherhood. We would probably have numerous duplicates of all information, but it was better to have too many copies rather than not enough.

Finally, I cleaned my desk, making sure everything was neat and tidy for our return. Something felt off. Herne had said there were things he couldn't tell us, and while I didn't like to seem paranoid, it felt like they were directly related to me. When I was finished in my office, I headed out front where Angel was finishing up packing a box of documents.

"Are you ready?" I asked.

She nodded. "I don't mind telling you, I'm nervous. I've never been too far away from home, let alone traveling to another world. But it's more than that." She paused, then glanced around. "I'll tell you on the way home."

As we stacked up everything that we were going to take in the corner, I glanced around the office. For some reason, it felt like we were headed on a major quest, like we were heading out on the long road, like Frodo to Mordor. Only I prayed we wouldn't be facing a foe like Sauron. And I prayed we would be home a whole lot sooner than it had taken Frodo to get back to the Shire.

ONCE WE WERE IN THE CAR, I TURNED TO ANGEL. "ALL right, what's going on?"

"I'm worried about you," she said bluntly. "I told you that I had a premonition while Herne was talking. You're walking into something big, Ember. It's huge and it's scary and it's dark and I'm terribly afraid for you." She paused, then lowered her voice. "I'm afraid you'll get killed."

I kept my eyes on the road. "I wonder if this has to do with that recurring dream I've been having for weeks."

In the dream, I was standing in a wide field as the stars twinkled overhead. As I stood there, a flaming arrow came soaring toward me and landed at my feet. I reached down to look at it, and saw that it was made of gold, and the fire clinging to it was magical—clear and pure and sacred. Then the sun began to rise behind the distant mountains, and as I looked up, I saw the dark silhouette of a man standing against the sky with a spear in one hand and a shield in the other. As I stood there, terrified, I looked down and saw that the arrow had turned into a sword, and I realized that I was going to be facing the man in battle.

"I think it does," she said. "Could the man be Nuanda?"

I caught my breath and eased onto the graveled parking space that stretched the length of our property. We had room for up to six cars, which was helpful when everyone came over for a party. As I turned off the ignition and leaned back against the seat, I could feel something stirring in my blood.

"Yeah. It could be."

As we stepped out of the car, Angel said, "I forgot to tell you, I've got the gift certificate for Joffrey."

"Why don't you take it over to him?" I was feeling almost dizzy. Angel's premonition had stirred up my own fears.

As I headed inside, I felt a pull to go out into our garden. I opened the sliders and stepped onto the patio. The rain had eased up, and it was partially cloudy, a welcome change from the constant drizzle. Huddling against the chill, I sat on the bench nearest the roses, staring out over the second lot that was our garden. We planted a lot of perennials, though none of them were up yet. But the juniper bushes were still green, and the fir and cedar trees, of course, had kept their needles. The beds where we intended to plant vegetables were so much mud right now. Pawprints told me the neighbors' cats had been wandering through. We didn't mind, considering we kept Mr. Rumblebutt inside at all times. I wanted the neighbor cats to feel safe around my home.

As I sat there, three crows winged down to land near me on the ground. They were cawing loudly, and I looked up to see a raven circling overhead. Ravens and crows didn't always get along, especially when it was nesting season. I leaned down, my elbows propped on my knees, and looked at the crows.

"Is that raven bothering you?"

One of the crows let out a shriek. Then a bevy of them came flying in, chasing the raven away. They all settled into the yard, waiting. I realized that I hadn't filled the birdfeeders in a week, and they were empty.

"Hold on. I'll get your food."

I headed back to the small shed that was offset on the back of the house. It was only big enough to hold a few things, like gardening implements and birdseed, but it did the trick for what we needed. I pulled out a bag of birdseed and trudged my way through the mud over to the birdfeeders, taking them down one by one and refilling them.

Not only did the crows come to feed, but we had several pairs of Steller's jays that liked to hang out in our yard. And of course, we had grosbeaks and finches and a lot of the other birds around the Pacific Northwest. I had even seen a pileated woodpecker a few months back, though I hoped he would stay away. The last thing we needed were holes in the house. As I stowed the birdseed away, the crows fell silent, and I turned to find Angel behind me.

"Joffrey was ever so grateful. He asked if we needed any help with the house and I told him we were going to be away for a few days, so could he keep an eye on it. He was happy to help."

"Good. I've never been so grateful to Herne for catching Ray as I am now. If he was still on the loose, I'd be afraid to leave. I would have to board Mr. Rumblebutt to make sure he was safe and hire someone to house sit."

"What do you think Cernunnos did with Ray?" Angel asked as we headed back inside and I closed the sliders.

"I don't know. I'm not sure I *want* to know. I'm just grateful that he won't ever bother me again." I let out a sigh as I looked around. "I'm not really looking forward to this. Beyond your premonition, I just don't feel like taking a trip. But I guess we don't have a choice."

"What kind of clothing should I pack? Is it perpetually warm over there?"

I shook my head. "No. Remember, Herne said it's winter over there right now. Think snow and cold. I'd pack jeans and T-shirts and tunics that you can move in. In terms of fancy dress, for when we go before the gods, I usually just end up in my jeans and whatever I happen to be wearing, but it sounds like there's going to be some dance or ball or maybe a formal dinner. I'd take the fanciest dress you have."

She frowned. "You mean like something that I'd wear for a wedding?"

"No, I'd say more something you'd wear for a dance. It doesn't have to be long, but it has to be nice."

As we headed upstairs to pack, I tried to keep my mind off of Angel's premonition. It wouldn't do any good to dwell on something that I couldn't change. But all the way through the afternoon, as we discussed outfits and function and form, in the back of my mind I played over

Angel's warning, and I mulled over the dream that I kept having. The two were linked, I knew it in the core of my being. But how they were linked, I wasn't sure. And just what we were walking into was anybody's guess.

ANGEL AND I DECIDED TO MAKE THE EVENING A SPECIAL one, given we were headed into what could very well be a shitstorm. She made clam chowder and biscuits for dinner, while I played with Mr. Rumblebutt. I called Joffrey and asked him if he could also pick up our mail for the next few days. I also made sure that Angel had told him the arsonist had been caught, so he shouldn't worry about Ray coming back after him. I liked putting people's minds at ease when I could. Next, I put in a call to Raven.

"We're headed to Annwn for a few days. I'm not sure when we'll be back, but I wanted to let you know." After a beat, I added, "I think it's a dangerous mission. If something happens, Ronnie Archwood is watching over Mr. Rumblebutt. I doubt if both Angel and I will..." I wasn't sure how to say it, so I paused, running through the options in my head.

"It's not likely that both you and Angel will be hurt, but on the off-chance you are, I'll make sure Mr. Rumblebutt's okay. I promise." She forced a smile into her voice— I could tell—and said, "Whatever you're facing, I hope you make it through with as few bumps and bruises as possible. Good luck."

As I hung up, Angel called me to dinner. As we ate, I told her what Raven had said.

"In no way do I think that *you're* in danger," I said. "But it occurred to me that you can never tell what's going to happen. If something happens to me, I know that you'll take care of Mr. Rumblebutt. But if by some chance something happens to both of us, I don't have a backup. Raven seems as good as any, and I know she takes good care of her ferrets and Raj."

Angel nodded. "You know, I was thinking. I should make a will and grant custody of DJ over to Cooper, should anything happen to me. I'll take care of it when we get back."

After dinner—which was wonderful—we curled up on the sofa and caught up on several episodes of *The Underhill Staff*, a period drama that we had fallen into watching. It was in the same vein as *Upstairs, Downstairs* and *Downton Abbey*, only it was set in a Fae household, with shifters being the staff.

Finally, it was nearing midnight.

"I guess we can't put off the inevitable. Let's go to sleep." I stood and stretched, then gathered up Mr. Rumblebutt to carry him upstairs.

"I'm actually looking forward to seeing Annwn," Angel said. "But I'm nervous, because of the premonition I had. I wish we were going on a vacation instead."

I let out a sigh, then gave her a reassuring smile. "Tell you what. When we get back—and let's just assume we *are* coming back—we'll go on a vacation to Annwn. Just for fun. I'll ask Herne to take us to all the pretty sites there. How about that?"

Angel nodded. "Sounds good. I'm going to take you up on that. Okay, I'm going to check the doors and turn off all the lights. You go on up."

As I ascended the stairs, holding Mr. Rumblebutt in

the crook of my arm, I realized there was a knot in the pit of my stomach. It had been there ever since Herne had told us we were headed to Annwn. Yeah, something was waiting for us, all right. I just didn't know what it was, and that was what made me the most uneasy.

CHAPTER THIRTEEN

The next morning, rain loomed as we waited for Herne to pick us up. Angel sent a text to Rafé, letting him know we were heading out.

"I'm going to miss him," she said, sighing.

"You two are getting on pretty well." I shaded my eyes to keep the wind from stinging them. It was chilly, but Herne asked us to be outside so we could just take off.

"We are, though I'm cautious. Rafé is wonderful, but he really doesn't understand much about the human condition." She paused, then pointed down the road. "That's Herne, isn't it?"

As Herne eased his Expedition into the drive, I saw that he had already picked up everybody else.

"I guess we're last on the list, huh?" I joked as I slipped into the front passenger seat, which the others had left open for me."

Viktor was in the second seat along with Talia, and Yutani was tucked away in the back with a bunch of gear.

He jumped out, stowing our gear for us, and then held out his hand to Angel, helping her to scramble in next to him.

I leaned across to give Herne a quick kiss. "Morning."

"Hey, gorgeous. Good morning." He glanced over his shoulder. "All set back there?"

"We're good to go," Yutani said.

As we pulled away from the drive, I glanced at Herne. "Are we headed over to Quest Rialto's?" She was the portal keeper I knew best.

Herne shook his head. "No, actually. There's a portal that's closer—we recently installed one that's not far from my place. It's on Culbertson...my father bought a house there. It's at 1010 Culbertson Drive, just past Sherwood Road Northwest. There are two huge oaks on the land, and they made a perfect place to set up a portal. Gage, a bear shifter, is watching over it. I can park my car there for days and it will be all right."

Traffic was still heavy but we managed to reach Carkeek Park, where Herne's house was, in about fifteen minutes. Another ten minutes through yet more heavy traffic and we reached Gage's house. The house was nice, and I thought it made a great perk that portal keepers generally had free rent thrown in with the deal.

The area was heavily wooded and near to the Sound, and the breeze came in off the water, bringing the smell of brine and decaying kelp with it. I shivered as I opened the window and took a deep whiff. Those smells—seaweed and saltwater decay—always spelled home for me.

As we pulled into the driveway, a huge bear of a man walked over to the car. Sometimes, it was difficult to tell what kind of shifters people were, but in the case of bear shifters it was easier. Most of them were burly, or stout if they were women, and while they could be short, they tended to be tall. The men almost always wore thick beards, and the women were full-busted and full-figured.

Gage was at least six-four and he must have weighed close to three hundred pounds. He greeted us as we tumbled out of Herne's car, gear in tow.

"Herne tells me you're all his crew. Welcome, welcome friends." Gage's mood seemed jovial enough, but I had the distinct feeling he was watching us, sizing us up.

"Sure enough are," Yutani said as he shouldered his pack.

Herne shook hands with the bear shifter and introduced us. "Gage, this is Talia, Ember, Angel...that's Yutani, our computer whiz, and this is Viktor."

"How do?" Gage shook each of our hands in turn. "You all be careful over there, you hear? I gather there's an upswelling of sub-Fae crossing over here, and they have to get through somehow. Lord Cernunnos thinks there may be a natural portal in the area, so I've been tasked to look for it."

"That means the traffic may be heavy on the other side, in Annwn, as well," Herne said.

"Yeah, that's the thought. I'll keep your car safe. If you give me a key, I can drive it into my garage to protect it." Gage held out his hand.

Herne dropped a key in Gage's hand. "Take care of her. We'll be back in a few days."

He motioned for us to follow him and we went around back of the mammoth house. It really wasn't that big, I thought, just tall and narrow. Behind the house, in the backyard, we found the oaks. They were scarlet oaks, like several other portals I had seen, and they were crackling with energy, the sparks flowing off them like water off a duck's back.

Herne paused as we neared the portal. "Everybody but Angel's been over in Annwn before. The portal won't hurt you, Angel, though it will feel weird…as though your body is shifting in all directions at once. Try not to panic, because it will just take a few seconds and you'll find yourself back together again."

Gage approached the portal and held out his hands. A brilliant light shot from his palms toward the center of the oaks, and within seconds, a vortex appeared between the trees, like a web of energy that was flashing brightly.

Herne motioned to me. "You and Viktor go through, then Talia and Yutani, and I'll bring Angel with me, since she's new at this. Take your gear with you."

I nodded, turning to Angel. "It will be fine. Don't be afraid." I slung my pack over my shoulder, along with my purse, and then took a deep breath. Next to me, Viktor followed suit, donning his backpack. He handed me a walking stick, which I was grateful for, given I always forgot to bring one and inevitably, I would end up needing it.

We approached the vortex and I caught my breath. It made it easier to go through after letting out a big breath, so I held it for a moment, then let the air whistle through my teeth and walked into the portal. Next to me, Viktor did the same.

WALKING INTO A PORTAL IS A LITTLE LIKE WALKING INTO A Cuisinart, except the blades don't sever you in half, they just scramble you up. Maybe it's more like walking into a blender, I suppose.

Either way, the moment I stepped through the vortex, I felt like I was stretching a million miles, from the tip of my head to the bottoms of my soles. Then, every atom in my body seemed to vibrate and dance, and I was in a dozen places at once. The next step brought me out of the vortex and I squeezed through, stumbling out into a dark woodland laden with snow.

As I stepped aside from the entrance to the portal, I looked around, taking note of where we were. Unlike the forests that surrounded Cernunnos's palace, the trees here were massive oaks and maple, devoid of their leaves. The undergrowth was sparse, here and there a berry bush, and some bracken and fern, but there were wide walkways between the trees, and it looked more like a well-tended estate rather than a wildwood.

The portal stood to one side of the trail. While the trail also had snow on it, it was compacted, with what looked like wagon tracks carving through the snow and ice. The snow wasn't deep, perhaps eight or nine inches, and over-head, the sun glimmered down, cold and frosty, but it cast a glow of light across the field. The terrain was so different than what I was used to that I couldn't help but gape at the barren beauty of the landscape. I imagined that this must be what parts of the East Coast looked like back home, where most of the trees were deciduous and the forest floor was relatively easier to walk through.

Beside me, Viktor let out a low whistle. "We aren't in Kansas anymore, Toto."

"Seattle, either," I said laughing. "It's beautiful, but it seems so groomed."

"That's because we live in an area that has a lot of wild tangled into it. Even in the cities, the ravines in the parks are filled with a massive amount of undergrowth. I wonder where we're at? We certainly aren't near Cernunnos's palace, not that I can tell."

I shook my head. "I have no clue either."

The next moment, the portal shimmered again, and Talia and Yutani appeared. Both of them had been through the portals numerous times, and it only took them a moment to regain their equilibrium. They stepped to the side beside Viktor and me.

"Well, it's certainly chilly enough. But at least the sun is shining," Yutani said, glancing at the sky.

Yet another minute, and Herne and Angel appeared. Angel wavered, but Herne caught her by the elbow as she started to collapse. I crunched my way through the snow over to her side, but she was faring better than I expected.

"Are you all right?" I took her other arm, helping support her.

"Yes, I'm just a little dizzy. That's like the wildest carnival ride I've ever been on. I feel like everything pulled apart and then slammed together again." She shook her head, holding tight to my hand.

"We'll stand by you for a moment until you regain your balance." Herne looked around. "Everybody else okay?"

"Yes," I said. "Where are we? We aren't near your father's palace, are we?"

Herne shook his head. "No, actually. We're about a

quarter-mile from Brighid's palace. There should be a carriage coming to meet us soon. I gave them our approximate time of arrival."

Brighid's palace? That surprised me. I hadn't expected that we would be visiting her, especially not in Annwn.

"How far are we from your father's place?" I asked.

"I suppose, if you measure in miles, about a hundred fifty? Something like that. Most of the gods make their homes near one another. Cernunnos lives on the border of a massive wild forest, but that forest runs parallel to a lot of the gods' homes, including Brighid's. In a sense, his place is the last civilized domain in Annwn, at least this part. Annwn's a massive realm, and the home of the gods occupies only a fraction of it. Think of it as another world entirely, connected to your realm, but separate."

"Is it like a different dimension? Like a parallel universe?" Angel let go of my hand. She wavered a little, but seemed capable of standing on her own.

"Not if you're thinking overlapping universes. Annwn does not mirror Earth per se. But the two are connected, like neighbors, only Annwn lives in a different dimension than Earth does. It's as if your neighbor Joffrey's house was in a different dimension. It's not on top of your house, but it's still connected to your land, in a sense." Herne frowned, then laughed. "Any discussion of parallel universes and dimensions is fraught with the chance of driving you crazy. Nobody really knows how it all works. Not the gods, not scientists, not metaphysicians. We just know that it does work. Although some of your scientists are really beginning to understand how vast the universe is, in terms of multiple dimensions and realms. But they always want to put limitations on them. Eventually, they'll realize that they only understand a fraction of what there is to know. Hell, not even the gods know most of what there is to know about the universe. No god is omnipotent, though a few crazed buggers think they are. And none of us really know what's out there."

As he finished speaking, a noise sounded from up ahead. We looked up. In the middle of the trail, a carriage was rounding the bend. The carriage was built of white wood, like birch, and it was decked out with ornate bronze and brass trim. There were green velvet curtains in the windows.

The carriage was drawn by eight magnificent white horses, each wearing bronze and green bridles and blankets, and bells that jingled as they clopped along.

The horses looked to be Andalusians, and they held their heads up proudly as the driver guided them along. The driver of the carriage was dressed in a rich green cloak, and a white tunic and pants. His hair was flaming red, bound back in a long braid, and two guards who looked enough like him to be brothers sat on either side of his bench.

They drew to a halt in front of us. The guards jumped off of the carriage, kneeling before Herne, bowing their heads before they rose once again, shoulders back in attention.

"Lord Herne, Lord of the Hunt, in the name of the Lady Brighid, we welcome you to Brigantia. Please come with us. The Exalted One awaits your arrival."

One of the guards opened the carriage doors, and they unfolded a short set of stairs. Then the two men stood on either side, waiting to usher us in.

Herne motioned for us to get in first. As I approached
the guards, they held out their hands to steady me as I
stepped up into the carriage. It was roomy inside, with
more than enough room for the six of us. Like most
carriages, there were two long seats facing each other, and
they were covered in the same green velvet of the men's
cloaks and the blankets on the horses. I took a seat by the
opposite window, wanting to be able to see out as we
drove along.

Angel joined me next, and then Talia. The three of us
sat on one side, while the three men sat on the other.
Once we were all inside, the guards folded up the stairs
again and firmly shut the carriage doors. They climbed
back atop the carriage to flank the driver and we took off,
heading down the road the way the carriage had come.

I peeked out the window. As we rode along, the trees
began to thin out, the white fields covered with snow. At
one point, we caught sight of a herd of deer who stopped
to watch as we were passing by. I glanced over at Herne
and he smiled tenderly as he looked at them. At that
moment, I suddenly wondered if he could talk to the deer.
We never really discussed it much, but I wonder just how
much he knew about their daily lives. Not *these* deer in
particular, necessarily, but in general.

As the trees thinned out, we rounded yet another
curve in the road. Up ahead, the road led to a massive
castle wall, surrounded by what looked to be a thriving
village. I wasn't sure what I had expected, but a part of me
had thought that we would find Brighid living inside a
castle made of silver or gold. But this was solid stone, and
the castle rising from behind the wall looked to be at least
five stories high. The fortress sprawled across the open

land, looking like it might be able to house a small town inside its walls as well.

As we passed through the village, it spread out on either side of the road. People stopped to watch us as we passed by. Most of them looked tidy and fit, and several of them waved at the carriage. Children were running through the village, dashing here and there, and I realized that the villagers weren't human. They were Fae, with some elves mixed in.

"That's right," I whispered to myself.

Herne looked at me quizzically. "What?"

"I just noticed that the villagers are Fae, although I see a few elves as well." I glanced back out the window. "Brighid is a goddess of the Tuatha de Dannan, isn't she? Like Morgana?"

"Yes, Brighid is a goddess of the Light Fae. Only she herself doesn't discriminate between Light and Dark. Morgana is a goddess of the Dark Fae who stayed over in our realm. While they are of the same stock, the Fae here call themselves the Tuatha de Dannan, although they do—as always—make the distinction between Light and Dark. You think the skirmishes are bad over on Earth? Over here, TirNaNog and Navane are constantly at war. And I do mean *war*."

"Do you have any agencies over here like the Wild Hunt that try to keep peace between them?" Angel asked.

Herne shook his head. "Over here, they're free to do as much damage to each other as they want. The fallout isn't going to hurt anybody who isn't already part of it." He scratched his head. "That's why the Wild Hunt was formed, and the other agencies. While in some cultures the Fae don't fight each other as much as others, we needed agencies around the world because the Fae live everywhere. So we approached the gods of the other pantheons and asked them to help."

"So there are actual wars raging here?" Viktor said.

Herne nodded, a bleak expression on his face. "Yes, and magic is used as a weapon. While they can't annihilate Annwn, like the possibility of nuclear war over in your world, the damage is stark and harsh, and the death toll will just keep rising through time. But the Fae here breed fast, and there is never an end to willing soldiers signing up."

He paused for a moment, then added, "I believe both TirNaNog and Navane—the cities in Annwn—have mandatory military service. Make no mistake—they're truly out to destroy one another. The only time they ever fight on the same side is when they're fighting the Fomorians. If you think it's bad back over on Earth, you haven't seen anything until you've seen the Fae go against each other here."

We fell silent at that, and I glanced out at the village again. They looked so peaceful, and so happy. "What about the Fae under the watch of Brighid's Castle, or some of the other goddesses of Fae? Do they ever go to war?"

Herne shook his head. "They are the exceptions. It's a given that if you live in a village watched over by one of the gods, you are protected by that god or goddess, and you are not allowed to start any fights unless the gods specifically order it. The queens of TirNaNog and Navane —the cities here—have accepted this."

"What happens to one of the Fae who might want to be a pacifist?" Angel asked.

"A few who do choose a more pacifistic route, or who want to intermarry, specifically seek out positions within the gods' villages. That way, they have protection, and they don't have to go to war. And some take off on their own. Rogues and loners, mostly. But that can be problematic if they happen to meet a warring party from one of the other sides. For example, if a raiding party from the Autumn's Bane happens on a solitary Light Fae family, there's not much hope. It makes sense to band together, if you have any sort of vulnerability."

We fell silent, watching out the window as the path disappeared under the wheels of the carriage. If we had been in a car we would have been to the castle by now, but the carriage made good time and the horses were fast.

As we neared the castle, heading toward the entrance, I saw a large number of guards standing outside the gates. I wondered if that was usual, but decided to ask later because Herne told us to get ready. We gathered our gear, and as the carriage clattered through the massive gates of the castle wall, we entered a wide square.

Inside, the castle rose at least one hundred feet into the air. Inside, there were wide lawns and snow-covered rose gardens, as well as a small grove of trees. Behind the castle, a row of houses had been built against the wall, probably for the servants. What looked like a hedge maze spiraled in the northeast corner of the grounds. We were higher up in elevation than the labyrinth, and I could see the top of it crusted over with snow, the greenery peeking through.

In front of the castle rose a massive holly tree, and cardinals, crimson red against the snow and the greenery, fluttered around the boughs. Ten large steps led up to a stone walkway, which led into the castle. There was a ramp on one side. People were scurrying around, scarcely taking note of us as they went about the day.

The carriage made a beeline for the castle, pulling up in front of the massive structure. A moment later the guards opened the door, once again helping us as we stepped out into the courtyard. It was cold, probably around thirty-one degrees, and I cinched my jacket tighter around me, slinging my backpack over my shoulder. Angel scooted closer to me, her eyes wide.

"We really *are* in a different world, aren't we?"

I nodded. "Follow the rules. Remember, all the laws back home can't help us here. Do what you're told." I glanced over at Herne, waiting for him to take the lead.

"Are we all ready? Do you all have your gear?" he asked, shouldering his pack.

We nodded, almost in unison.

"All right. Follow me then."

As Herne moved forward toward the doors leading into the castle, there was a sudden flurry of activity and four footmen appeared, along with several maidservants. Behind them, a large, imposing woman turned the corner. Like many of the others, she had blondish hair, and her eyes were ringed with thick black liner. She was beautiful, but I had a feeling that she took no guff from anybody. She stepped forward, and the footmen and maidservants parted, making way for her. As she stopped in front of Herne, she curtsied low.

"The Lord of the Hunt does us honor with his presence." As she stood, she met his gaze, ignoring the rest of us. "I am Lady Aimee, and I am milady Brighid's assistant.

I was sent to greet you and take you to your quarters. Her Ladyship will meet you for luncheon."

The footmen immediately took our gear from us and they followed behind us. The maidservants followed them. It felt like we were checking into a theme hotel, I thought, as we followed Aimee into the castle.

CHAPTER FOURTEEN

*T*he inside of the castle was as beautiful as the outside. Massive tapestries covered the walls, embroidered scenes of battles and forests and events that I knew nothing about. They were exquisitely woven as my gaze darted from scene to scene.

The castle itself was brighter than I had expected, yet another surprise. I had expected it to be dark and gloomy but lights glimmered from wall sconces, looking like brilliantly tinted LEDs, only instead of bulbs, there were sparkling spheres that darted here and there within the glass. Some were pink, others blue and pale green, and still others pale yellow.

I turned to Herne. "The lights? Are they Lightning Flits?"

I remembered the orbs from Cernunnos's palace. Lightning Flits were created from shattered lightning, and while they weren't alive in the sense that we were alive, they darted here and there, or stayed put as ordered. If you put them in a sconce, they would stay if you told them to. They almost seemed sentient, but Herne had assured me they weren't.

Herne nodded. "My father supplies most of the gods with their Lightning Flits. He seems to be best at catching lightning bolts. But if you really want to talk about somebody who's not only able to catch a bolt but conjure one up at will, go to Olympus and watch Zeus."

Angel's jaw dropped, and she hastily closed her mouth. Then, coughing delicately, she asked, "Watch Zeus? Does he give demonstrations?"

Herne snorted. "You know what I mean, but yes, there are times when the gods from different pantheons meet and talk. I tell you one thing, though," he added, lowering his voice. "I suggest that you hope you never catch his eye. You, Ember, Talia…any woman. All the rumors are true. Zeus is a predator when it comes to women. And Hera gets extremely pissed when he flirts, especially with mortals. Zeus has long been known to force himself on unwilling women, and nobody can do a damned thing about it. Which is one reason I won't have anything to do with him. My father doesn't like him, either."

My stomach lurched. "Rape culture."

"You know the gods aren't immune to stupidity. Or to cruelty." Herne gave me a dark look, then shook his head. "That's why I suggest that we stick together. I have no clue who else might happen to be staying in Brighid's Castle, and the last thing we want is any sort of incident that we can't control or fix."

My giddy mood took a nosedive. Herne was right. For all we knew, Brighid could have visitors who would happily harm us, and if they were powerful enough, there wouldn't be a thing we could do about it.

Aimee led us to a staircase, which we began to ascend. It was a side staircase, but still wide enough for four or five people to go abreast, with room to spare. She led us up to a landing, then turned, and led us up two more flights of stairs. By the time we got to a long hallway, Angel was grumbling.

"They need elevators."

I nodded. Even though I wasn't hurting, I would have happily jumped in an elevator at this point. "I totally agree."

Talia let out a cackle. "You two are far younger than I am, *far* younger. And you're complaining about a few steps?" She wasn't even out of breath.

Aimee turned back to glance at us, a sneer on her face. "I apologize if this is taxing for you." By her tone of voice, the apology was only a formality.

"Not at all," Herne said, giving us a look that said *shut up*. "We're fine."

Aimee led us down to the hall to a suite of rooms. There were three. She stopped in front of the first, and turned to Herne. "The Lady Brighid bids you and your consort to stay in this room."

Startled, I glanced up at her. Usually when Herne and I were out of town on a job we stayed in separate rooms to keep things on a professional level. But apparently Brighid didn't care about that. The footman closest to me, who was carrying my gear, moved forward, along with another who handed him Herne's backpack. The footman opened the door and entered, followed by one of the maids. Aimee ushered us in with a wave of the hand.

"If you find anything amiss, or need anything, just tell

the footman or the maidservant and they will attend to your needs. I'll be back to fetch you before lunch."

I paused at the door, watching as she led the others down the hall. The next suite was for Angel and Talia, and the one after that for Viktor and Yutani.

I glanced around the room. It was beautiful and spacious, with a bath to one side and a sitting room to the other. The bed itself was a huge four-poster, draped in green and white linens, with a green velvet bedspread. There was a loveseat, a few chairs including a rocking chair, a table and four dining chairs, a desk, and a bookcase full of books in the room. A giant fireplace crackled merrily, but the room still held a chill that the fire couldn't seem to touch.

The maid and footman unpacked for us while I glanced into the bathroom. There was a toilet with a chain attached to it, and a large marble bathtub.

"Does the tub have running hot water?" I asked the maid.

She shook her head, dipping into a curtsey. "If you would care for a bath, I will have hot water brought up for you."

I shook my head. "Maybe later. Thank you."

Herne turned to the footman. "I assume that bell over there summons you?"

The footman nodded. "Yes, your Lordship. Is there anything else we can do for you and your lady?"

"Since I doubt it's long till lunch, no, I think we're fine." Herne waved at them, and they curtsied and departed. As the door shut behind them, he turned to me.

"Do you like the room?"

I nodded, feeling overwhelmed by everything. "It's

beautiful. Huge. Although running water would make a nice addition."

Herne laughed, opening his arms. "Come give me a kiss, you greedy wench." As he enfolded me in his embrace, I felt better. I felt protected when I was with him, especially since we were in his world, not mine. He rocked me back and forth, nuzzling my neck. Finally, after a moment, he pulled away. "While I'd like to keep this up and see where it goes, we're probably not far off from lunch. Change into one of your nice dresses. It will be formal."

"You should tell the others, then. I doubt if Angel and Talia will know that."

He nodded, waving at me as he headed toward the door.

"I'll be back in a moment," he said. "Go ahead and dress."

As the door closed behind him, I went over to the dresser where I found my things neatly placed. My dresses were hanging in the armoire. I had brought two— one an elaborate gown that I had bought when I figured out that I'd probably have formal occasions where the gods were involved. The other was a pretty wrap dress, warm enough for the winter but with embroidered embellishments against the teal blue. As I began to change clothes, it occurred to me just how strange my life had become. Pushing the thought from my head, I focused on changing clothes and fixing my makeup.

Apparently I was going to join the *ladies who lunch* brigade.

WHEN WE WERE ALL PROPERLY ATTIRED, AIMEE ESCORTED us down the stairs. Herne was dressed in the formal colors of his father and mother's courts. He was wearing a pair of deep blue trousers with an ornate green tunic, cinched by a silver belt. Over that, he wore a cape. It was black with embroidered swirls of sparkling gold and silver. A bronze brooch held the cape shut, and he was wearing black leather boots, highly polished.

He had plaited his hair back into a long French braid, entwined with silver and blue ribbons, and he wore a circlet around his head. The circlet was bronze, with oak and maple leaves vining around it, and sparkling emeralds and sapphires inset into the leaves. He looked like a king, I thought, and I felt terribly underdressed.

He held out his hand, and I placed my fingers in his as we descended the stairs. The others were behind us, and they were all dressed to kill. Angel looked absolutely stunning in an orange sheath dress, belted at the waist with a thin brown leather belt. Talia was wearing a purple swing dress with a silver belt. Viktor and Yutani were both dressed in suits. Compared to them, I measured up, but none of us matched Herne's extravagance.

I leaned close to Herne, hoping Aimee wouldn't hear me. "Are we dressed up enough? I mean the rest of us? You look great."

"Don't worry," he whispered, leaning down to nuzzle my ear. "You look beautiful, and so do Angel and Talia. Viktor and Yutani look great. Everything's fine." But as he said the last, a veiled look crossed his eyes, and I once again felt on edge.

Aimee led us into a long hall, where a massive table sat ready for lunch. It was covered with a light green cloth, and china dishes and crystal goblets were placed around the table. I tried to count the number of settings but couldn't tell how many there were from where we stood. At the end of the hall, a large seating area with lounges and sofas gathered around the fireplace. Flames crackled in the hearth, but like the fire in our bedroom, they didn't seem to take the edge off the chill.

It occurred to me that if all castles were this drafty, I was grateful I lived in a modern house with a thermostat that could be easily adjusted.

There were people gathered in the seating area, and I recognized Cernunnos and Morgana, along with Brighid. Another man sat with them, obviously a god by his glamour. He had fair hair and a strong, firm jaw. He was dressed in white and gold, with a sword that looked like it was made from gold hanging from his belt. As Aimee led us over, Cernunnos and the man stood, as did Brighid and Morgana. Herne dropped to one knee and I followed suit, curtseying deeply. Behind us, the others did the same.

"You may rise," Brighid said.

She was as I remembered her from over on the Olympic Peninsula, as tall as Cernunnos, with copper hair that fell in waves down to her ass. She was pale as cream, with vivid green eyes. Brighid again wore a gown of velvet, only this time it was burgundy. Last time I had seen her she'd been clad in green. This gown was gathered at the waist with a golden corset, and the ends of her sleeves draped down to the ground. Her voice echoed like chimes on the wind as she greeted us.

"Welcome, my fair friends. Welcome, Lord of the Hunt. So we meet again. Events are moving in both our worlds." She turned to me. "Ember Kearney, do you remember the promise you made to me?"

I nodded, trying to find my voice. "Yes, Lady, I do. And I honor it. As long as my Lady Morgana has no objections." I blinked, realizing that the promise I had given Brighid was being called in. I owed her a favor but somehow, I hadn't really expected her to call in her marker.

"Good. But first, we break bread and enjoy a meal together. Solemn discussion and long thoughts can wait until after luncheon. Let us eat and enjoy each other's company, before we discuss the events to come. A last chance to be merry before we must face the future."

I was silent, as were the others. I glanced at Herne, but his expression was unreadable. But I knew that he already had some idea of what was going on.

"Where are my manners?" Brighid said. "You know Cernunnos and Morgana, of course. But please allow me to introduce you to Lugh the Long Handed."

The man in the white and gold outfit turned to us and I felt a sudden flutter in my throat as Herne reached forward to take his hand. I could say nothing as they spoke, but as I looked up I felt Cernunnos's gaze fixed on me. I looked at the Lord of the Forest, and he gave me a solemn stare in return. He almost looked sad, and the nerves I had been feeling over the past couple of days exploded in my stomach. I felt faint, and started to waver.

"Come," Cernunnos said holding out his hand to me. "Let me escort you to your chair."

I took his hand, my fingers dwarfed by his massive palm, and allowed Herne's father to guide me over to the table. He was half holding me up, and as we approached the chair with my name on a card next to the plate, he leaned down to whisper in my ear.

"I know you are afraid, and right you are to be. But I have faith in you. And so does my Lady Morgana. And our son Herne will be here to help you along the way as much as he is allowed. Don't be afraid, Ember."

As I sat down, I realized that he thought Herne must have told me about what they had discussed. I started to explain to him that I didn't know what he was talking about, but at that moment Brighid stood at the head of the table and rang a bell. The servants began to carry in lunch as we began to eat. And all I could do was sit there, wondering what I was about to face, as they filled the table with the most wonderful-smelling food in the world.

LUNCH WAS EXQUISITE, I COULD SAY THAT MUCH ABOUT IT, with smoked pheasant and freshly roasted beef, and very thinly sliced cold ham, and salmon, freshly caught and cooked with dill and lemon. The table was covered with tureens of soup, and platters of roasted squash and pota-toes, and baskets of freshly baked bread that filled the air with a yeasty smell that made my mouth water.

Between each course the servants handed around sorbet, light and cleansing on the palate. And then, for dessert, bowls of cold stewed fruit and a rich assortments of cakes and pies. I felt as though we had just come through a lavish Thanksgiving feast by the time we finished.

As dishes made the rounds, I kept wondering what the

hell I was in for. Cernunnos had spooked me and I was antsy all the way through dinner. Morgana was engaging Talia in a discussion, while Cernunnos was talking to Herne and Viktor. Brighid was talking to Yutani, but I noticed that Lugh hadn't spoken to anybody. Or at least, not more than a few words. I glanced over at Angel, who was sitting across the table from me. I had the feeling she was doing her best to go unnoticed. I tried to give her an encouraging grin but it came out forced, and she just stared back at me and shook her head.

After everyone had eaten their fill, Brigid stood once again. "Shall we adjourn to the fire? We have so much to discuss." Before anybody could say a word, she snapped her fingers and several servants came running. "Clear away the dishes and food. Bring us wine—a light honey mead."

The head waiter bowed. "Is there anything else, my lady?"

"Chocolates and nuts and dried fruit." She led us back over to the overstuffed seats. I sat down next to Herne and took the chance to whisper, "Your father thinks I know whatever it is you wouldn't tell me. He was encouraging me not to be afraid of what I was facing."

Herne raised his eyebrows. "That's my father, all right. I don't think he believed I could keep my mouth shut, even though he ordered me to." He motioned for me to be quiet as the servants once again gathered around us, pouring tall goblets of mead, and setting bowls of nuts and fruits and chocolates on the center table.

I glanced at the flames. A few moments later, Brighid began.

"Welcome to my home, and thank you all for coming.

There are two subjects we need to discuss tonight, and we'll tackle the larger one first. We've told Herne this. Your friend Raven already knows because of her mother and she'll be working with you on this."

I perked up. This sounded interesting.

"Do you remember Herne telling you that Corra, the great serpent oracle of Scotland, had woken?" She didn't wait for a response. "She has warned us that an ancient evil is rising. A creature out of the ancient age of Greece has begun to stir. His name is Typhon, and he is the father of all dragons. He brings darkness and danger with him."

I blinked. This was something new, all right. I glanced over at Herne, who was staring solemnly at Brighid. Morgana and Cernunnos both had grave expressions on their faces. Whoever this Typhon was, this was serious business.

"Typhon carries the powers of Tartarus in his blood, for Tartarus was his father."

"Who's Tartarus?" Angel asked.

Cernunnos glanced at her, a look of approval on his face. "Well you should ask, if you do not know. Tartarus was at the core of the world when it was born. He is one of the primordial ones, along with Chaos and Gaia. He's the father of pain. Together with Gaia, he engendered Typhon, a monstrous entity. While dragons of today are fearsome and some are up to no good, Typhon is the worst, following in his father's path rather than his mother's. He fuels the dead, allowing them to escape from the Netherworld."

"Dragons. Okay. I wish I hadn't asked," Angel said, grimacing.

I stared at the gods, dinner no longer sitting easy in my stomach. "We're going up against a dragon?"

"Not exactly. But Angel is correct—it's best to fear Typhon. Do not underestimate his powers," Brighid continued. "You will not be fighting him—you'd perish in seconds if you showed up to confront him. But when he rises, the spirit world will be in turmoil, and the dead will walk among us. They'll break out of their graves, and I'm not talking just on the spirit realm. I'm talking zombies, and ghouls, and wights. The powers of the undead will be greatly increased. This will be a war like none other. Typhon feeds on fear, and the dead will naturally gravitate toward him, for he exists within their world."

"So we'll be picking up after the collateral damage," Viktor said.

"Correct, you'll be taking care of as much of the fallout as you can. So will the other agencies—Mielikki's Arrow, Odin's Chase, all the others. This war cannot be fought directly, and it may continue for a long, long time until the gods figure out how to drive him back into his slumber. For one thing, Tartarus will be encouraging his son, and some of the other gods who are less…caring about humans, let's put it that way. So it will come down to god against god."

"So, can you clarify? You mean Typhon can affect the Netherworld?" Talia asked.

Brighid shook her head. "No, I'm speaking of the Aether. The realm where the restless dead exist. Raven will be fighting, along with a number of other necromancers that we can pull in. So will her mother—Phasmoria—and the other Bean Sidhe ruled by the Morrígan."

"And there's nothing we can do to stop him from

waking up?" Talia asked. "What about Zeus and Hera? Will they help?"

"They've already tried and failed. That's when they brought this to the attention of the Council of Gods. And Corra woke at that time. Typhon will wake, there is no doubt of that," Cernunnos said.

"But how can he be defeated if even the gods can't touch him?" It seemed hopeless to me.

"That's something the Council of Gods will have to figure out. But for now, be prepared for when we call you. In other words, you're going to be hunting around graveyards a lot." He shook his head, looking rather disgusted.

"A question," Angel asked. "Will Typhon be able to influence vampires? Are they at risk for being caught up in this?"

Morgana frowned. "That's actually a good question. What do you think?" She turned to Cernunnos.

He pursed his lips, thinking. After a moment, he shrugged. "I don't know. If Typhon *can* affect the vampires, that puts the entire Vampire Nation at risk, as well as the human community. The vampires have integrated themselves fully into society. I can't imagine what would happen if Typhon were suddenly able to exert his influence over them."

That silenced us all. The thought that the entire Vampire Nation could be affected by this was terrifying. Cernunnos was right in that the integration of the vampires into society had been so successful that if we had to somehow pull at the threads, so to speak, the process would be extremely messy and dangerous. I wasn't even sure it *was* possible.

"Do you have any idea of how long we have until Typhon's active?" Viktor asked.

Brighid shook her head. "Not long, that we know, but we can't pinpoint a time. All we know is that he's reaching a conscious state and when he does, he'll let loose on anything and everyone that stands in his way. He'll be hungry for energy and since he feeds off fear, we think he'll instigate as much havoc as he can."

"It's because of this that we must take care of the matter of Nuanda as soon as possible." Herne turned to me. "This concerns you, my love." He looked back at Cernunnos. "She doesn't know anything yet. I did as you asked and kept silent."

Cernunnos coughed, looking chagrined. "Well then, I'm proud of you, son. Brighid, would you? It's your volley."

I straightened my shoulders and turned to Brighid, waiting. Considering what we had just found out, I felt numb enough to hear what was coming next.

CHAPTER FIFTEEN

"*E*mber, I'm calling in my favor," Brighid said. "And the reason that you're the one I'm asking goes back to yet another favor, one your mother asked of Morgana. For that, I turn the floor over to her. Please set the stage, Morgana."

Morgana leaned forward, her silvery eyes glittering. "To be succinct, your mother knew that she and your father were going to die. She foresaw it. She came to me shortly before they were killed, asking me for protection for you. She knew they couldn't escape the fate your grandparents had planned for them—it was woven into their tapestries. I agreed to help, but I wasn't sure how to ensure that you would survive the assassination. I approached Brighid, asking her for assistance."

I was getting awfully tired of destiny. She seemed like a first-class bitch.

Brighid picked up the conversation. "When Morgana came to me, the only way I could ensure you'd be safe was by asking the Weaver to weave a destiny into your tapestry that required you to reach adulthood in good health. And the Weaver agreed. Neither Morgana nor I realized what it involved until this business with Nuanda arose, and then it became clear. Nuanda carries the shield of Longlear, correct?"

I nodded. "Yes, he does."

"One sword, and one sword only can cleave through the shield to expose the one wielding it. And I was the one who forged that sword thousands of years ago. It's known as Brighid's Flame. I created it so that once it was fully tempered, no god could wield it. This protected Lugh from angry rivals. But it also meant that only mortals could carry it. I wove a magic into its making that only a Fae maiden could shoulder the sword." Brighid held my gaze.

"And I'm Fae."

"Yes, you are Fae, and you're female." Brighid motioned to Lugh. "Tell them how you came to lose Longlear."

He cleared his throat. "I was carrying it when I came to a lake. The grotto was beautiful and quiet, and I thought I'd have myself a bath. I disrobed, and went swimming. When I returned to shore, my shield was missing. I had placed my spear next to a large tree, and I suppose Nuanda overlooked it, thank heavens." He paused for a moment. "I later found out that Nuanda had been following me. He hates me because the Tuatha de Dannan accepted me, but the Fae won't accept him."

"That's what we figured out," Yutani said.

"Nuanda isn't a god." I held Lugh's gaze.

"Exactly. The Tuatha de Dannan wouldn't have accepted me either if I'd been mortal. Anyway, Nuanda has my shield, and it will protect him from harm unless someone can break the shield. And that requires Brighid's Flame."

I caught my breath, sitting back. "So I have to go up against Nuanda?"

Brighid nodded. "I asked Corra, the Oracle. She confirmed it."

Scratching my chin, I asked, "Does she predict that I win the battle?"

"That, alas, is not for us to see," Lugh said.

I glanced at Herne, who was staring at me with open concern. I blew him a silent kiss as I mulled over the situation. It was up to me to break the shield. Which meant, I would be face-to-face with Nuanda, and therefore, the most likely to strike him down.

"All right," I finally said. "Give me the sword."

Brighid and Morgana exchanged glances again.

"All right, I saw that look. What's up?" There was something more they weren't telling me. "Just put all your cards on the table, please. Tell me everything I'm up against."

"There's a little problem," Brighid said. "I don't have the sword. And I can't get it. I hid it for safekeeping, but to be honest, since it's the only hope we have of removing Nuanda's protection, we can't entrust just anybody to bring it back. There's too much riding on this mission."

I frowned. "So where *is* the sword?"

Brighid glanced at Cernunnos, who said, "In a forest that the gods are no longer welcome to enter. We've decided to send Yutani and Viktor with you. Bear in mind, the sword was hidden eons ago, before the forest got so persnickety." His dark eyes flashed as he spoke.

"All right," I said slowly. "Is the forest over here, or is it over on Earth?"

"Here," Morgana said. "The forest is called Y'Bain. It's the oldest forest in Annwn, and one of the most magical. You're going to chance running into a lot of sub-Fae, as well as other creatures. That's why I want you to take Serafina with you. She's used to the forests over here, and she'll protect you if you wield her with confidence."

A bow as a bodyguard made about as much sense as anything else did at this point.

"How far into the forest is the sword, and how will I know where to look?" I wanted something to take notes with. "Does anybody have a pen or pencil and a pad of paper?"

Brighid rose and crossed to a sideboard, where she withdrew what looked like a spiral-bound notebook and a gel ink pen. I laughed aloud, thinking that at least there were *some* things we did better on our side of the portal than Annwn.

She handed them to me. "Here you go. And before you say it, yes, we *do* covet a number of things from your world." Her eyes sparkled and her smile was filled with her warm and gracious nature. Brighid was truly a beautiful goddess, inside and out. Just standing near her made me feel good. It was something about her aura.

I took the notebook and pen and began jotting down notes. When I caught up, I motioned to her. "Go ahead. I'm ready."

"We will start you out on a path into the forest of Y'Bain. Follow that path until you come to a massive fairy ring. The path splits at that point. It does continue on the other side of the ring, but if you pass through the ring, you'll end up going through a portal to some of the ancient burial mounds belonging to the Ante-Fae. Over here, the Ante-Fae are more coordinated, and they do have hidden cities in the forests and jungles."

I shuddered, not wanting to think about what those cities would be like. Raven was wonderful, and so were some of her friends, but we had also met some Ante-Fae who were deadly and cruel, and who made my skin crawl.

"*Check.* Do *not* set foot inside the fairy ring."

"When you come to the fairy ring, you will take the left-hand path—the one to the west, and it will eventually curve to the north. Oh, around that area, you have a really good chance of encountering will-o'-the-wisps. They're more powerful over here than they are in your realm, so try to avoid them if you can."

"Oh, this is just getting better and better," I mumbled.

"Excuse me? Did you ask something?" Brighid said.

I shook my head. "Nope." Sometimes, discretion was the better part of valor.

"Once you turn north, the trail is clearly marked so continue to follow it until you come to a lake. Lake Discover, too, has its dangers. There are a number of water Fae in the area, and as you know from your own blood, they can be deadly."

Water Fae. Be cautious, I scribbled down.

"On the opposite side of the lake, you will find an ancient well—the Well of Tears. A guardian watches over it. She's what we call a Lamentation. I'll give you a marker to give her. Once you do, she'll allow you to retrieve the sword from the well. If you don't give her the marker, she'll fight you and I guarantee, she'll win."

"Lamentation. *Check.* Marker. *Check.* Don't lose it. Okay, continue."

Brighid stifled a laugh. "Once you have the sword, return as quickly as you can. I would provide you with horses to use in the wood, but they all run in fear from that forest, so I'm afraid you'll have to go on foot. It should take you no more than two days to reach the lake and the well."

"Two days in, two days out. I assume that includes resting at night?"

Brighid nodded. "Yes. We'll supply all the gear you need. However, I warn you now: do not, *under any circumstances*, build a fire in the forest. The trees are alive and they're ancient. They don't appreciate unwelcome guests. And to them, anyone who does not live within their shelter is an unwelcome guest."

I took a deep breath, reading over the instructions. Then it hit me what day it was. "Tomorrow's Imbolc, your feast day, Lady. Does that play any significance in terms of the trip?"

Brighid shook her head. "No. And normally, I would bid you to stay and celebrate. It's a merry day here in my castle. But there's so much riding on this that you should start out this afternoon. My guards will ride with you to the edge of the forest. You'll camp outside for the night and get a bright and early start tomorrow morning."

"Brighid's correct," Cernunnos said. "You should start today."

"Do you have any other questions?" Morgana asked.

I looked over the list of instructions, trying to think of anything that might be useful. "How will I know where the sword is? You said that it's near the well?"

"*In* the well, actually. You'll understand once you actually come to the Well of Tears and give the Lamentation her marker. The well was sacred to me at one time, used to bathe those who were in mourning. My priestesses guarded it, until the forest drove us out. The Lamentation is the spirit of one of those priestesses."

"Sometimes, even the gods are in danger from the natural forces of the world," Cernunnos said. "I rule the forest and even this woodland doesn't care for me. Y'Bain is alive and sentient. It's very much a hive mind. So take care not to injure any part of it, build no fires inside, and steal no wood or rock. To do so will only rain trouble down on your heads."

And with that, I had my marching orders. Yutani, Viktor, and I remained silent as a burst of conversation rose around us.

AN HOUR LATER, BRIGHID'S SERVANTS WERE GOING through our gear with us. Yutani and Viktor were overseeing the operation, while I stood next to Angel and Talia. The task ahead loomed large, and I thought about Angel's premonition that I wouldn't be coming back.

"Promise me you'll be careful," Angel said, resting her hand on my arm. "I don't want to lose you. You're my best friend. You're the only sister I've ever really had."

"I don't want to lose me either," I said. "I'll do what I can to be careful, but they're right—this seems like our only chance to take down Nuanda. I have to get that sword. And after that, I have to face him with it. I don't think I care much for destiny," I added. "Sometimes not knowing what lies in your future seems a lot more palatable than having it spelled out for you."

"You'll manage," Talia said. "You faced worse before. Kuveo was no picnic. And neither was the Cailleach. At least Nuanda's mortal, once you get the shield away from him."

"Sure," Angel said. "You can do this, and we will be right behind you, supporting you."

"Hell, I'd go on the trip if I could, but they seem to feel that you'd be better off with Viktor and Yutani," Talia added. "But whatever I can do, all you have to do is ask."

"Me too, you know that." Angel wrapped her arms around me, giving me a tight hug. "Just come back alive, in one piece."

I glanced up to see Cernunnos crooking his finger at me. He was standing next to Morgana and Herne. As I approached them, Herne reached out, wrapping his arm around my shoulder. He pulled me close to him, and gave me a quick kiss on the cheek.

Cernunnos grinned. "You know we'd send our son with you if we could. But his presence would do more damage than good. The forest doesn't like the gods. Y'Bain would admit me, given I rule over all woodland areas, but it wouldn't be friendly. I want to talk to you about Y'Bain. I want you to know what you're walking into."

I nodded, gazing up into those brilliant gold and green eyes. Cernunnos stood seven foot two, with the most massive muscles I had ever seen. He was strong, without an ounce of fat on him. Narrow braids the color of a raven's wing fell to his thighs, and his skin was a golden tone, almost olive, with tattoos of serpents winding around his forearms. He was dressed formally today, wearing a pair of brown trousers, over which he wore a hunter green tunic and a golden belt. A green and gold cape flowed from his shoulders.

Cernunnos was the perfect match for Morgana, who was dressed in an indigo-colored gown, gossamer and sheer. Beneath the bodice of the dress, I could see her pale, round breasts, and she was wearing a pale silver underskirt. Her hair was bound up with silver combs, and tendrils fell in loops and curls around her shoulders.

"Tell me what to expect, then." I leaned against Herne, wanting to stay within the safety of his arms as long as I could.

"The forest of Y'Bain is the oldest forest in Annwn. It spreads far and wide across the realm, and at one point it touches my own forest. It's the wellspring from which this realm was born, the most ancient of forests, and it's taken on a life of its own. The soul of the forest is crafty and cunning, and has grown so strong that it seldom listens to anyone save itself. Those who live within it are protected as long as they follow the rules. Brighid already told you to light no fires within it, and I must stress that. Fire is the enemy of the forest. If you let a stray spark fly from your fingers, not even I could save you."

"You said it's sentient?"

"Y'Bain has developed a hive mind. Each tree, each bush, each blade of grass belongs to the hive. Take no wood, light no fires, pick no fruit, unless you are invited. The Fae who live within are ancient and treacherous, as wily as the Ante-Fae over in your realm. They are not governed by the laws of the great cities. In fact, neither TirNaNog nor Navane ever sends soldiers into the forest. They learned the hard way how easy it is to lose troops among the shadow of the trees. I cannot impress this enough: the moment you walk into those borders, you are alone."

More nervous than ever, I glanced anxiously at Herne. "I wish you could come. I know you can't, but I wish you could. I'm frightened."

"You can find me through the waters." Morgana stepped forward and tipped my chin up so that I was looking into her eyes. "There are numerous water elementals in the lakes. You can find me through them. They also guard the streams. If you need help when you're near water, call on them. They tend to remain unaligned. And the streams of Y'Bain are numerous, and wind around through the woodland."

Viktor cleared his throat. "I think we're ready."

I turned Cernunnos. "Is there anything more we should know?"

"Travel by day, make camp by night, and keep watch. Trust no one that you encounter. Make as quick a pace as possible, and the moment you have the sword, start your return. We'll be waiting for you. That's the best advice I can give you. The fate of the Fae in your realm depends upon you, Ember. What happens between you and Nuanda will set the destiny of both Light and Dark Fae in your world. Be safe and take my blessing with you."

Morgana kissed my forehead. "A kiss for safety as well. My love travels with you, and my magic. You can do this, Ember. I have utmost faith in you. Use whatever powers you need to in order to bring back Brighid's Flame."

I turned to Herne, trembling. "I'll do what I can. And if something happens —"

He shook his head, trying to shush me, but I waved away his protest.

"No, please listen. This is a dangerous mission and I'm not sure how we'll come through. I'll do my best, but I can't make any promises. If anything happens to me, I want you to help Angel. And take care of Mr. Rumblebutt. Help DJ. And remember me." I was almost in tears, because deep in my heart, I was terrified. Angel's premonition had wormed its way into me and I wasn't sure whether the fear I was feeling was hers or my own.

Herne held my hands in his. "Ember, you *will* come back to me. I love you so much. And I wish I could take this on my own shoulders. I'll go with you to the edge of the forest, and there I'll wait until you return. Never forget my love, and make good use of Serafina. She likes you, and her aim will be true for you. Remember that I made her, so a piece of me goes with you."

He leaned down then, pressing his lips against mine, and I tried to memorize every moment of the kiss, the warmth of his lips against mine, the feel of his skin against mine. When he finally let go, I shouldered my pack and took the walking stick Viktor held out to me.

"Can we wait with you?" Talia asked Herne.

"Yes, I figured you and Angel would want to wait with me so I asked them to gather camping gear for us. Brighid's guards, along with several of Father's guards, will wait with us." Herne motioned, and ten stalwart Elven guards marched out, in full leather armor.

Lugh stepped forward, extending his hand to me. "Good luck. The others have faith in you, and I see why. Bring back the only weapon that can cleave Longlear. I will not be sorry to see it broken, given the circumstances."

And that was it. There was nothing more to say. After we dressed for the road, we trooped out into the courtyard where horses waited for us, more of the beautiful white Andalusians that we had seen driving the carriages. We would ride as far as the edge of the forest, and then leave our horses with Herne and the others. I glanced into the sky. It was cold and the snow crunched under our feet, but at least we had a clear afternoon in which to ride.

We set out, with Brighid, Cernunnos, Morgana, and Lugh the Long Handed waving.

I kept my eyes on the road ahead of me. I was frightened, yes, but a swell of excitement rose up, and I could feel the Autumn Stalker side of me rejoicing to be on horseback, riding toward the woods, out on a hunt.

CHAPTER SIXTEEN

*S*hortly after sunset, before it was full dark, we approached the outskirts of the forest of Y'Bain. The tree line stretched as far as we could see, and the trees were tall and thick. The forest was a mix of conifers and deciduous, tall fir and cedar mingling with oak and maple and birch. Unlike the forest we had passed on our way to Brighid's Castle, this woodland was dark and thickly overgrown, the foliage dense below the trunks of the tall trees. There was a dark feel to the forest, and even from several miles away, while the forest was still a dark blotch on the horizon, I could sense the energy.

When we were about a quarter-mile away, the guard stopped. The lead guard—his name was Hale—stamped his feet in the snow as he clapped his hands to get warm.

"If we camp here for the night, we'll be able to have a fire. Any closer and his Lordship Cernunnos forbids it. To be safe, we make camp now." He motioned to the other four guards and they dismounted, helping Angel and Talia and me down from our horses. Viktor's horse, a massive stallion, knelt to allow him to scramble down.

"He's well-trained," I said to Hale.

"Aye, that he is. He is one of Lord Cernunnos's personal mounts. He can bear the half-ogre's weight without a problem." Hale looked around, then put his fingers to his lips and whistled. The other guards immediately beelined to his side. "Set up camp, and build a fire. Then make dinner."

The guards jumped to work immediately, setting up the camp in a smoothly choreographed pattern that told me they had done this time and again. Yutani and Viktor went to help them as I trudged out into the snow, arms crossed over my chest as I tried to keep warm.

As I gazed up into the sky, stars began to twinkle across the darkening panorama. They were brilliant here, with no light pollution to obscure their path.

A storm was coming in from the east, moving at a good clip, so we would probably have cloud cover by midnight. I didn't mind, considering the clouds would hold in the warmth. There was a crispness to the air and it practically sliced through my lungs, it was so cold and clear.

I was wearing a pair of jeans, a turtleneck sweater, and a jacket that Raven had given me. She had several like it, and I had begged one off of her. It was charmed so that it used my body heat to keep me warm. Lightweight, it was easy to move in, and one of the best gifts I had ever received. I wasn't toasty warm, not at these temperatures, but I was definitely far warmer than I would have been if I had worn one of my uncharmed jackets.

As I exhaled, my breath formed clouds in front of my

face, and I shifted my scarf to cover my nose and mouth. I watched the forest, shivering as I noticed a faint green glow rising from it. The entire skyline surrounding the tops of the trees lit with an olive glow. It had to be the magic inherent within the forest. Y'Bain was most definitely alive, and I had the uneasy feeling it knew we were out here, waiting on the outskirts.

Herne came up behind me, wrapping his arms around my waist as he pressed against my back. I looked up, and he leaned around to kiss me, reaching up to shift the scarf away from my lips.

"What do you think of my world?"

"It's beautiful," I said. "But it frightens me. There's a wildness here that you don't find over in my realm. I'm sure we still have places like this, but nothing quite so grand or intense."

"Actually, you *do* have places like this. They tend to be remote, far away from human interference. The top of Everest will never be tamed, and the volcanoes of the world have this same wild sense. And there are some forests and parts of the jungles that are still hidden from mankind, still thriving and alive on their own. But yes, my realm is far more rugged and wild than yours."

I pressed back against his chest, grateful that he was here. "Do you really think I can do this? Do you really think I retrieve Brighid's Flame and go up against Nuanda?"

"I have faith in you. And Cernunnos and Morgana and Brighid have faith in you. The Weaver would not have given you the challenge if she did not think there was a way for you to meet and win. *No one* faces insurmountable tasks in life, not when it comes to destiny. When you are fated to meet something, there will always be a chance for you to win. Perhaps a slim chance, but there will always be hope."

He turned me around to face him. "Ember, every day you amaze me in what you are capable of. And every day, I fall a little more in love with you. I don't know what it is that brought us together. I don't know whether we were fated to meet or whether we just happened on one another. But whatever the reason, I bless the day we met."

His eyes were glowing in the dim light of twilight. He truly belonged here. This was his realm, his home, and here, he was among the others of his own kind—the gods. I caught my breath again. It was hard enough to find love in the world, but to find love with one of the gods? I had never imagined this could happen.

As he leaned down to kiss me, pulling me close, every care in the world faded, leaving me in the present, awash in his love. He buoyed me up and gave me the hope that I needed to face the morning.

A moment later, Hale called to us. As we turned, a fire crackled in the center of camp, and a stew pot hung over the fire. I could smell something cooking and my stomach rumbled.

Herne laughed. "Let's get you back to the fire, and get some food inside you. Although after lunch today, I'm surprised you're hungry."

I laughed in returned. "I'm mortal, remember? I need food regularly, and being Fae, I need more food than usual. Humans are lucky in that they don't have to eat nearly as much to keep going."

"Well then, come on. I don't want you to starve." He wrapped his arm around my waist.

As we ambled back to the fire, the others were gathering around it, huddled with blankets around their shoulders. One of the guards was passing around what looked to be enameled campfire cups and again, I grinned. Yet another small victory for my home. And the tents were also from one of the large camping store outlets. Yes, there were definitely some things that we did better and I was grateful to see the gods acknowledged it.

I spent my last night in the tent with Angel and Talia. Herne, Yutani, and Viktor were bunking together. And the guards were sleeping in yet another two tents, five standing watch and five asleep at a time. It was cold, but the guards had heated rocks in the fire, and tucked them beneath the feet of our sleeping bags, wrapped in towels. The sleeping bags were from REI or some other store like that and they were actually comfortable and warm. They were mummy bags, which gave me a touch of claustrophobia, but they kept the cold air out except for my face.

"Are you asleep?" Angel whispered from my right side.

"Not yet. It's so quiet out here that it's hard to sleep. I'm so used to all the sounds of the city," I said.

"Me too. But I have to tell you, this is a beautiful place. I'd like to bring DJ here sometime—not to the forest, that would be too dangerous. But to Annwn. I think he'd love it."

"You're probably right. I bet he would love it. We can talk to Herne some time. Maybe we can take a company vacation—a camping trip—and bring him." A few Lightning Flits lit up the inside of the tent just enough to see and give us a warm comfort.

"Annwn feels a cold place to me," Talia said. "Beautiful, but rugged and isolated. I think I've become so used to the city that I wouldn't know what to do with myself if I had to move out to the country." She paused for a moment, then said, "What do you think of this Typhon business? I've heard of him, of course. He comes from the pantheon of my world. But for something so ancient and dangerous to awake…everything will change, you know. It has to."

I had pushed thoughts of Typhon out of my head, in order to focus on the coming quest, but now the future loomed heavy. Even if I was able to take down Nuanda, that only meant we were clear for the next round of danger. And *that* would make the battle we were fighting look like child's play.

"I don't know what to think," I said. "They said that Raven knows about this as well. Her mother must have told her when she came to visit. We haven't had much of a chance to talk since then, or I'm sure she would have told us. But it sounds like we'll all be fighting in this battle, each in our own way. Perhaps we can unite the Fae in TirNaNog and Navane—at home, at least—to fight with us."

"I wonder if they'll tell the United Coalition about this. If so, then perhaps we can enlist people from all walks of life to do what they can. We have to hope that Typhon won't be able to control the vampires. *That* would be an incredibly complex and delicate situation."

"You can say that again," Angel said. "If he can control them, nobody's safe." She paused, then asked, "Can vampires turn the Fae? Or harpies? Or shifters?"

"It can happen," I said, "but it's rare. It's not often that one of the Fae or a shifter falls prey to them. But it *has* been known to occur, and when that happens, the vampire is far more powerful than if they were just human to begin with."

Vampires tended to prefer human victims, because they were easier to overpower. Vampires were strong, usually stronger than most shifters or Fae, but it was much easier for them to track and take down humans.

While they were proscribed by law from killing for their food—by an amendment to a treaty forged between the Vampire Nation and the United Coalition—that didn't prevent the lone vamp from going rogue. However, the Vampire Nation was quick to hunt down those vamps who violated the laws, and they staked them, usually dragging them in front of other witnesses since filming the execution would be useless.

There was too much to be lost by allowing rogue vampires to cause havoc. The Vampire Nation controlled a large percentage of the country's financial institutions, and they owned Wall Street. Something about the process of being turned heightened their mathematical abilities, and they had an excellent sense for anything to do with numbers and accounting, which led to rules forbidding them to enter casinos as guests. However, a number of vampires actually owned casinos around the world.

"I don't know if I've ever met a vampire other than Charlie," Angel said.

Charlie Darren was a member of the Wild Hunt Agency—the most recent agent taken aboard. But he was spending most of his time taking accounting classes. It'd been his major when he was human. We had first met him during another case, and Herne took a liking to him. He was paying for Charlie to finish college, and when Charlie did, he would take over our books and become our official accountant. He was turned when he was just nineteen, and he still had a newness about him that was both naïve and nerve-racking. His sire had been rogue, and the VN had tracked him down and staked him, which put Charlie at a disadvantage within the vamp community. He was a good sort, and we all liked him even though we didn't see him very often. He also caught up on entering data for us when we were overwhelmed with cases.

"You probably have," I said. "Vampires easily can pass in society when they choose to, and I'll bet you when we've been out clubbing at night you've met a few."

"We better get to sleep," Talia said. "You have a long day tomorrow, and a long journey ahead of you. You need your rest."

And with that, we burrowed down in our sleeping bags, but it was a long time before I was able to fall asleep. Finally, the muffled silence around me took hold, and I let myself tumble into a troubled slumber, filled with uneasy dreams.

The next morning, Viktor, Yutani, and I headed into the forest. We kept our good-byes short, because otherwise it would have been far too easy to give up and turn my back on the whole mess. So, at first light, we ate breakfast and then rode to the tree line, along with Herne and one of the guards. As we dismounted and handed the reins to them, I blew Herne a kiss. With one last reluctant look back at the distant campsite and the fire, I took a deep breath and led the way beneath the tree covering.

CHAPTER SEVENTEEN

*T*he forest immediately closed in around us, and even only a few yards in, it was difficult to see the opening behind us. I shivered, glancing up at the trees. They loomed large overhead, towering out of sight. The oaks and maples were bare and I could see the remains of birds' nests in the lower branches. The forest of Y'Bain was teeming with life. Everywhere I turned, I could hear the rustle of animals in the bushes—or what I hoped were animals. Birdsong filled the air, low and haunting, as though the birds were calling out, "A storm is coming!"

The path we were on was wide enough for two to go abreast, two arms' lengths apart. A horse could have traversed the trail easily, but given the horses refused to come near the woodlands, we were on foot. The trees around us seemed to loom large and dark, blocking out much of the sun and shrouding the path. The snow blanketing the land reflected what light came through, giving an eerie glow to the forest.

Viktor and Yutani had fallen silent, walking as unobtrusively as they could. And I was following suit. It was as though we could escape notice if we went on tiptoe, if we crept through the forest.

Y'Bain rose up around us, like a shroud. It felt as though the forest went on forever, with no beginning and no ending. I blinked, trying to remember how long we had been walking. It wasn't dark yet, but it seemed as though we had been traveling all day. My thoughts began to echo in my head and, mingling with them, I realized I was hearing whispers, the sounds of someone calling my name. I tried to focus on the voices but the moment I did, they vanished, and then—when I ignored them again— they started back up. Finally, feeling like I was playing some macabre game of cat and mouse, I turned to the men.

"Do either of you hear someone calling your name? I could swear it's audible, but when I focus, I only hear someone in the back of my mind, like they're a long, long ways away and my name is echoing on the wind." I stopped, realizing how odd that sounded, but Viktor regarded me gravely, and Yutani immediately began to look around us.

"I don't hear anybody calling, but I hear the sound of someone singing. It's a man's voice." Viktor looked around nervously. "Kelpie, maybe?"

"This forest is riddled with streams, but I don't hear singing. Maybe it's because I'm not listening?" I turned to Yutani. "What about you?"

"This forest is one big creature, and it's watching us as we pass through. At any moment, I expect something to sweep down from the trees to capture us." His eyes were somber, and he was wearing his deadman's hat, which gave him a dangerous, handsome look. "I feel an energy within the borders of this forest that reminds me of my father. Chaos incarnate, and a temper that can swing either way depending on what we do."

Yutani's father was the Great Coyote. We—including him—had only recently found out about his parentage, and no one knew exactly what to think about it, except that Coyote had dogged Yutani's heels all of his life and thrown him into situations that had caved in beneath him. Until Herne had taken him in, Yutani had been nomadic, wandering from town to town, working for tech companies here and there as the years progressed.

"We should reach the lake by tomorrow evening, which means we'll have two nights to camp. Given it's… what time is it?" I asked.

"We've been traveling about four hours now, so it's nearing noon. I suggest we take a break for lunch, but don't make it long. We'll want to continue on as far as we can before dusk falls. We can use flashlights, but no fire, remember, so we should make camp in about five hours. I don't want to chance veering off the path if we try to travel after dark." Viktor held my gaze, and I realized he wasn't making a suggestion so much as giving an order, which suited me just fine. I really didn't want to be in charge of this trip.

"All right. Let's stop right here—there are a couple logs to the side. We can eat and rest for fifteen minutes, and then be on the move again." I motioned to a couple of fallen logs.

As I carefully brushed the snow from the tops so we could sit down, Viktor shrugged off his pack and sat down, opening it to find our food. Brighid's servants had provided a dozen large dinner rolls, a dozen hardboiled eggs, a thick roll of salami, and a small wheel of cheese for our trip, along with apples, cookies, and nuts. We also had a couple large water bottles each—the guards had encouraged us not to drink the water within the woodland. Viktor pulled out his knife and carved off wedges of cheese for us, then a thick slice of salami, while I handed an egg, a dinner roll, and an apple to Yutani, and then the same to Viktor. The cookies and nuts we would keep for snacks.

I broke open my dinner roll and sandwiched the cheese and salami into it for a makeshift sandwich. Then, I peeled the egg and dinner was ready. As I bit into the sandwich, the rich, mellow flavors of the cheese blended with the sharp edge of the salami and I relaxed, the food warming my spirits.

"I don't even care that we're going to be eating the same thing for the next few meals. This is so good. Brighid's cooks know what they're doing," I said between bites.

Viktor nodded. "That they do."

Yutani glanced around the forest. The turnout we had stopped at was small—back home it would have been large enough for one campsite. "I wonder how far this forest goes. If it's the biggest forest in Annwn, it probably stretches out for a thousand miles or more."

"Cernunnos was right, though," I said. "It's one giant hive mind. You can feel it beneath the surface, if you focus. I can almost feel the heartbeat of the forest beneath our feet. It's like this tingle, almost like being shocked by a frayed cord. I'd feel a lot better if we could have a—" I paused, not even sure if the word should be spoken out loud under the boughs of the trees. "F-I-R-E. That's funny, I'm even afraid to say the word out loud here."

"There's good reason for that. The forest is listening to us even now," Yutani said. "I can feel it, too. Its eyes and ears are everywhere. It may not know English, but it knows intent. And the forest is crafty, and cunning. I wouldn't want to be lost in here."

"I suggest we eat quickly and get a move on. We don't want to be here any longer than we have to." Viktor took another big bite of his sandwich and wiped his mouth on his sleeve.

I nodded, turning back to my own food. All around me, the forest moved, thinking whatever long, dark thoughts it held. I hoped it would keep them to itself.

When we were finished, I dusted my hands on my jeans and stood, stretching before I picked up my walking stick and returned to the path. Viktor and Yutani joined me.

"If anybody has to go to the bathroom, I suggest behind that bush right there," I said, pointing to a nearby bush. "And I suggest you go now, so that we can pick up the pace and make as much distance as we can before nightfall."

Yutani took advantage of the bush first, and then Viktor, and I went last. Another luxury that Brighid's servants had provided was toilet paper from our realm. It was definitely a long sight better than rags or leaves. I washed my hands using the snow before pulling on my gloves and again and returning to the guys.

"All right, let's go," I said, setting the pace at a good brisk walk, the fastest we could manage through the snow. The weather had held, and I myself hoped it would cloud over before night because it was going to be damned cold without a fire, and a clear sky would make it even worse. The jacket I was wearing—the one Raven had given me—helped, but it sure wouldn't stave off temperatures that were below freezing all night long.

As the shadows crowded in overhead, the sun slowly lowering in the sky, I realized we had been walking for about three hours without speaking. Everything felt muffled by the snow and the susurration of the constant breeze blowing through the forest. I tried to think of something to break the silence, but it was as if all thoughts of conversation had fled, and the only thing that existed was our never-ending hike through Y'Bain.

Another half-hour and it was growing dark. While we were in the waxing half of the year now, the light still faded quickly in the January night, and it seemed like a good time to begin looking for a camping spot. I was going to point this out when we came to a T in the road. Straight ahead, poking through the snow, stood a ring of red-capped mushrooms that were almost knee high. The road continued on beyond them, but I remembered all too well what Brighid had told me.

"We've reached the faerie ring. Make certain you don't step over the borders of it. We have to turn left here."

"We should find a place to camp. It's growing dark and you remember what they said about walking through the forest after nightfall," Viktor said. He pointed off to the right, about ten yards away from the ring. "There's a bit of a clearing there that would probably make for a good campsite. What do you think? Camp, or take a chance in order to put distance between us and the faerie ring?"

I wanted to continue. The last thing we needed was to

camp next to a portal. But the light was fading quickly and it felt like danger lurked everywhere.

"I don't know. I'd hate to have night fall while we're still on the path. They warned us not to forge ahead during the dark. I have the feeling the paths here may shift at night." I thought for a moment, then gave him a nod. "All right. As much as I don't want to camp near the portal, let's break for the night. We only have about half an hour until it's fully dark and it will take that long to set up the tent."

We scoped out the campsite first, making sure there were no animals around or traps that we could see. Yutani and Viktor set up the tent as far away from the faerie ring as possible. It was large enough for all three of us, and as I stepped inside to help lay out the bedrolls, I was surprised by how warm it was. It wasn't shirtsleeve warm, but the chill from outside didn't seem to penetrate the walls.

"Well, that's a surprise," I said. "I wonder if they enchanted this so it stays warmer?"

"Is there a way you can tell?" Yutani asked.

I placed my hands against the polyester walls of the tent and closed my eyes. Sure enough, just below the surface I could feel the comforting flow of magic. I wasn't sure what kind it was, but it infused itself through the material. I wondered whether it extended its reach to protection magic as well, but I wasn't going to bet on it.

"It definitely has magic woven into it. But we still need to take shifts. The tent may keep us warm, but I don't know if it can protect us. Whoever is on watch can sit right outside of the rain flap. I suggest using your sleeping bag to drape around your shoulders. I'll take first watch, if you like." I picked up my sleeping bag and unzipped it, figuring that it would help above and beyond the jacket I was wearing.

"I'll call second," Yutani said. "I'm good with just four or five hours of sleep a night."

"Wake me up for third," Viktor said. "When do you want to eat dinner? It's not like we have to cook."

I was always up for a good snack, but I also realized that we weren't even into the mid-evening hours yet. "Why don't we wait for a couple hours? If we're not going to travel during the dark, then we have a long evening ahead of us."

"I thought of that," Viktor said. He pulled out a couple LED battery-operated lights. They illuminated the tent so that we could see easily. He also brought out a deck of cards. "Anybody up for gin rummy?"

Yutani snorted, but he sat down on the floor of the tent and motioned to Viktor. "Okay, deal them out. By the way, I also brought an e-reader. So if anybody wants to read, I've got a huge selection of books on it."

I joined them, and we played five straight games of rummy, then shifted over to poker, using nuts as poker chips. I was winning when my stomach let out a loud rumble.

"What time do you think it is now?"

"Probably around seven-thirty. Dinner?"

I nodded. I was getting a hunger headache. "Yeah, I'm hungry."

Once again we made sandwiches, along with eggs and apples. This time, we added in a couple cookies as dessert. Brighid's servants had been generous with the cookies, but I knew we could easily eat them all in one sitting, and

I wanted to make sure we had something saved for snacks along the way.

An hour later we were all yawning. I longed for coffee —I had a caffeine headache already. Fumbling in my pack, I looked for something that I had figured I would need. I pulled out one of several bags of chocolate-covered espresso beans.

"Seriously, you're going to caffeinate up *now?*" Yutani asked.

"You better hope I do, or I'll fall asleep on watch." I poured a handful into my palm, and made quick work of them. As the ping of caffeine hit my system, I felt ready enough to go out and keep watch. "You guys get some sleep. Yutani, I'll wake you up in a few hours. Although I have to say, time seems very odd to me here."

Viktor handed me his watch. "Here. I set the alarm for three hours."

"I'm not putting this on, because I could kill it if I did. I stop watches. But I'll put it in my pocket." I slid the watch into the pocket of my jacket, and then, pulling my sleeping bag around my shoulders, I stepped out of the tent into the chill.

The sky was still clear, with stars shimmering down from overhead. It made the entire forest glow, although I wasn't sure if some of that glow wasn't the aura I had seen the night before. Y'Bain was beautiful in the darkness, with the snow reflecting under the light of the stars.

I settled myself on a small log that we had carried over next to the tent. I readied Serafina and unsnapped the binding on my dagger in its sheath, so that I could grab it out at a moment's notice. I nocked an arrow into Serafina, readying the bow for use, and then settled in to watch.

Yutani had offered me his e-reader, which was backlit, but I had turned him down, preferring to keep as alert as I could. The caffeine was racing through my system now, shoring me up, and I felt like I could hear every sound echoing through the forest. It was an odd cacophony, a concert of clicks and whistles and rustles and the occasional *thump* of snow falling off the trees to the ground. After a while, I settled down, my nerves smoothing out as nothing happened.

About halfway into my watch, however, I had the sensation that we were being observed, that something out there was watching me, waiting. While we had felt like this all day, the feeling was growing stronger and I was beginning to get uncomfortable. I shifted, looking around, trying to see if there was anything nearby that I could catch sight of.

Ember— Ember—come here. The words seem to sing through the air, a faint melody on the wind.

I straightened up, looking around. At first, I saw nothing, just the snow and the dark silhouettes of the trees. But then, across the clearing at the other end of the campsite, I began to notice faint orbs of light hovering in the air. They paused, still glowing, orbs of pink and blue, of green and gold.

Just Lightning Flits, I thought, starting to relax.

But then they started toward me, not floating aimlessly like Lightning Flits usually did, but as though they were directly focused on me.

Ember— Ember—come play with us.

I stiffened. These were no Lightning Flits. Catching my breath, I stood, readying Serafina.

"Who are you?" I asked, trying to keep my voice low so I wouldn't startle Viktor or Yutani.

But the orbs didn't answer, they just kept coming at a slow, steady pace.

I paused, mesmerized by their beauty. They were lovely, and they felt so welcoming. I paused, thinking that perhaps I should lower my bow, but then some part of me deep inside reared up, furious. Without thinking, I sent an arrow singing toward one of the orbs.

"Get back," I ordered. Now, I knew what they were. From some memory locked deep inside, I realized that we were facing a group of will-o'-the-wisps.

"Get away, *now*." Then, I called out, "Viktor! Yutani! Will-o'-the-wisps."

The will-o'-the-wisps paused, waiting. It felt like we had approached a standoff. As I stood, the tent rustled behind me, and Viktor and Yutani came rushing out.

"We have will-o'-the-wisps."

"I'm not entirely sure how to deal with them," Yutani said, standing by my side, staring at them. "I've seen them before, but I've never had to fight them. How do you deal with corpse candles?"

I thought for a moment, running through what knowledge I had of the creatures. They were forest *devas*, not true Fae the way most people thought of the Fae. They weren't sub-Fae, either. They were dangerous to anyone and everyone who crossed their paths, and they hunted in packs.

"They don't like light or fire." As I said the last, the forest shifted around me. *Crap*. Apparently I had to spell the word after all. "We don't have the option of…F-I-R-E, so what do we have in the way of light?"

Viktor pulled out his flashlight, shining it in their direction. That caused them to shift around, and it was obvious they didn't care for it. Yutani popped back in the tent and then returned with Viktor's LED lights. He turned them on, and set them on the log next to us. That halted any additional forward movement from the will-o'-the-wisps.

"What do we do now?" Viktor asked.

"How long of a lifespan do those lights have?" I asked.

"About two hundred hours and I put fresh batteries in before we left. More than enough if we need to leave them on all night."

"All right, that will keep them at bay. But another problem is that they can lure you away. They can affect me. I heard them calling me to come play. I was about ready to run off with them until my father's blood rose up. The Autumn Stalker blood in me recognizes them, apparently, and prevented me from falling into their trap. Oddly enough, I don't think that my Leannan Sidhe side can protect me from them, though. But you two are prime targets. We need to drown out their ability to speak to you. Anybody got any music?"

"Yeah, but it will wear my phone down. I don't think it can last a morning," Viktor said.

I groaned. There was only one other option as long as they were around. I was going to have to sing.

"Guess what? You're in luck, boys. I'm going to sing. And whoever takes over, as long as the will-o'-the-wisps are here, will have to pick up where I left off. Because these creatures can hypnotize you even when you're asleep."

"We can't go without sleep, not for forty-eight hours,"

Viktor said. "All right. Do you think you can sing for a while?"

"Bring me my bottle of water. I just have to continue until they get bored and go away."

Viktor set up another LED light inside the tent so the will-o'-the-wisps couldn't enter, then he brought me a bottle of water. Feeling nerve-racked, I motioned for them to go back to bed. I kept my arrow trained on the will-o'-the-wisps while I began to sing.

Illuminated by the LED lights, I sang my way through several songs by Gary Numan, then tried rapping a couple Beastie Boys songs, then mangled a couple songs by The Kills. Finally, the will-o'-the-wisps seemed to get bored of me and they withdrew into the woods.

I kept singing for another twenty minutes, making certain they weren't sneaking around behind the tent, trying to get in that way. But after a while the forest fell silent, and when the alarm went off, I was more than ready to wake up Yutani to take my place.

As I snuggled inside my sleeping bag in the tent, I could hear him singing, and I wasn't sure what song it was but it was haunting and ancient, and I realized that he had an excellent voice. Feeling strangely secure and comforted, I closed my eyes and fell asleep, not even waking when Viktor and Yutani changed places.

CHAPTER EIGHTEEN

*W*e were on the road again by first light, giving the faerie ring a wide berth. The will-o'-the-wisps hadn't returned, and I was grateful to whatever impulse had made Viktor bring the LED lights. The clouds had socked in and it felt a little bit warmer, although I could smell snow on the horizon. That crackle of ozone filled the air, the way it always did preceding a snowstorm.

"It would be a whole lot easier if horses would cooperate in the forest. We would be at the lake by now." I felt grumbly, especially after the will-o'-the-wisps, and my throat hurt from singing so much. I loved the forest, and I tried to respect it, but Y'Bain had other ideas. Annwn seemed a far bigger and scarier place than any place back home.

"If wishes were shares of VN stock, we'd all be rich." Viktor laughed, glancing my way.

"True that," Yutani said.

VN stock—the official stock of the Vampire Nation's

financial holdings—was soaring on the charts. I had actually invested $3,000 to buy three shares, and it had doubled in the past month. I was hoping it would go higher, and all things looked good. Although if Typhon was actually able to control the vampires, everything would go crumbling to the ground. *Maybe I should sell*, I thought, suddenly feeling leery about the possibilities.

I paused, suddenly aware that I could hear water up ahead. "We can't be to the lake yet, can we? I hear water." But I could feel the water, too.

It was alive and thriving, and the energy of it flowed past me like a wave rolling in from the ocean. My Leannan Sidhe side rose up, responding to the energy. Given my Light Fae side was steeped in water magic, it was no wonder that I responded to it.

"No, we're not due to hit lakeside until afternoon. But I hear it too," Viktor said. "It's coming from around the bend up there." He nodded toward the bend in the road, which angled sharply to the north.

"This must be the shift that Brighid told us about. Toward the north." I cautiously rounded the bend, Viktor and Yutani close behind me. Up ahead, breaking across the path, was a swift stream, churning along with whitecaps frothing atop the water. It looked deep. Deep enough that I didn't want to try crossing it.

"Well, how are we supposed to get around that?" Yutani asked. "It's far too deep to wade through, not with the speed of that current."

"Is there a bridge anywhere?" I looked around, trying to spy a crossing nearby. There didn't seem to be anything in sight, although as we approached the shore, I saw the remains of a splintered log. It quickly became apparent that there had been a small footbridge over the water, but it had either been swept away or broken.

"What do we do now?" Viktor asked, staring at the remains of the bridge. He glanced around. "I could cut a small tree to fall across the water, but somehow I think cutting a tree in this forest would be akin to lighting an F-I-R-E."

"Yeah, we're not cutting any trees down. But is there anything around here that we could drag over? A fallen log that's wide enough and long enough?"

The stream was about four yards wide. However, it was hard to see where the bottom was, it cut such a deep channel. And looking both left and right showed no end in sight.

"The only way to find out is take a look," Viktor said.

We began to look for a log that was already down and would be long enough to cross the water, but not so heavy that we couldn't lift it. Luckily, Viktor was incredibly strong, and Yutani had a wiry strength going for him as well. I was strong enough, but I couldn't match either one of them. It was slow going, picking through the woods right near the path, especially since most everything was covered with snow.

"This is the first time I've ever wished I was a bird shifter instead of a coyote shifter," Yutani said. "I could fly across with the end of a rope, and we could create a rope bridge."

"I wish you were a bird shifter, too, right now," I said, brushing the snow off of a log that looked like it might be promising. "Viktor, what do you think about this? It looks long enough. Do you think we could lift it?"

Viktor walked over to one end of the log and knelt to

take a look at it. He tentatively tried to lift it, grimacing a little, but he was able to get it off the ground.

"It's heavy, but it's definitely long enough, and I think the three of us might be able to drag it over there. My suggestion is that we get it over to the edge, then lift it up and push it so that it falls across the stream. It's not very wide, so we'll have to be careful on the way over."

Under Viktor's guidance, Yutani and I grabbed hold of the front end of the tree, while Viktor pushed on the back. It took some doing, but we were able to lug it over next to the stream without too much of a problem. As we stood, sweating, Viktor eyed the stream, then the tree.

"We're going to want to stand it on end, and tip it so when it falls, it will fall toward the other side of the stream. We'll have to be careful or we could knock it into the stream and all our work would be for nothing. I want you two to pick it up and help me prop it on my back. First, though, let's tie a rope around it, so we can keep some control over it when it's upright."

I grimaced. My faith that we were going to be able to do this right was in short supply. Now that we were at this point, it seemed incredibly tricky to maneuver the tree across the stream. But we had no choice and it was a senseless waste of energy to move it like we had unless we were willing to give it a go.

Viktor threaded a rope around it, tying it in a tight knot about two-thirds of the way up the trunk. Then Yutani and I lifted up what had been the top of the tree as Viktor crouched beneath it, shouldering the weight on his back.

Yutani and I took hold of the ropes, one of us on either side of the tree, and held them taut, doing our best to steady it. Grunting, Viktor began to walk backward, levering the tree up off the ground. Yutani and I held the ropes as tight as we could, doing our best to take some of the weight off Viktor. When he got halfway up, he quickly spun, his massive arms pushing the tree even further.

I was doing my best to hold steady on my side, ready to let go if Viktor lost control of the tree and it launched itself toward the stream. The last thing we need was for either Yutani or me to be dragged into the water. Viktor was doing his best to adjust the tree's position, the strain showing on his face. Finally, the tree was pointing toward the stream.

"I'm going to give it one more shove. When I do, *let go of the ropes.* Make sure that you're not entangled in them. Actually, make sure that you aren't tangled up now. You need to be able to drop them at a second's notice."

I glanced at the rope. It was wrapped around my forearm so I untangled it, still trying to hold on as best as I could. I made sure that it wasn't circling around my legs or feet, and that when I let go, it would be free to fly.

"I'm ready," I said.

"Me too," Yutani called out from the other side.

"On the count of three I'm going to give one final shove and then jump away. When you hear me say *two*, let go. Understand?" Viktor glanced my way. "Ember?"

"Understood. Let go on the count of two."

"Yutani?"

"I hear you. I'm ready."

As Yutani and I waited, Viktor gave one final grunt.

"One." The tree shifted and moved forward another few inches.

"Two." It felt like the tree was beginning to waver. It

was upright now, listing toward the stream. I dropped the rope and jumped away, and so did Yutani.

The next moment Viktor called out, "Three!" and gave one final shove before jumping to the side. He landed in the snow bank next to the path as the tree teetered, then fell.

I held my breath watching, hoping that it would be long enough. Sure enough, we had estimated correctly because the tree fell toward the stream, the top six feet of it landing on the other side. I let out a cheer, and so did Yutani. Viktor picked himself up from the ground, dusted the snow off, and crossed his arms with a satisfied look.

"Well, damned if that didn't work." He looked proud of himself.

"Sometimes it's nice having a half-ogre on the team," I said, clapping him on the back. "Way to go. We did it, so now I guess we have to cross the stream."

The tree wasn't that wide, but at its narrowest, it was still a foot in diameter. But it was wet, slick from the snow and moss that had grown on it. And the rushing stream below could be awfully mesmerizing.

"So how do we want to do this part of it? Anybody have any more rope?" I asked.

"I have plenty," Viktor said. "The guards packed several lengths of the special rope that Brighid's people weave. It doesn't break easily, and it's very lightweight."

I eyed the rope hanging off the other end of the tree, down toward the water. "It's not like the Elvish rope in *Lord of the Rings*, is it? I hate to leave that rope there."

"I don't think so, unfortunately. Fiction rarely mirrors reality, even when we'd like it to." Viktor pulled out another length of rope. "Who wants to go first? Whoever does can take this rope across with them, and they can tie it off on a tree on the other side to steady the way for the other two."

"I'll go first," Yutani said. "I'm nimble on my feet. And I'm stronger than Ember so I can help steady it easier. I'd rather not tie it off on another tree over here, though, because we don't want to leave another rope behind. Why don't I go first, then Viktor, you come across. And then Ember can tie the rope around her waist and that way, if she falls, we can catch her."

Yutani practically skipped across the log without missing a single step, or even wavering. Once on the other side, he held the rope taut, and I held the other end. Viktor didn't want to lash himself to the rope just in case he fell. His weight could probably pull me off my feet. But he held tightly to the rope, cautiously crossing the tree step by step. For such a large man, he was graceful in his movements, and he made it to the other side without incident.

Then it was my turn. I wrapped the rope around my waist, tying it off with what I hoped would be a sturdy knot. Then, placing a foot on the trunk, I tried to avoid looking down. But I couldn't help it. I had to see where my feet were placed, to make sure that I was stepping onto the actual trunk and not onto thin air. I turned my walking stick sideways, holding it the way a tightrope walker held a balancing rod.

Halfway across the tree, I felt myself beginning to panic. I knew that if I fell they would catch me, but that didn't seem to help. There was something about the frothing whitecaps below my feet that kept me mesmerized. I could hear voices coming from them, whispering for me to *jump, just jump.*

Feeling myself starting to respond, I took a deep breath and raced ahead, praying I could cross the remainder of the tree without falling. At the very end I stumbled, but Yutani was there, and he grabbed hold of me, dragging me onto solid ground. I buckled onto my knees in the snow, seconds away from a full-blown panic attack.

"You're safe, you're safe now. Ember? What happened?" Yutani wrapped his arms around me, bracing me as he pulled me up to stare him in the face. His eyes were dark, glowing with the light of the Great Coyote. In an uncharacteristic move, he reached out and brushed my hair back away from my face, sliding his fingers along the curve of my cheek.

I shuddered, a chaotic whirlwind of feelings resting rushing through me.

"I… I was in the middle, and all of a sudden I couldn't move. I heard voices whispering for me to jump. I was about to obey when I realized my only chance was to run the rest of the way, to get away from the voices." I held Yutani's gaze, still feeling flustered and anxious.

"You're all right now. You're off the tree. Can you stand?" He cupped my elbow, helping me to my feet.

I still felt winded, and suddenly embarrassed, as though he had seen me naked. I tried to look away, wanting to avoid his gaze because, if he looked me in the eye, I was afraid he might spark off feelings that I really didn't want to explore. I had never been attracted to Yutani, although I found him a handsome man, but now, he was holding me up and I realized that I was as aroused as I was afraid. As I turned, I caught his gaze once again, and the intensity of his look suddenly shook me out of my embarrassment. I pulled away, thrusting my hands in my pockets.

"Thank you. I'm all right, I'm fine now."

"Are you sure? Can you go on?"

I nodded, not wanting to say anymore.

Yutani gave me an odd look, then gathered up the rope and untied it from my waist. I turned away as he stood next to me, fiddling with the knot. After he wrapped up the rope and gave it back to Viktor, we headed out again. I took the lead once more, distancing myself a little from the men, trying to sort out my feelings.

Ever since I had been with Herne, I had only had eyes for him, and I was deeply in love with him. Oh, I had flirted a little, all in fun, with Viktor and Yutani, and once in a drunken stupor, with Kipa, who had the good graces to help Angel pour me into bed. But other than that, I had never felt the pull to kiss another man.

You're forgetting, a little voice in my head said. *Don't forget when you were using your Leannan Sidhe powers, when you were tracing down the iron bones. You tried to entice several men then.*

Oh crap, I thought. That was right. My mother's blood had risen up, before I learned to control it, attempting to trap and seduce men. I could feed off of their energy. Was there something in the woods that spurred on that side of me? Worried now, I decided I needed to tell Viktor and Yutani about what happened. A little embarrassment was worth their safety.

I turned, waiting for them to catch up with me. "We

need to discuss something, and we need to discuss it now."

Viktor looked worried. "What's going on?"

Yutani gave me a long look, then said, "It's your Leannan Sidhe powers. They've come to the surface again, haven't they?"

I nodded. "I think they have and I don't know what set them off. How did you know?"

"You're the boss's woman," he said, his eyes somber. "I seldom allow myself to think in those directions about any woman who has a partner. When I realized that my mind was wandering along roads it should not go just a few minutes ago, I knew something was wrong. And then I remembered up on the mountain, when you tried to lure me in."

"Right. That's what I thought of, too. You're going to have to watch me, because I think there's something in this woodland that stirs that side of me. I've heard my name called several times, then something trying to lure me into the water. There's something out here of which I need to be wary."

"That's an understatement," Viktor said. "Cernunnos wasn't joking when he said Y'Bain is dangerous. Let's get a move on. We should be to the lake within a few hours. But I have a feeling we're going to have to make camp before we find the well."

That I *didn't* want to hear. The realization that some-thing was activating a part of me that just loved to trick men to their death, that fed on life energy, was frightening enough. That I had responded to Yutani was even more frightening. If something happened that went beyond our control, Herne would probably understand, but it would throw a real wrench in all of us working together, and that was the last thing I wanted.

We were on our way again, and this time I kept up a steady chatter, trying to keep myself from falling into a trance as we walked. I knew I was most susceptible at that point. But after a while, the conversation lulled once again, and I found myself drifting in my thoughts.

We were approaching what looked like an opening in the woods—the path had narrowed and the trees were thick on each side at this point, when once again I heard my name being called. I tried to turn around, to warn Viktor and Yutani, but before I could, I felt an overwhelming urge to race forward on the path, to run through the trees into the opening ahead.

I tried to stop myself, tried to put a brake on the impulse, but I couldn't. Someone was calling me and I *had* to answer. I had no choice in the matter, so my body answered for me. I dropped my bow, quiver, and pack, then broke into a run. I stumbled along the path, toward the opening in the trees. Faintly, from behind me, I could hear Yutani and Viktor calling, but their voices were faint, so distant I couldn't even hear them anymore, and my sole focus was on what lay in the clearing ahead.

As I cleared the opening, I found myself on the shore near a lake. And by the lake were two tall, absolutely gorgeous men. They were standing there with hair the color of spun platinum coiling down their backs, and they were stark naked, gloriously muscled, and absolutely beautiful. All I could think about was needing to be with them, letting them have their way with me.

As I approached them, once again I could hear Viktor

and Yutani shouting from behind me. Irritated, I ignored their calls, wanting them to back off and leave me alone.

"We've been waiting for you. You're one of the Leannan Sidhe, aren't you?" one of the men asked, in a voice so deep and resonant that it sent chills through my entire body.

A smile broke across my face as I was about to answer him.

But suddenly, they closed in on either side of me so that I couldn't get away. The enticing looks on the faces turned into deep sneers, vicious and predatory, and their nails lengthened into talons. They looked like they were shifting, but I couldn't tell into what.

One of them grabbed my wrists, and I realized how incredibly strong he was. He began dragging me toward the water, his brother helping him, and I suddenly realized that I had fallen into a trap. That single slice of understanding pierced through the glamour, and I knew precisely what I was facing.

I had been caught by the aughiskies, a vicious form of waterhorse shifter, and they were about to feed on me— or worse. Screaming, I tried to break free, but then they had me in the water, and the icy chill of it was seeping through my clothes as they tried to drag me under.

CHAPTER NINETEEN

I could hold my breath quite a while, but struggling to get free made it harder to focus. At that moment, one of the men pressed his lips against mine, and air began to flow into my body. But he was kissing me, hard, almost violently. His partner was yanking at my jeans, trying to get them off of me, and right then I realized that they weren't just intending to feed on my energy.

Oh crap. A brief memory flickered into mind, from some entry I had read in a bestiary somewhere. All aughiskies were male, but they could mate with several forms of water Fae. They captured human women to feed on, luring them into their deaths. But nixies and naiads, undines and the Leannan Sidhe—all of these could inter-breed with the violent waterhorse shifters. Female children would follow their mother's blood, but the males would become aughiskies and return to their brethren, no matter how long it took them.

They obviously didn't realize I wasn't full-blooded. If they found out, they'd just kill me right there. I pushed against the one who was holding me tight and tried to kick the other. But they were incredibly strong, and I realized that I was running through my air supply by trying to escape. As long as my attacker was kissing me, I could breathe. So, even through my revulsion, I relaxed into the kiss long enough to throw them off guard.

As I tried to calm myself, I remembered what Morgana had said.

I focused on the lake, searching for any water elementals that might be nearby.

There were several, one who was sending out an alarm, and it occurred to me that the water elementals might not like the aughiskies. The one I had tuned into seemed anxious, and I forced all of my will into contacting it, projecting feelings of danger, that I needed help. I focused the energy of my magic into my thoughts, trying to establish a connection that might save my life. Even if Viktor and Yutani made it into the lake, they weren't equipped to fight on the aughiskies' home turf, so if I was going to survive, it was up to me.

The aughisky who was kissing me slid his hands over my naked butt. My other attacker had managed to yank my jeans off.

I started to panic. I had to get away *now*. I appealed to the water elementals once more, focusing all my panic and fear into my thoughts.

The next moment a great swell of water rose beneath us, pushing us up and out of the lake. Startled, my attacker let go of me, and I dove away from him, back into the lake where I began to swim like mad as I tried to reach the shore. I couldn't even glance over my shoulder—that would take too much time—but I kept imagining them behind me, catching up to me. Aughiskies were excellent swimmers. Water was their home turf.

As I raised my head, I saw I was reaching the shallows of the lake, and Viktor and Yutani were there waiting for me. They waded out and grabbed me under the arms, dragging me out of the water.

I glanced over my shoulder to see that the water elemental had swept the wave high into the air and it was still holding the aughiskies over the lake. They were fighting to free themselves but the water elemental coiled around them, tendrils of lake water holding them captive.

I let out a cry, furious. I wanted them *dead*. I must have been projecting my thoughts, because the water elemental rose even farther, looking like a massive wave, and it slammed the aughiskies far onto the shore, near us.

"Give me Serafina!" I held up my hand. Viktor slammed the crossbow into my grip and I swung around, seeing that he had nocked an arrow for me. I aimed directly at the one who'd been kissing me and pulled the trigger, feeling a delicious victory as the arrow lodged into his chest. The other aughisky was running, trying to reach the lake, but Viktor handed me another arrow and I smoothly fitted it into Serafina, swinging my aim to target the remaining shifter.

Without an ounce of hesitation, I pulled the trigger, and the arrow flew swift and true, hitting my target. He, too, dropped to the ground without a sound. I stood there, naked—all my clothes had been pulled from me—

panting as the bloodlust that had thundered through my body began to fade.

After a moment, Yutani quietly began to dig through my pack.

"You'd better get dressed," he said, handing me underwear, a spare pair of jeans, a bra, and a shirt. Viktor headed over to check on the aughiskies. I silently accepted the clothes, shimmying into them. I didn't have another coat with me, but Yutani stripped off his parka and handed it to me. Beneath his coat he was wearing a denim jacket.

"Won't you be cold?" I asked.

He shrugged. "We can take turns if we need to. I should be all right. And if worse comes to worst, we can cut up one of the sleeping bags and make a cape out of it." He paused, looking at me with those dark eyes of his. "Are you all right?"

I nodded, still angry. "Yeah, I am. But I lost my dagger." I wasn't sure what else to say. The blood was still raging through my veins, and I wasn't sure whether my drive for vengeance was spurred on by my mother's blood, my father's blood, or just me in general. After a moment, I said, "They didn't manage to do anything."

"What were they?" Yutani asked.

Viktor returned then. He had cleaned off my arrows and now he handed them back to me. I stuck them in the quiver and hung it over my shoulder. In my hand, Serafina was practically vibrating, and if I had to give an emotion to the bow, I'd say she was doing a happy dance.

"They're dead. You got nice clean shots on both of them. I searched them, but there wasn't much there."

"They are called aughiskies," I said.

"O-hə-skees?" Yutani repeated.

I nodded. "They're a form of waterhorse shifter."

"You mean like the hippocampi? Surely they aren't related to Rhiannon and the Foam Born pod?" Viktor said. He looked incredulous.

The Foam Born pod were a group of waterhorse shifters—hippocampi—whom we had helped out earlier in the year. Only *they* were nice.

I shook my head. "No. There's more than one type of waterhorse shifter. These are far more dangerous, and quite frankly, the only good aughisky is a dead one. They lure human women to their death. They must have thought I was full-blooded Leannan Sidhe, because they were trying to rape me. They impregnate water Fae from other races, and if the child comes out male, it's almost always aughisky and it returns to the fold."

I looked around nervously. "They can charm female water Fae as well as female humans. We need to find the well and get away from this lake. You two need to watch me. If I seem like I'm ignoring you and try to head toward the lake, do whatever you have to in order to stop me. Where there's one, there's probably more, and I might not be able to get away a second time."

"If I remember right, Brighid said that the well was on the other side of the lake. Which means we need to skirt around it." Viktor glanced at the sky. "Dusk is falling. I'm not sure I want to take that chance."

"If you want to wait until morning, then whoever is on watch is going to have to keep an eye on me, and I'm not going to be able to stand watch. Also, consider this.

There's bound to be more than just those two. If they figure out that their brethren are dead, they're going to come looking for whoever killed them." I shivered, thinking of the possibilities.

Yutani zipped up his jean jacket. "How long can they stay on land? Are they like, for instance, the hippocampi or the Leannan Sidhe? Can they exist out of water for long?"

I thought for a moment, trying to remember what I had read about them. "See, that's the problem. I don't know. If they can, a raiding party could come up and overwhelm us. And I guarantee you, they're strong. If they drag us into the water, they'll drown us for sure. I'm not certain how many are usually in a *skoll*—that's what you call a group of aughiskies—but there have to be more than two. Especially in this forest."

Y'Bain was a lot like Australia. It seemed to attract the deadliest creatures. While I wasn't sure how I knew, I was positive there were definitely more of the waterhorse shifters in that lake. I took a good look at the water. It wasn't a massive lake, but it was at least a mile wide and probably three miles long. There was plenty of room beneath the surface for a number of water breathers to live.

"But do you want to travel in the dark?" Viktor asked. "I'm not being facetious. I'm asking you a very real question, and I want you to think it over carefully."

I glanced at the sky. The sun was setting, but there was still some light to go by. And clouds were coming in, thick and heavy with snow. I could smell it in the air. The night wouldn't be too dark, not between the illumination of the clouds and the snow on the ground. Plus, we had flashlights. And if we kept the lake within our sight, we shouldn't risk running off into the wilderness. Then again, who knew what else was out here? Cernunnos had warned us specifically against traveling during the dark, and when the Lord of the Forest gave you a serious warning, it was best to listen to it.

"I'm not sure what to do. I suppose that we should wait until morning. Cernunnos was adamant about traveling only during the daylight hours. But I'm serious, guys. You're going to have to watch me tonight. The aughiskies can get into my head, and it's not easy to keep them out." I gave them an anxious look, terrified that we would be attacked in the dark. "We should retreat into the forest again. We shouldn't be out on the lakeshore when dusk falls. I don't know how much sleep we can afford to get. If they creep out and sneak up on us during the dark, we're as good as gone. I welcome suggestions."

"We could camp high up in the trees. It would be harder to reach us, and we'd have more of a warning." Viktor glanced up at one of the nearby oaks. Its bare branches were thick and sturdy, but the thought of actually climbing one of the trees of Y'Bain made me even more nervous than I was of the aughiskies.

"Let's back away from that suggestion. Given the forest is watching us, do you really want to tempt fate by crawling up the trees?" I was mulling over the possibilities when a noise behind us caught my attention. I whirled, staring at the entrance to the forest, wondering what the hell we were in for now. I raised Serafina, nocking an arrow just in case. Viktor pulled out his sword, and Yutani brought out a pistol grip crossbow as well, fitting an arrow into it.

As we waited, there was a rustle in the trees, and then, out from the trees stepped a band of Dark Fae. For a moment, I stared at them, uncertain as to who they were, but then something in me stirred, and I knew. I knew in my core that I was facing a group of my father's people.

THERE WERE AT LEAST TEN IN THE PARTY, AND ALMOST ALL of them were carrying bows and arrows. They had a certain look to them, dark and swarthy, with a glint in their eyes that I recognized because I felt it within myself. It was the glint of the hunter, the glint of the predator. I stood, my arm outstretched, the arrow targeted on the leader.

"*Daug tergath frei janeer so pointe?*" the leader said, speaking in Turneth, the Dark variant of Faespeak, the language of the Fae. He had asked who we were and what we were doing.

I stared at him for a moment, then replied, "*Frei aliath dek Cernunnos o Morgana o Brighid, dek onet uo kestiar.*" I told him the truth—that we were on a quest for Cernunnos, Morgana, and Brighid. I waited, wondering if the fact that I was tralaeth would cause a problem.

The leader stared at me for a while, then raised his hand to his companions and they lowered their bows and arrows. He was a handsome man, with a rugged jaw, and long hair caught back in a braid that fell to his knees. His eyebrows were arched, and his mustache thin, but delicately groomed. He didn't look particularly muscled, but I didn't trust appearances in this case. He was probably stronger than he looked.

He looked me up and down, frowning, then glanced at our flashlights. "You are from the other world?" he asked, still speaking in Turneth.

I nodded. "We're from Earth. I serve both Cernunnos and Morgana." I stressed the *both*, feeling like it might serve as a shield. "We mean no interference. I'm looking for something, and once I find it, I will leave this forest. Can you tell me how many of the aughiskies are in that lake? We were attacked earlier." I nodded my head toward the bodies lying on the edge of the shoreline.

He snorted, staring at the naked waterhorse shifters. "More than we need around here. Are you making camp on the shoreline for the evening?"

I slowly nodded, wondering if we could strike some sort of a bargain. Although that might be as dangerous as sticking around where the aughiskies could find us. Members of the Autumn's Bane weren't known for their hospitality.

"We weren't sure about traveling in the dark in Y'Bain."

The leader took a long look at my bow, then at me again. "You have our blood flowing in your veins. You are, however, a tralaeth."

I was surprised that he'd even *admit* that I had Dark Fae blood, when he recognized me as half blood. "I may be a tralaeth, but I am proud of both my heritages, and I have been through the Cruharach."

He shifted from one foot to the other, considering my words. After a moment, he said, "We have heard of a half breed wandering the woods. Rumors say that she bears the protection of Cernunnos, Morgana, and Brighid. Rumors also warned that any hand raised against her will be met with swift and deadly retribution. I would venture to guess that you are this woman?"

So *that's* why they hadn't attacked us. The aughiskies wouldn't give a damn about any such rumors, but any sane group of travelers with a sense of self-preservation would listen well.

I nodded, lowering my bow. "I am Ember Kearney, and yes, I am the one you've heard tell of. These are my companions, Viktor and Yutani. We're searching for the Well of Tears. Can you show us the way?"

The leader let out a small laugh, then bowed. "I am Unkai, chieftain of the Orhanakai band of the Autumn's Bane. We can lead you to the well tomorrow morning, but until then, we must break for camp. It's far too dangerous to traverse these forests in the dark, even for my people. I propose that we make camp together, and we can trade stories till morning."

I looked at him, hesitating for a moment. "You would make camp with me, a tralaeth?"

"You're a tralaeth guarded by powerful gods, and you bear our blood in your veins. Not all of the Fae stand with TirNaNog or with Navane. There are those of us who choose our own path, and our own companions."

A surge of relief swept through me. Making camp with a large party would be so much easier—and safer.

"Bravery, courage, and cunning are far stronger quali-ties than just purity of blood," Unkai continued. "To traverse these woods with just three in your party? That speaks to bravery. To destroy the aughiskies? That speaks to cunning and courage. Come, let us make camp and break bread."

Unkai motioned to the others and they quickly set about making up camp for the evening. I returned to Viktor and Yutani, motioning for them to join in. As we set up our tents toward the forest, away from the lake, I filled them in on what I had learned.

"Keep your eyes on them, don't be complacent. For now, we will accept what they say at face value, but we're still keeping watch during the night." I turned as Unkai called me over.

They were setting up a feast, and it looked far better than what we had to eat. Of course, not even the Autumn Stalkers were building a fire, so the food was cold, but it was good and there was plenty of it. We sat with them, eating roast beef and bread and cheese, fruit and nuts, into the evening hours. As it grew dark, Viktor brought out our LED lights, and Unkai's eyes lit up as he looked at them.

"So this is the magic of your world?" he asked, letting out a sigh. "We have heard tales of your world, of course. But none of us have ever been there."

"I love it there, but it is vastly different than here and there are far more people. And far more rules," I added, hoping to stave off any requests for an invitation to visit. "There is far less freedom over there than there is here."

Unkai looked a little disappointed, but shrugged and leaned back.

None of the others spoke to me, but they listened and watched, and I could tell they were taking in everything we said. Unkai must have noticed me staring at them, because he reached up and snapped his fingers. A moment later, a woman joined him. She was wearing the same garb as the others, and she, too, carried a bow.

"This is my woman. Her name is Liera." He put his arm around her shoulders then, and I noticed a gentleness between them that I hadn't expected.

I nodded to her. "How do you do?"

She blinked. A moment later, she said, "I do well, Ember Kearney." There was a tinge of jealousy in her voice, and she looked me up and down, frowning.

I happened to glance at Unkai, and realized that he had quite the glint in his eye. I wasn't familiar with the customs of the Autumn Stalkers, but I didn't want to give them any ideas.

"I'm tired. I've had a long day. I think I'll get some rest. My guards will be watching," I added, pausing for a moment before continuing. "They'll be watching... Just in case the aughiskies return."

Unkai stared at me for a moment, then laughed. "Message received. You will sleep undisturbed."

I returned to the tent and told Viktor and Yutani everything that had passed between Unkai and me. "Keep watch. I feel that they'll be true to their word, especially since they know that I'm being watched over by three powerful gods. I have a feeling they may believe that I have more power than I actually do, and I didn't do anything to dissuade that notion. But it never hurts to keep on guard. And if you see me trying to head toward the lake, stop me."

Viktor took the first watch as I curled up in the tent with Yutani. I was missing Herne horribly, and I wanted to be out of the forest and home. Y'Bain was a terrifying place, and our companions were just as frightening. I couldn't wait to find the sword and get back to Brighid's palace, and then return home. I couldn't sleep, and tossed and turned for a while until Yutani tapped me on the shoulder. He held out his arm and, feeling sheepish, I rolled into it. He curled it around me, keeping his fingers on my shoulder, and I finally fell asleep.

CHAPTER TWENTY

*U*nkai was good to his word. When I woke in the morning, I realized I was fully refreshed—as refreshed as I could be—and I scrambled out of the tent to find breakfast sitting on a rock next to Viktor. He nodded for me to sit down and eat.

Unkai's people had given us dried fruit, bread and meat, cheese, and what looked suspiciously like a variety of potato chip. I took one.

"These taste a lot like potato chips."

Viktor nodded. "So I noted. But I can't speak your people's language, and I wasn't able to ask anything about them."

I glanced around. "Where's Yutani?"

"He's having a conversation—of sorts—with one of the Fae. I'm not sure how they're communicating, but they are." He pointed over at a clearing on the shoreline, where Yutani was showing one of the Autumn Stalkers what looked a lot like a tai chi move.

I raised my eyebrows. "Well, at least they're getting along."

"I have to say, they're not what I expected them to be. I expected... I don't know... More feral?"

"So did I, to tell you the truth. In a way I feel they're more honor-bound than my grandfather was, by far." I let out a sigh, looking around.

The morning looked overcast, but the scent of snow had backed off. Hopefully it would wait until we returned to Brighid's Castle, but with a two-day hike, I doubted the possibility.

"I really want to get out of here," I said. "I wonder if we can convince Unkai to travel with us back to the edge of the forest. Maybe I can promise them some sort of reward in turn for helping us. I'd feel a lot safer in a big group."

"I'm not so sure about that," Viktor said. "They've been true to their word so far, but I don't trust them. I do agree with you on wanting out of this forest, though. Promise me you'll never drag me back in here again?"

"You'll have to ask Cernunnos to hold that promise," I said. "I'm not the one who asked you to come."

We finished breakfast, and I approached Unkai. "Can you show us the Well of Tears?" I asked, after the obligatory morning greeting.

He gave me a solemn nod. "My people don't like that area. We'll hang back, and let you go in. There is a spirit in there, near the well, and she disconcerts my people."

"She's a Lamentation. A guardian." I looked him straight in the eye. "I need to talk to her. I wanted to ask you something, and whether you say yes or no, it's fine. I won't take any offense. But I wondered if you would consider waiting for us, and then escorting us back to the edge of the forest? We were set upon by will-o'-the-wisps the first night, and then the aughiskies yesterday. While we were able to fend them off, my companions and I just want to get the hell out of Y'Bain after we finish our task."

Unkai held my gaze for a moment, staring at me steadily. "And what could you offer for such a favor?"

"I'm not sure what you want. I'm not sure what's valuable to you. Food? Money—gold? What do you value that would be worth your time and trouble?" I wasn't sure I really wanted to hear the answer, but I knew better than to offer blind payment.

For a moment I thought he wasn't going to answer, and then, the edge of his lips curled up in a cunning smile and he let out a laugh. "There is one thing that I will take as payment. I wish to visit your world, Ember Kearney. And I want a guide when I get there."

I tried not to let my dismay show on my face. Inwardly, I was beating myself up for being so stupid. I let out a little laugh and glanced sideways at Viktor, who was standing nearby.

"One moment," I said to Unkai. Without turning my head, I switched over to English. "He just asked me to be his guide when he comes visiting over in our world. That's his payment for seeing us to the edge of the forest. What do you think I should say? Now that I've started the deal, it seems rude to stop midway and say no." I kept my voice light, smiling as I spoke.

Viktor broke into a coughing fit so loud that I worried that he was choking. One of the Autumn Stalkers brought him a jug of water, and he drank deep. As he wiped his mouth and turned back to me, he raised his eyebrows and I realized it had been a ploy.

"Are you all right?" I asked, forcing concern into my voice.

"Yes, I'm fine," he said thumping his chest and nodding. "You're a fool if you accept."

"And we could be in trouble if I don't." I paused, then walked over to him and patted his back with a concerned look. "Tell you what. I'll tell him that I will help him as much as the gods allow. Think that will go over?"

"Let's hope so," Viktor said, straightening up and clearing his throat once again.

I turned back to Unkai. In Turneth, I said, "I'm sorry for the interruption. My comrade was having some difficulties. Where were we? Oh yes, talking payment for your services. I can make you this promise. I will be your guide as much as the gods will allow me. Since I am pledged to them, I have to do their bidding. I can only make deals to that extent."

Unkai stared at me with a steady gaze. After a moment, he snickered.

"Do tell. Very well," he said, shaking his head. "We will guide you to the edge of the forest. I do hope that I'll have the chance to visit you in your world, however." With that, he called for his people to break camp, and within less than ten minutes, we were packed and they were leading me to the Well of Tears.

We skirted the lake, and there was no sign of any more aughiskies. The focus of the Autumn Stalkers was so intense that I could feel it all around us. We wore their aura like a shroud, and it surrounded us as we crept through the bushes that lined the edge of Lake Discover. No one talked, and we followed suit, trusting that they knew the area better than we did.

As time passed, I began to notice a change in Serafina. She felt alive in my hands, and I sensed an excitement coming from her. Slowly, not sure exactly what I was doing, I reached out with my thoughts to try and communicate with her.

Can you hear me? I waited for a moment.

There was a shift in the bow's energy.

After another beat, I thought, *My name is Ember. You're Serafina, and Herne the Hunter made you. Can you hear me?* And again, I waited. Just as I thought that I wasn't going to get any answer, a very soft voice crept around the edge of my thoughts.

I'm here. It's been a long time since someone picked me up.

I know. But I have you now, and Herne the Hunter has given me permission to use you. You have an incredible aim, and I want to thank you for your help. I wasn't entirely sure exactly what thanking the bow would do, but it was obvious that it was no inanimate object. There was a sentience in this bow, and an intelligence.

Yes, I understand that you are my new person. Trust me and I will guide you to a true aim.

I paused, mulling over what Serafina had just said. She could increase my aim and ability. I wondered what was in it for her, but then brushed aside the thought. Herne had made her, had brought the wood to life, and it was infused with his energy. I could trust this bow, even though it had belonged to my great-great-grandmother. Morgana had cleansed it, and I had claimed it. Serafina was mine.

Unkai glanced back at me, and then at the bow in my hand. He motioned for me to join him at the head of the group. I picked up my pace, wondering what he wanted.

"It's a beautiful bow," he said.

"It should be. Herne the Hunter made it. And he's given me leave to use it. My great-great-grandmother used it until her death. It was passed down through the family and eventually came to me." I left him to think about that.

"And your great-great-grandmother was…?" He left the question unfinished, but I knew what he was asking.

"Yes, she was one of the Autumn's Bane."

Unkai nodded, as if slowly digesting what I had just told him. After another moment, he asked, "So are any of that side of your family still living?"

I paused, not sure what to say. "A great-uncle, as far as I know. My grandfather killed my father for loving my mother, and he would have killed me, too." I looked directly at Unkai. "Apparently, my existence stood against everything he believed in."

"Was he very invested in the court of TirNaNog?"

I nodded. "He was friends with Queen Saílle. I belong to neither Court. Neither will claim me, nor really want anything to do with me."

Unkai let out a soft laugh. "Their loss. And your grandfather's loss as well. Does he know you have the bow?"

Here it was. A subject that I couldn't seem to avoid, no matter how hard I tried.

"I killed my grandfather. He tried to kill me, so I sucked out his life energy. My mother's blood is strong in me as well. Usually one side takes precedence during the Cruharach, but I came through with powers from both bloodlines." I stared at him, defying him to say anything against me. But he surprised me.

"There is no shame in defending yourself, even when it's against one of your elders. And as I said, my people have little to do with the court of TirNaNog here. We have no interest in the politics between the two great courts. We live for ourselves. We are the Autumn's Bane, the stalkers of the forest. We make our own rules."

Before I could say anything, he pointed ahead as we rounded the lake.

"There, some half a mile ahead you will find the Well of Tears. We will walk with you for a few more minutes, then wait for you. My people will not approach that space."

I gave him a nod, grateful that Unkai seemed to be a reasonable person. I knew that my people were ruthless. In fact, they preyed on stray villagers and were known as plunderers, much like the Vikings had been back in our realm. But apparently, they did so without regard for petty politics. That didn't necessarily make them better people, but I knew where I stood.

I turned back and motioned to Viktor and Yutani. "Come up here. We're nearing the well."

As they joined me, I shaded my eyes with my hands and looked ahead. Sure enough, about half a mile in the distance on the shore of the lake, I could see something glistening. It was a structure of some sort, and even from here I could feel the energy of Brighid emanating from it.

I turned to Viktor and Yutani. "You need to wait here. I can't explain why, but if you try to come with me, you could get hurt."

"What about the aughiskies?" Yutani asked, looking worried.

I frowned, just now realizing he was wearing a cloak over the jean jacket. "Where did you get that?"

"From Unkai. He didn't say anything, but he fingered the material on my jacket, gave me a disgusted look, and a few minutes later, one of the hunters brought over a cloak and handed it to me. It's warm, that much I'll say for it. Oddly enough, it smells like cinnamon bark." He held up his arm and sniffed the sleeve. "Yeah, cinnamon, and… smoke. Bonfire smoke."

"It must have been stored with some of their other things," I said. "All right. You can come with me to that pair of fallen logs, but you have to wait there."

The path leading to the well rose in a gentle gradation, only about ten feet, but at the top of the rise, there were two fallen logs, one on either side. They buttressed the path like gates, and while I couldn't put it into words, I knew that nobody should cross beyond those logs except for me. I panicked for a moment, thinking the marker Brighid had given me for the Lamentation had gotten lost in the water, but then remembered that I had stored it in my pack, not my jacket. I dug through my pack, took a long swig of water, and then found the talisman.

It was a triskelion, formed in brass, about three inches in diameter, and it was engraved with a number of runic symbols that I didn't recognize. I turned it over in my hand. The symbols were engraved on both sides.

"I'm ready," I said, hoisting Serafina and making certain my arrows were within easy reach. My dagger was gone, but Viktor had provided me with another, so I took a deep breath and turned away from them, heading up the rise.

Viktor and Yutani followed me as far as I would allow,

then stood to the side, flanking the logs as I passed between them.

IMMEDIATELY, I FELT A SHIFT IN THE ENERGY. EVEN THE aughiskies wouldn't be able to manage here, I thought, so strong was Brighid's claim to this place. The well was about ten yards away, and it was low to the ground, only a few feet high. The snow was almost gone. As I turned I saw that, in a circular pattern, the ground was mostly bare. It was as though an invisible dome arched over the area containing the well. I knelt by the stones forming the sides of the well and leaned over the edge, staring in.

The water was near the top, but the well seemed to sink into the ground, far deeper than it looked from the outside. I tried to gauge how deep it was, but the ripples kept shifting. I knelt, leaning far over the edge, searching for the sword, but saw nothing but rippling water.

A movement caught my attention and I looked up to find myself facing a magnificent specter. She was hovering off the ground in back of the well, and as translucent as sheer silk, but I could still see every detail.

Tall she was, with long flowing red hair, and eyes as fierce as any tiger's. She was wearing a long gown that looked to be pale green. Her expression warned me to be very, very careful. This spirit had the ability to kill me if I didn't watch my step.

I slowly backed away from the well and straightened my shoulders. Without a word, I held up the talisman that Brighid had given me.

The Lamentation stared at me for a moment, then

slowly turned her attention to the marker. She leaned her head back and let out a wail that echoed through the forest. It must have reverberated for miles. Then she moved back, held out her hand, and swept it over the top of the well.

As she did so, the entire circle we were in shifted. I blinked as the rippling on the water stilled. A faint light began to glow from within the well, growing stronger with each moment. It started out as pale green, then deepened into a leafy peridot, and finally, it was radiating pure gold. I squinted against the light—it was so bright—and gasped as it came flying out of the well—a round sphere that was as golden as the summer sun. It rose above the well, then cracks formed against the surface as another light inside began to seep out. This light was pure—clear and white, the light of truth and of illumination.

As I watched, the light shattered the last of the sphere and the Lamentation let out a joyous cry. She turned to me, then she vanished into the mists, disappearing from sight.

I looked back at the well. There, in the shallow water, was a sword. I slowly knelt beside the stone exterior, gazing down into the water. I could see the bottom now—it was about five feet down, and covered in moss and algae, with a decidedly brackish scent rising from it.

Just below the surface of the water, a glint of metal caught my eye. I leaned closer, reaching into brush aside the floating moss. About a foot and a half down from the surface was the hilt of his sword. I hesitated for a moment, wondering whether I should just reach in and pull it out. I could see other things down in the water, too. Goblets and necklaces, the shimmer of gold and silver.

But I wasn't here to claim those items, whatever they were. I'd been given one charge, and one charge only. Intuition told me to leave everything else where it lay.

As my fingers slowly approached the hilt of the sword, a flutter in my stomach told me that the Lamentation was back again, watching. I glanced over my shoulder and sure enough, there she was. Only now she didn't look so terrifying. She was smiling, and she glided to the other side of the well and knelt, watching me.

I looked at her, wondering if she could hear me. "The Lady Brighid sent me. You know, right? From the marker?"

She nodded, and placed her palm over her heart. Her smile widened.

A sudden thought crossed my mind. "You're the priestess Brighid was talking about?"

She ducked her head, then looked up again. With a gentle nod, she placed her hands on the side of the well, still holding my gaze.

"And this was a holy spot for Brighid, wasn't it?"

Again came a nod.

"The other things in there, I'm to leave them, aren't I?"

Again, she indicated agreement.

"Do you have to guard them as well? Do you have to stay here until they're all gone?"

I felt sorry for her, wishing she was free to move on. But the look she gave me wasn't one of frustration or impatience. No, as I watched her, a look of forbearance crossed her face, and she sat back, leaning against the tree that was nearest the well. The trees showed through her, but she didn't seem to notice that. She merely waited for me to continue.

I wrapped my hand around the hilt of the sword, and it was solid in my grasp, the metal cold from the icy water of the well. I slowly withdrew the blade, standing up as I did so.

The sword was dripping with moss, but the cross-piece and hilt were bronze. The sword hummed in my hand, and I held it up, trying to shake the moss off. There was a bright glow to the sword, and it felt as though with any movement, I could conjure fire out of it. I brought it up, sweeping the blade from side to side, feeling the heft and weight of it.

The Lamentation jumped up, shaking her head. She motioned to the trees, and then to the blade, and then shook her head again.

"Oh, Brighid's Flame can actually conjure flame, can't it?"

The Lamentation gave me yet another nod, a wary look on her face.

I stopped slashing the sword around, lowering it as I examined the metal. There were fine etchings all over the blade, beautiful scrollwork, and I had the feeling that Brighid had inscribed those runes herself. She had made the blade, she said, and I was the first to touch it in eons. I looked around for a sheath, but saw none, so I fastened the sword to my belt as best as I could. I turned to the Lamentation.

"Thank you for all of your help. Trust me that the sword will be used for good intent." As I turned away, I felt an icy chill on my shoulder and I looked back. The Lamentation had moved close behind me. I wasn't sure what she wanted to tell me but she looked at me for a moment, intently, and then smiled again, and let go.

As I headed back down the incline away from the well, I turned back to look for the Lamentation one last time, but there was no sign of her. Just the well on the top of the slope. I wondered about the other items in it, but they were not my quest, and not my story to follow. I turned back and crossed between the logs that formed the portal. Viktor and Yutani were waiting for me, as were the rest of the Autumn Stalkers.

"I've got the sword," I said. "We need to return to Brighid's Castle now."

And just like that, Unkai motioned to his people. As one they turned, and began leading us back through the forest. No one asked to see the sword. Not even Viktor and Yutani.

CHAPTER TWENTY-ONE

*O*ver the next two days, Unkai and his people led us back to the entrance of Y'Bain. During that time, we didn't learn much more about the Orhanakai, other than that they had lived in Y'Bain for thousands of years, but I developed a growing respect for Unkai. He was tough, but fair, and he treated his band of hunters with respect and the expectation that they would do their best for him. His wife—or rather, woman—I had no idea of their marriage customs or even if they had any—was an integral part of the group, though she kept to herself. Unkai had confided to me that she was one of the best hunters in their band, and that was one of the reasons he had chosen her.

By the time we arrived at the entrance to the forest, it was nearly nightfall, and I was genuinely sorry to see them go. While I still wasn't sure if they were entirely trustworthy, I did sense a strong element of honor running among them, and they were also a good deterrent to will-o'-the-wisps and the other surprises the forest had thrown at us.

"Remember, you promised to give me a tour of your home when I come to visit," Unkai said as we stood at the edge of the forest.

I nodded, no longer trying to deflect the subject. If he managed to get himself over to our realm, I'd happily show him around. "I remember. Until then, be safe, and may hunting be abundant." I kept trying to remind myself that they not only hunted for food, but they enslaved people, but the thought seemed so alien from the hunters we had traveled with that I decided just to shelve the matter.

He saluted me and, before they turned back at the forest's edge, said, "I hope that what you found was worth the journey, and that it brings you peace."

I held his gaze for a moment, almost blurting out why I wanted the sword. But something stayed my words. Regardless of whether I felt like I could trust him, the truth was, I didn't really know him. And not knowing him meant that I didn't know who he was aligned with or who he was connected to.

"Thank you," I said. "I hope so too."

And then, as Unkai turned back to Y'Bain, Viktor, Yutani, and I stepped out of the forest, into the open plain.

ON THE WAY BACK TO THE PALACE, HERNE RODE BY MY SIDE. The storm had socked in, and the snow was blowing like crazy. We were all shrouded in cloaks. The guards had brought extra. As the horses picked their way through the massive flakes, the night took on a surreal silvery tinge and it felt like we were walking through a whiteout, even though we were still on trail.

"You seem quiet," he said. "How was the trip?"

I hadn't told them much, not yet. The forest had sent me spiraling inward, and meeting Unkai's people had made me rethink my feelings about myself, and my father's blood.

"Dangerous. We had to fend off will-o'-the-wisps. And…" I glanced at him, hoping he wouldn't go charging off to avenge my honor.

"And what?"

"I was almost captured by a couple of aughiskies. Thanks to Serafina, they're dead." He began to sputter but I held up my hand. "Stop. They weren't able to harm me. I called on a water elemental while they had me in the water, and it didn't like them, so it came to my aid. Once I was back on land, I was able to get hold of the bow and I put arrows through both of them. That's when we met Unkai and his people."

Herne let out a slow breath, it whistled through his teeth like wind through dry leaves. "I wish I could have gone with you. But the forest wouldn't have been so friendly, and even with what you experienced, it could have been far worse. And it would been, had I been there. Tell me, what did you think of Unkai and his band?"

He sounded almost like he was familiar with who they were. I tilted my head slightly, trying to formulate my answer.

"I found him surprisingly helpful. And surprisingly congenial. Do you know who he is?"

Herne nodded as he chucked to the horse, gently

guiding it back to the path when it started to wander off to the side. The stallion responded to him as though he was its mother.

"Actually, I've met Unkai several times. Once in a while he comes out of the forest, near my father's palace. We've had several long talks about Y'Bain, and the energies that run deep within the wood. He's unlike a number of the other Autumn Stalkers. His people don't take prisoners very often. The Orhanakai are, in a sense, both more feral and yet more humane than the rest of the Autumn's Bane. He's a good sort, and you can trust him for the most part."

"I had that feeling. It was odd, but I felt like he's truly a man of his word. They showed us no reason to doubt them, although I had to promise to guide him around Seattle if he ever comes over to our realm." I laughed. "Somehow, it strikes me as odd to think of him as wandering around the city streets, but if anybody can adapt, I imagine it would be him."

We reached the castle before midnight, and when the guards saw us, they hustled us in, helping us down from our horses and scurrying us into the main chamber, where we found a huge fire crackling in the hearth. Even though the cloaks had done a fairly good job of keeping us warm, it felt so good to sit down by the fire and hold up my hands to the flickering warmth.

"I will summon the Lady Brighid," one of the guards said, motioning to the others. "Have servants bring them food and wine."

There was a flurry of activity as we were stripped of our cloaks and given food and drink. I was carrying the sword, wrapped in a length of cloth, and I set it across my lap as I bit into a hunk of cheese that had been melted across a great slab of soft bread. I was tired of bread and cheese, but this was at least warm and hot, and the mulled apple cider that they pressed into my hand was also hot, leaving a trail of warmth to glide down my throat. I realized, too late, that there was a good spike of brandy in it, and the drink went straight to my head, leaving me a little giddy.

Shortly after we had eaten, Brighid, Cernunnos, and Morgana entered the room. As they took their seats, Brighid leaned forward to me. Her eyes were light, and her gaze was fastened on the cloth-wrapped sword on my lap.

"You managed to find the sword." It was a statement rather than a question.

I nodded. "We encountered a number of difficulties along the way, including some will-o'-the-wisps, but we made it to the lake and I found the sword. The Lamentation accepted the marker and opened the well to me." I paused, wanting to ask Brighid if there was any way she could relieve the guardian of her status, to give her rest. "The guardian seems extremely tired, and very lonely."

"It's her job," Brighid said. "She understands her duties, and accepted them after her death. Don't worry about her, child. She isn't unhappy, and while, yes, she's melancholy, that's simply the way of Lamentations."

"May we see the sword?" Cernunnos asked.

I slowly stood, still a little giddy from the brandy and apple cider, and tired from the trip. As I unwrapped the sword, winding the material away from it, I was surprised to see how brightly the blade gleamed in the dim light, even given the years it had been in the well and the moss that was still hanging off of it. I gazed at the runes that covered the blade, feeling as though I should understand them.

Brighid let out a soft cry, a smile lighting up her face. "It has been so long since I have seen my Flame. I regretted having to let it go, having to curse it so that no god could ever touch it. But it is still as beautiful as the day I forged it." The fondness in her voice seemed to resonate within the blade, and it tingled in my hands.

I held it up, and the moss fell away, shedding like water. Brighid held her hands over it, not touching the blade, and whispered an incantation below her breath. I couldn't make out the words but as she spoke, the tarnish seem to vanish, boiling off of the sword in a mist.

As the fog around the sword dissipated, the metal shone with a brilliance I hadn't expected. A moment later, it looked newly made, as though it had never spent thousands of years deep in a well.

With one hand, Brighid touched my forehead, her other hand still hovering over the blade.

> *Soul to blade, blade to soul,*
> *let these events now unfold.*
> *Hilt to hand, hand to hilt,*
> *now a bond shall be built.*
> *Metal to flesh, flesh to metal,*
> *so the magic, it shall settle.*
> *Voice to thought, thought to voice,*
> *so the blade shall make her choice.*
> *Those who witness shall remember,*
> *that I bind this blade to Ember.*

As her words faded away, I felt something happening between me and the sword. The hilt resounded in my hand, pulsing as a faint bluish glow began to surround the blade. I watched, unable to avert my eyes, as the glow brightened to an almost blinding flash.

The energy spiraled up the blade, into the hilt, through my arm, and I dropped my head back, feeling the power of Brighid's Flame as it washed through me, a wave of energy that crested as it reached my crown chakra.

There was something so right about holding the sword, something so true to my nature, that I never wanted to let go. I gasped as Brighid stepped away, and I moved back, out of reach of the others, and flourished the sword, slashing her through the air.

She felt light as a feather in my hand, the weight of the metal no longer an issue. And she hummed brightly, as though she were singing to me as I maneuvered her in first one position, then another. I laughed, my weariness falling away as I fell in love with the blade, and the blade seemed to fall in love with me.

"What did you do?" I asked, finally finding my tongue.

"The sword is yours. I bound it to you. If anyone ever attempts to take it away, the sword will find its way back to you. And it will not function for others, unless they are your friends trying to help. You can never be hurt by this blade. Even if you accidentally hit yourself with it, Brighid's Flame will not cut your skin. Her tip will not pierce your heart. No one can use your weapon against you. And trust me, Brighid's Flame will slice through the shield of Longlear."

The mood grew somber again as she mentioned Longlear. I lowered the sword and returned to my seat, placing the blade across my lap as I leaned back against the sofa.

"I need a sheath. There didn't seem to be one in the well." I glanced over Brighid, not wanting to sound greedy.

"There is a sheath for the sword. I will have it brought to you in your room. Take care of my blade for me—she's one of my favorites. She'll stand you in good stead when you need her." Brighid looked over at Cernunnos. "How long do we have before Typhon rises? We must take care of Nuanda before then."

Cernunnos shrugged. "I have no clue. It won't be long, but we have at least a few weeks. Perhaps a couple months if we're lucky. Ember, you must summon Nuanda. I suggest that you summon him on the full moon. That's two weeks away. That will give Herne time to train you with the sword, because you're the only one who will be able to wield it against him."

Part of me wanted to take care of it in the morning, to just get it over with. But Cernunnos was correct. I had no clue of how to handle a sword. It wasn't the same as a dagger, and definitely not the same as a bow.

"How will I summon him? How do I contact him? And where will we fight?"

"You will fight here, in Annwn. As to summoning him? We'll teach you how," Morgana said, turning to Lugh the Long Handed. "You know, right?"

Lugh nodded. "Yes, I'll teach her how to summon him. And yes, you must fight him over here so that as little damage is done in your realm as possible. I will do what research I can on him during the next two weeks. Meanwhile, learn to use the sword and try not to worry. It won't be easy to cleave through Longlear, especially since your opponent is half giant. But there are tricks and ways to throw your opponent off. The more you can unbalance him, the better chance you have of taking him down. And make no mistake, Ember. You *must* kill him. There's no room for mercy. When he dies, the Brotherhood will fall apart. But as long as he lives, they will gather around him."

I stared at the sword on my lap. The thought that in two weeks I would be fighting against Nuanda, in hand-to-hand combat, terrified me. But even as the fear raced through my body, a reassuring pulse echoed from the hilt into my hand. Brighid's Flame was trying to reassure me, to let me know that she would do her best. And right now, I needed all the reassurance I could get.

AFTER THINGS WERE SORTED OUT, WE WERE ESCORTED TO our rooms. After taking a long bath, I fell into bed next to Herne. I lay there, my arm across his bare chest as he crooked his arm around my shoulders. I nuzzled him, too tired to do anything except lay there, but I luxuriated in the feel of him next to me.

"Can you really teach me to fight with the sword in two weeks?"

He stretched his other arm under his head, and leaned over to kiss my forehead. "I think so. You already know how to fight with the dagger, and you're pretty good at martial arts. It shouldn't be too difficult, especially if the sword is as light as you say in your hands."

"It's as though the weight just drifted away when she

bound it to me," I said. "I've never felt connected to a weapon like I do to Brighid's Flame, although Serafina runs a close second. Is it odd that I think of them as entities, rather than just objects?"

"Not at all. They *are* entities. They each have a consciousness of their own. Most of the weapons and artifacts created by the gods do. We put a little bit of ourselves into each creation, so there's a little of me in Serafina, and there's a little bit of Brighid in Brighid's Flame. These aren't just run-of-the-mill weapons that you can walk into a store and buy. You'll need to treat them with the respect they deserve. Polish the sword weekly, make sure it's sharp. As for Serafina, you'll want to polish the wood with a fine oil each month. Don't toss them around, and make sure they have a place of their own in your home."

I nodded, my cheek against his chest. "I understand. Treat them like I would a valued member of my family, basically." I paused, then asked, "Do you think I can take down Nuanda? Do you really believe that I can do this?"

He adjusted the covers, pulling them up over my shoulders. I felt so safe in his arms that I never wanted to leave, never wanted to move from the spot.

"I think you can. And you know I'm not one for hyperbole or overexaggeration. I think you can defeat him. But you're going to have to train hard the next two weeks, harder than you've ever trained for anything except, perhaps, the Cruharach. Mostly, you need to stop second-guessing yourself. You need to learn to trust your instincts. Those are the two spots where you could trip and fall. Too often, I think I trust your instincts more than you do."

He shifted, pushing himself up so he was sitting against the headboard. I followed suit, pulling the covers up around my shoulders as I stared at the fireplace across the room. The fire was burning brightly, but the room was still chilly. Both Serafina and Brighid's Flame were on the divan near our bed. Brighid had sent one of her servants to me with the sheath for the sword. It was a dark crimson leather, handworked in stone. The fittings on it were bronze, and it had a matching belt specifically made to carry it.

"I think I've been unsure of myself most of my life," I said. "I don't know where it started. Maybe it started in grade school when the kids bullied me for being a tralaeth. Or maybe it was when my parents were killed, and my world felt like it was shattered. I don't know. Somewhere along the way, I lost my confidence in my decisions. But one thing I'm sure of, and I know this to the core of my being, is that I love you. And honestly, that frightens me."

Herne paused for a moment, then asked, "Why are you afraid of loving me?"

"I don't think I'm afraid of *loving* you. I think I'm afraid of somehow losing your love. I've never felt this way about anybody before, I've never been deeply in love with anyone. And then, when I do fall in love, it's with a god. How do I process that? How do I handle these bouts that come over me where I feel unworthy? I mean, when a god falls in love with you, how can you measure up? I guess I keep thinking that any day now, you'll look at me and see the real me, all my faults and foibles, and you'll think: *Why did I ever choose her?*"

Herne let out a long sigh, but he didn't sound irritated.

"I suppose I can understand. I mean, I've never felt that way, but I can empathize. But it's important for you to remember that while yes, I am a god, I feel similar emotions, and I can love the smallest of things. And I'm not saying *you're* someone small. I'm just saying that if I can appreciate the beauty of a daisy or a bluebell, if I can listen to a bird singing and feel a sense of peace, why can't I love someone who isn't a goddess? Love doesn't understand rank, love doesn't understand caste or hierarchy. Love transcends gender, and it transcends money, and it transcends just about everything there is. So for me to fall in love with you—I don't see that as unusual. All I know is that when I met you, I lost my heart to you." He took my left hand, and tapped the ring on my finger. "I gave this to you as a promise of my love. I'm not about to take it back. My love for you stands, and I just hope that your love for me will stand. Ember, I'd be so lonely without you, and so miserable."

He gathered me in his arms then, holding me tight as he kissed me. My weariness fell away as he slid me back down into the bed, rolling between my legs. As I opened myself to him, I found myself crying.

"What's wrong?" He asked softly, kissing away my tears.

"Nothing's wrong. Just make love to me. I'm tired, but I need you inside me, I need you to fill me up, swallow me whole with your love."

And so, as the fire continued to crackle away, Herne made love to me, and for a little while I was able to forget about Nuanda, and the coming fight.

CHAPTER TWENTY-TWO

*A*ngel and I stared at the house. We'd been gone for six days and the drive home from the portal, after being in Annwn for so long, seemed almost surreal. Our cars were safely in front of the house and nothing looked out of the ordinary as Herne eased onto the gravel. Angel and I scrambled out of Herne's SUV, gathering our gear before we waved at everyone and headed inside.

"I'm so glad to be home," I said, unlocking the door.

"Me too," Angel said.

We dropped our packs by the door, and I scooped up Mr. Rumblebutt to give him a kiss on the head when he ran over, glaring at me.

"I'm sorry we were gone so long, but you love Ronnie," I said before he jumped out of my arms and, pointedly snubbing me, turned his back.

"You've got a lot of apologizing to do," Angel said with a laugh. She paused, then added, "Something happened in the forest, didn't it? Beyond finding the sword?"

I hadn't told her about the aughiskies yet. We hadn't

really had time to sit down and talk. "Yeah, but save it till after we've had showers and changed, okay?"

Frowning, she nodded. "All right."

An hour later, we were clean, wearing comfy clothes, and in the kitchen. I could hardly wait to get my hands on a latte, and she wanted her tea. We finally sat down at the table, drinks and cookies in hand, and I cleared my throat.

"All right. Here's what I haven't told you yet. You were right, I almost didn't make it out of Y'Bain. There's a form of water Fae known as an aughisky. They're waterhorse shifters, but not like the hippocampi." I licked my lips, then told her what had happened. I had already realized that I didn't like talking about it because I had felt so helpless, and the thought of what might have happened sat like a lump in my stomach.

When I finished, Angel slammed her hand against the table. "It never fails. It doesn't matter where you go, it's always a danger, isn't it?" She looked at me, her eyes registering a fury I seldom saw in her. "Isn't there anywhere in this world or in any other world, where women are safe from assault?"

I shrugged. "Unfortunately, I don't think so. But they're dead. I shot them both with Serafina. At least those two will never attack another woman. I didn't even want to talk about this because it makes me so angry, and because when I managed to get away from them, all I wanted to do was to kill them. And I did. I wanted to make them suffer for what they tried to do to me."

"At least you got away. For that, I'm grateful. And I thank whatever water elemental it was that you summoned." She let out a long breath, reaching for her purse. "I think that's what I was sensing—the danger from the aughiskies."

"Promise me something," I said.

"What is it?"

"The martial arts classes you're taking? You'll double down on them. Make certain that you can disarm an attacker. Don't be squeamish. I mean, there will always be times when we're outnumbered, or our opponent has a gun or something that we can't fight. But promise me that you'll do everything you can to learn how to keep yourself safe. If we can't change the world, we can at least try to make sure the freaks won't ever get a chance to attack anybody again. I want to put the fear of the gods in them."

"Oh, you have my promise on that. I'm actually doing really well. I'm coming up for the test for my yellow belt. And I think I'm going to pass." She gave me a bright smile, shaking her head. "Who would have thought? Me, Angel Jackson, who used to be a pacifist, is actually going for her yellow belt in karate!"

"Way to go! We'll celebrate when you get it. I'll come watch your test, if that's allowed."

We grudgingly gathered our packs and began to empty clothes into the laundry. The house needed cleaning, and so—like most magical moments—our trip ended with doing dishes, washing clothes, and dusting. Because reality consisted of cleanup, even after victory.

THAT EVENING, ANGEL WAS SUPPOSED TO GO OVER TO Rafé's, but he called to warn her he had a cold and told her she probably shouldn't come. So she and I were sitting around the living room, eating pizza, when her phone rang again. She pulled it out, then frowned as she glanced at the caller ID.

"Damn it, it's DeWayne."

"Oh hell. What the fuck does he want?"

"I guess we'll find out," she said, answering.

She listened for a moment, then let out a loud shout. "I *told* you to leave me alone... No, I will not! The *only* reason you're calling me is because you're after money. I told you there was nothing left after Mama J. died, and even if there was, you'd be the last person to get your paws on it. Don't ever call me again or I'm calling the cops." As she punched the end-call button, I thought she was going to throw her phone across the room. But she stopped short of that.

"He still trying to find out where DJ is?"

She nodded. "At least he still doesn't know whether Mama J. had a girl or a boy. He doesn't give a damn. All he wants is money, the loser."

He hadn't been heard from until the past couple months, when he called Angel, sniffing around to see if there was any money. Mama J. had died close to a year and a half ago in an accident—she was struck by a car on her way over to Angel's place. But DeWayne didn't give a fuck about his kid. He could do a lot of damage if he managed to get in contact with DJ, however, so we were doing our best to keep him in the dark.

"What are we gonna do about him?" I muted the TV, petting Mr. Rumblebutt, who jumped up on my lap.

"I wish I could send him over to Annwn, drop him off in Y'Bain. He's so stupid, he'd get himself killed and then he wouldn't be a problem."

I snorted. "That's not a bad idea, but somehow I don't think we're going to manage it. You should just change your number. I know it sucks, but it might be for the best."

She shook her head. "No, because then he might double down on trying to find out exactly who his child is. And we don't want that. As long as he's dealing with me, he's not harassing DJ."

"True that. All right, maybe we can talk to Herne and figure out something that will help. We could have Viktor pay a visit to DeWayne. Put some muscle on him to leave you alone. I'm sure Viktor wouldn't object." Being a half-ogre had its uses, and Viktor was always willing to help out a friend.

Angel laughed, shaking her head. "I'm not going to get Viktor in trouble. And I'm sure that he would end up with assault charges. Once he met DeWayne, he'd probably want to punch his lights out."

She muted her phone after checking for texts from DJ. "Let's just finish the night without any further stress. I'm tired of worrying about things. I just want to stretch out on the sofa, eat popcorn, and let the boob tube numb my mind."

And so, I turned the volume back up, and we binge-watched five episodes of DVR'd programs before heading to bed.

OVER THE NEXT TWO WEEKS, HERNE AND YUTANI TRAINED me hard. I came away with so many bumps and bruises from the swordplay sessions that every single inch of me felt like it had been beaten up. But I learned. They not only taught me sword fighting, but they taught me how to go on the offense.

"You can't wait for him to come at you. You can't let him push you into a defensive position. You have to take charge," Herne said, reminding me over and over that *I* was the one who had to lead the charge. "You're the one who's going to be summoning him. You're the one who's calling him out. You can't show weakness."

And so from dawn till sundown, I trained. Herne hired a masseuse to rub the sore spots away at the end of the day. The Wild Hunt took no cases during this time. Instead, all our focus went into getting me in shape. Angel cut the junk food out of my diet, fueling me with as much high-quality protein and carbs as she could. And Marilee, my magical mentor who had guided me through the Cruharach, drilled me on my water magic when I was too tired to lift the sword.

As I fought, as each session progressed, I developed more of an affinity with Brighid's Flame. The sword felt natural in my hand, and near the end of two weeks, she felt as at home in my hand as a dagger, or as Serafina.

At one point, Marilee took me to the side. "I know how important it is for you to learn how to use the sword. But I have a hunch and I need you to pay attention to this. Your Leannan Sidhe side—that's what's going to help you in the very end. *She* will keep you alive. Don't be afraid to let her off the leash."

I let her words settle, then let out a slow breath. "It's going to take more than one front to destroy him, isn't it?"

Marilee shrugged. "I can't answer you for certain, but

yes, I think it will take a mix of blade *and magic*. But whatever it does take, you'll be the force behind it."

The days wore on, and I spent each night curled in Herne's arms, or cuddled with Angel and Mr. Rumblebutt, wanting to soak in as much of my life as I could. *Just in case*...I told myself. Just in case there was a slipup. Just in case I went down fighting. Just in case my destiny ended with Nuanda.

Finally, the day before the full moon, I was sitting in Herne's bed, trying to gather my equilibrium. Tonight, we would journey to Annwn, to Cernunnos's palace, and tomorrow I would summon Nuanda. And then...we would wait for him to respond.

"What if he doesn't come?" I asked. "What if he ignores me?"

"He'll come. He'll hear you. Trust me on that," Herne said. "Stop second-guessing yourself."

"Am I doing that again? Is that what I'm doing?" I pressed my lips together, crossing to the window to look out onto the dreary skies. It was pouring rain, but the snow was gone, all melted off. Mid-February was always a bleak time of the year.

"I'm afraid so," he said. "You have to go into this so resilient that if he manages to drive you back, you can come out swinging again."

I nodded, but my mind was a thousand miles away. I felt the need to walk by the water, to feel the energy of Morgana surround me. I might be going into battle with Brighid's sword, but I was rooted in the water, in the depths of the ocean.

After breakfast, I told him I wanted to be alone for a bit, and after he left, I drove myself down to the docks, parking on one of the side streets near Puget Sound. It was a rainy, gloomy day, chilly as most February days were, but I didn't care. The city had built a new pier that ran around part of the sound, before the ferry slips.

A few fishermen were lined up by the railings, trying their hand, although I wasn't sure what they expected to catch at this time of year. Most of them were old men, sitting on the benches on the edge of the walkway, staring out into the water. A few of them were smoking cigars, and one older man was sitting with a young boy. I recognize them as wolf shifters, so the boy was probably his great-great-grandchild, given how long they lived. The man tipped his cap as I passed, and I gave them a little wave. A solemn smile on his face, the boy waved in return, then turned back to his fishing pole.

The gulls were out, screeching as they flew over the water looking for scraps of food, and the waves of the sound were blowing against the boardwalk, fueled by a stiff wind. I finally came to a bench that was unoccupied, and I sat down, staring at the waves that lapped against the girders below. It was high tide, and the water reached almost to the edge of the boardwalk. I leaned forward, elbows on my knees, watching the silver sheen of the sound. It was drizzling but not raining full force at this point, and a melancholy resignation stole over me.

I sat there, trying not to think, just communing with the water. After a while, I sensed someone standing behind me. I turned around and saw Morgana, wearing a long velvet dress and a cloak. No one else was looking at her, but then again, she was able to pass when she wanted to.

"Scoot over," she said.

I made room for her on the bench, and she sat down next to me. She crossed one leg over the other, leaning back as she pulled her cloak around her.

"I know this all seems so unfair," she said.

I thought before I spoke, wanting to get the words right. "I don't so much feel like this is unfair, but it's a burden I wouldn't have chosen if I had the choice. Why *me*? Why can't somebody else carry the sword? And before you say anything, I realize it's woven into my tapestry. But seriously, couldn't the Fates have picked on somebody else?"

"They could have. But they didn't. And not even the gods can countermand the Fates. They're beyond our reach. We can appeal to them, but it usually does no good." She gave a little shrug, staring at the water. "It's choppy today. You know, the ocean can be as gentle as a ripple on the wind. And she can be mighty and fierce. She's more dangerous than any force on this planet. And you are part of her, as am I. I sense you learned much about yourself on this trip."

I nodded. "I learned about my father's blood. I learned that I enjoy being a predator when both sides of my heritage rise up. That scares me, but not as much as it would have before the Cruharach. At least now I feel like I can control it to some degree."

"You're born of two predatory races. Marilee wasn't at all off-base when she warned you to remember your mother's blood as well when you're fighting Nuanda. There are times when compassion and mercy have to go by the wayside. I predict that compassion is your greatest enemy in this situation. Don't feel sorry for the enemy. It's either you or him. There's no in-between. No other choice." She turned to me, her eyes luminescent, reflecting the silver of the sky and water. "When you come out of this—and I do believe and hope it will be *when*, not if— you'll be entering a new phase of your life. A new phase of your training."

"I'll still be working with the Wild Hunt, won't I?" I suddenly feared that I'd be pulled away from the agency, pulled away from Herne.

Morgana laughed at that point. "Of course. The Fae will still be after each other's blood, even more so than before because once their common enemy is removed you know they're going to be back at it. Typhon will be a rising threat. And my son would be bereft without you. He truly does love you, I hope you realize that."

I nodded. "Yes, and I hope he knows how much I love him. I never expected to fall in love with a god, and some-times I'm not sure how to deal with it."

Morgana gave me a soft smile. "I uttered those same words so many thousands of years ago. Remember, I am The Merlin's daughter, and my mother was Fae. I did not start out as a goddess. I'm one now, thanks to Cernunnos. I started out as one of the magic-born. I could have gone into the Force Majeure if I had chosen."

I wasn't sure exactly how to phrase what I wanted to ask next, but I finally decided to just blurt out the ques-tion. "How did... What did you have to *do* to become a goddess? I mean, I know Cernunnos elevated you to deityhood, but did you have to go through something like the Cruharach?"

Morgana turned back to stare over the rolling waves. "In a sense. I had to shed my mortal shell, I guess is the best way to put it."

"That makes it sound like you died," I said. "Like when someone is turned into a vampire."

"In a sense, yes. I did die, and was reborn as a goddess. It is a lot like being turned into a vampire, when I think about it. The body changes when you're reborn a god. Only I'm not one of the undead. Similar process, different outcome."

"Cernunnos didn't drink your blood, did he?" The thought of that made me queasy.

Morgana laughed then, shaking her head. "No, nothing like that. I can't tell you any more—it's something I'm not comfortable discussing. But yes, I went through a rite of passage. Now," she said, standing, "you should go home and spend the afternoon resting. You'll need all of your strength for tomorrow."

"Herne keeps telling me I'm second-guessing myself. I keep wondering how Nuanda will know that I'm summoning him? Will he hear me? Will he answer?"

Morgana offered her hand to me and I took it as I stood. "My son is correct. You need to stop second-guessing yourself, and you need to stop second-guessing the Fates. Nuanda will hear you, and he will answer. You should be focused on steadying your nerves for the battle. Not on whether or not the battle will occur."

And with that, she walked down the boardwalk as a wave splashed over the pier, spraying her with a fine mist. I blinked, and in that single second, she vanished. Feeling oddly calmed, I turned to make my way home.

CHAPTER TWENTY-THREE

We were standing on a hill, near Cernunnos's palace. Down the incline was a lake. Unlike Lake Discover, this lake was vast, so vast that I couldn't see the other side. The surface was still, with patches of ice here and there, and at one point I saw a stag walk out from the forest, onto the ice before it turned around and loped back down the shore. I had spent the night in a restless attempt to sleep, finally curling up with Mr. Rumblebutt on the sofa at three A.M. before I managed to drop off until six A.M. Once again, the entire agency made the trip, meeting Brighid and Morgana at Cernunnos's palace. Shortly after we arrived, Brighid drilled me on what I needed to do in order to summon Nuanda.

Now, it was time.

The palace was about three miles away, and everybody was gathered nearby to watch and wait. I felt like a gladiator, with the weight of my people hanging heavy on my shoulders. I stood near the crest of the hill, gathering my courage. It was up to me now, and while I didn't appreciate being funneled into this battle, at least it was about to begin. I just wanted it over with.

The wind whipped my hair around my face, and I paused to gather it back into a braid, which I coiled against my head. Fastening the braid firmly with two beautiful barrettes that Herne had given me—they were cloisonné, a beautiful black enamel with delicate flowers —I pinned my hair close to my head, not wanting to give Nuanda any advantage. Any loose hair, even a hanging braid, was a good handhold for an enemy to grab hold of.

Finally, I began to breathe evenly, a quiet sense of certainty washing over me. I glanced back at my friends, the gods, and Cernunnos's servants, who were all watching. Ferosyn was there, and I imagined he was prepared to help me should I end up injured, though it was a fight to the death and Nuanda wasn't going to leave me alive if he managed to cut me down.

I walked over to a flat area on the hilltop and used the sword to draw a circle. Stepping inside the circle, I inscribed a ring of runes—actually, it was an incantation written in Celtic ogham—around the ring, creating an inner circle. I had made the ring a good twenty feet in diameter. Finally, I walked to the center, driving the sword tip into the ground as I kept hold of the hilt. I could easily remove it, but the blade needed to be placed thusly for the spell of Summoning.

Finally, there was nothing left to do. It was time. I took a deep breath and, with my hands on the pommel of the sword, in a loud, clear voice, I sang out the enchantment that Brighid had taught me when we had arrived this morning:

You who would destroy my people.
You who bear the shield of Longlear.
I summon thee through the Aether.
Hear my command loud and clear.
You who are the one known as Nuanda.
You who are my mortal foe.
I summon thee to the battle.
Your force and power to overthrow.
The Fates have bound us one to one.
We must the call and summons heed.
There is no turning from this meeting.
From my summons, you shall not flee.

As the last of my words faded away, the skies opened up and a cold sleet began to pour, pummeling me. There was a loud crash as thunder broke through the skies, lightning jaggedly forking overhead. Still I stood, all too aware that I could become toast if one of the brilliant forks hit me.

But then, a mist began to rise in the circle and a silhouette shimmered into view. He was tall, a giant of a man, and he held a spear and shield. I flashbacked to my recurring dream. This was the vision I had seen, only instead of at a distance, I was now face-to-face with my adversary.

Out of the fog that wafted through the circle, stepped Nuanda. Half Light Fae, half Fomorian, he was easily seven feet tall, with hair the color of burnished wheat caught back in a ponytail. His beard came down to his chest. He carried a spear in one hand, the shield Longlear in the other, and a sword hung from his waist. His eyes glittered with anger and bloodlust, and he looked at me, then let out a laugh that reverberated across the hilltop.

"*You* are the one that the Fates sent to me? But I *have* seen you in my dreams."

I caught my breath, pulling the sword out of the ground and standing ready. "We've met in my dreams as well. It ends now, Nuanda. I give you one chance to stand down, to surrender. If you decline, then the battle is set and we fight to the death."

He lifted his spear, and brought it down, tip first, to skewer it into the ground. Then, withdrawing his sword from its sheath, he brought up his shield. "To the death, then. So it was ordained, and so it comes to pass."

And just like that, the fight was on. The most important fight of my life.

Nuanda glanced at the circle. "You've defined the battlefield."

I knew what he meant. Unless I crossed the circle, breaking it, we were locked within the magical ring, neither of us able to get out until one of us lost. If I came through victorious, I could break the circle. If I died, the circle would break on its own.

I wasn't going to insist on a fair fight. In a fair fight, I'd have no chance of winning. Instead, I gave him a nod and backed away to the edge of the circle. He moved to the opposite edge. I watched him carefully, trying to pick up any movement that might clue me in to any sign of weakness or hidden vulnerability. The half-giant moved with a remarkable grace. It was as though he had been doing this

his entire life and this was just the culmination of his life's training.

I held fast to my sword, trying to remember everything that Herne had taught me.

I wasn't wielding a shield because I couldn't manage both it and the sword as well. While I could handle the sword with one hand, I did much better with two, and right now I couldn't sacrifice quality for the extra protection.

At first, I found myself focused on breaking Longlear, but then realized that my main goal had to be survival. I had to *last* long enough to cleave through the metal.

The shield was beautiful, elaborately engraved with runic staves, and a circle of Celtic knotwork surrounded the edge, intricately embossed in the bronze. But Lugh had told me while we were eating breakfast in Cernunnos's palace to look toward the center. He had forged the shield in two pieces, then fused them together. The central point where the two halves merged would be the weakest spot.

Sure enough, as I eyed Longlear, I could see it—a thin line running down the center of the shield.

At that moment, Nuanda closed in, sword raised. He brought his sword down from his right shoulder and I deflected the blade with my own, swinging into a counterattack. I sidestepped to the right, wondering if Nuanda knew that I was carrying Brighid's Flame.

If he *didn't*, he might not guard Longlear as carefully. I tried not to tip him off, tried not to let my gaze linger on the shield.

He came at me again, bearing down as his sword whistled through the air, aiming for my head. He was tall enough to catch me at my throat if I wasn't careful.

Again, I danced back, repelling the attack as I caught his blade with my own. Once more he pushed forward and I deflected him. I tried to go on the attack, tried to grab the offense from him, because I couldn't get past his shield to hurt him. I had to break Longlear in order to have any sort of chance of winning. While I had years of fighting experience, he had decades of swordplay, and it was only a matter of time before I slipped up.

We engaged again, Nuanda swinging, and once again, I deflected the blow. Again and again, he drove me back toward the edge of the circle. I shifted, moving to the left, then to the right, trying to throw him off guard. An image of an old cartoon I'd seen played in my mind—Bugs Bunny running in circles to get away from Elmer Fudd. Nuanda was driving me around the circle, blow after blow.

The snow was falling hard now, and it was difficult to keep my footing on the new powder, slick over the compact snow on the hilltop. I slipped, almost going down before I managed to catch myself and duck away from a blow that could have beheaded me.

My arms were getting tired and I knew I couldn't keep this up much longer. I reached deep inside, searching for my father's blood, searching for the predator within. Within seconds, I felt the cunning Autumn Stalker within me emerge, and I coaxed her out, offering her the reins.

Within the blink of an eye, my mood shifted from slightly frantic to focused and determined. I gauged how far Nuanda was from me, and how close I'd have to be in order to hit the shield, all the while repelling the blows of his sword. I gave myself over to instinct, and the energy in the circle shifted as I drew on the powers of my ancestors.

Nuanda seemed to feel the change because he suddenly backed off a step, staring at me with narrowed eyes from behind the shield.

I chose that moment. He was unsettled and that meant he was off his guard as much as he was probably going to get. I raced directly at him, bringing Brighid's Flame down hard, landing the tip of my blade at the center of the shield. A massive roar, like rolling thunder, rippled through the air and Nuanda shouted as a crack began to form on the shield, brilliant golden light pouring out of it. The crack spiderwebbed across the surface, the light growing stronger. Longlear began to hum and I decided now was a good time to retreat. I darted away, averting my eyes as the light grew so bright that it was almost blinding. Nuanda dropped the shield and ran the other way, still confined within the circle.

The next moment, there was a deafening sound as Longlear exploded.

I turned, panting, brushing the snow off my forehead. Nuanda was staring at the shield, the look on his face scanning between anger and fear. He looked over at me, and then, rage winning out, came charging at full tilt, his sword ready.

I met his blow, redirecting the momentum of his swing, but he was full-on furious, and I knew I couldn't stand up against that kind of rage from a seasoned swordsman. I had to get away from him—had to defeat him some other way.

The lake. Get him to the lake...

The whisper rose inside me, and I didn't question

where it was coming from, I just followed orders. I broke through the circle, still holding Brighid's Flame, and skidded my way down the hill, half running, half sliding through the fresh snow. Nuanda thundered after me, a string of curses hailing down on my head.

I was panting, stumbling through the snow, running as fast as I could. The lake was right near the bottom of the hill, and I could easily imagine children rolling down the grassy slope during summer, then darting into the lake. But the pastoral scene vanished when I realized how close he was behind me.

Crap. What do I do once I hit the bottom of the hill?

You'll know what to do, came the answer.

As I skidded to a halt, a few yards from the frozen lake, I glanced around, searching for cover, but the bushes and trees were all a good mile or so away, and I couldn't see the other side of the lake. Whatever I did, it would have to be here. Maybe I could drown him, I thought, or drag him into the water where our swords would be useless.

Or maybe...but I stopped as an inner hunger rose up. I eyed Nuanda, suddenly aware of just how much life energy he possessed. He was ripe with it, swimming in it, and I wanted to drink him down, to suck every breath out of his body. Aware of what was happening, I gave in.

I turned to him. He was on level ground now, about five yards away, looking slightly confused by the fact that I had begun walking toward him. I smiled then, the most seductive smile I could, and he began to raise his sword, then wavered.

"You don't want to do that," I said, my voice gliding over the words like silk. "Put down the sword. We should talk."

He started to shake his head, but I repeated my words, trilling over the command, holding his gaze tightly with mine. I was dragging Brighid's Flame behind me as I sauntered toward him, coaxing him to drop his sword.

"I want you to stop, to listen to me. I'm your muse, Nuanda. Can't you feel it? I can lift you to great things. I can inspire you to take hold of the world and bring it down in flames. With me by your side, I can bring you everything you've ever dreamed of."

"Who...what...are you?" The words came slowly out of his mouth as his eyes glazed over. He lowered his sword, confusion flitting across his face.

"I'm your dream. I'm your muse. I'm your everything. You know you want me. You know what I can do for you. Can't you feel it? The bond between us? We're connected, and I'll always be with you." I coaxed him on, reveling in the desire that played across his face.

He couldn't look away—no man could, no mortal man. I had the power to bring kings to their knees. Even the mighty Fomorians couldn't resist me for long, not without magical protection. I was their dream, their muse, and now all I could think about was how much I wanted to slake my thirst, to fasten onto his life force and drink deep.

He slowly dropped the sword, shaking his head. "What's happening? What are you doing to me?"

"Nothing that you don't secretly long for," I said, whispering as I closed in on him. "You have always wanted this. The absolute adoration and worship that I can promise you, if you'll let me in." Deep inside, a voice whispered *Don't go too far...don't let her take you over all the way.* But I brushed it aside.

"What…I'm…" Nuanda dropped to his knees in the snow, trembling. "I need you."

The look on his face was stunningly beautiful. He was a gorgeous man, his lips full, his features chiseled against his pale skin. His eyes were those of a leader, but even leaders needed to be led at some point, to let down their barriers and expose their vulnerability.

I was right on top of him at that point, and I leaned down, pressing my lips to his, drawing a whiff of his breath into me. He jerked as I did so, but settled down, glassy-eyed as I subjugated him with my power to compel. I kissed him again, drawing off yet a deeper breath, suckling on his life force as I quenched my thirst. He began to struggle after a moment, but I pressed further, breath after breath, disarming him.

At last, I stood back and he fell forward, on his hands and knees before me. He didn't try to get away, so locked within my spell was he, and I drew on the powers of the lake to shore me up. I gazed down at Nuanda, the Mighty. Nuanda, the Warrior Who Would Be King.

"You would have destroyed *my* people. You would have destroyed *your own people* out of revenge. You're a coward, choosing to destroy innocents in your lust for vengeance." My voice echoed over the lake, caught by the rippling waves that lapped against the shore. The snow was falling heavily now, muffling everything around us.

Nuanda raised his head. He was crying. Confused, he began to shake. "Please, help me. Please? I need you. I need your power…"

I stared at him, disgust rising for his show of weakness. "You are *no king,*" I spat out. "You are *nothing*…a terrorist who uses others to instill fear and anger, a murderer. I sentence you now, Nuanda, to the same fate to which you have condemned far too many."

I raised Brighid's Flame. I was judge and jury here, I was the hand of Fate. This moment had been woven into my destiny and there was nothing to do but see it through. Herne's warnings came flickering back, along with the words from Lugh and Brighid and Morgana and Cernunnos. No mercy. No compassion. The fate of the Fae rested on my shoulders.

Nuanda's expression shifted from confused to fury as the power of my charm began to subside. But it was too late. Too late for him, and too late for the Tuathan Brotherhood.

"It ends here," I whispered, bringing the blade down with as much force as I could exert. "It all ends here, for good."

As my sword cleaved into his neck, slicing through like hot metal through soft butter, I held my ground. The blood began to spray, hitting me in spatters, but still I stayed my course. As Nuanda's head fell away from his body, a glassy look of surprise in his eyes, I watched impassively. Both my inner predators smiled, satisfied. I had done my job. I had fulfilled a destiny woven into my tapestry. And I relished the feel of his blood on my hands.

CHAPTER TWENTY-FOUR

*T*hat evening, we were sitting in Cernunnos's palace, goblets full of mead, a fire roaring in the fireplace. I was curled up next to Angel, Talia and Viktor were stretched out on one of the sofas, Herne was standing by the window, and Yutani was next to the fireplace, staring into the flames.

Cernunnos entered the room, followed by Brighid and Morgana. As we started to attention, Cernunnos held up his hand.

"That's all right, stand down. You've earned the right to rest. No curtseys necessary." As we took their seats, a bevy of servants filed in, carrying plates of finger foods and more mead. When they left, Cernunnos let out a satisfied sigh. "I've talked to the head of the United Coalition. They've already reinstated the Fae Courts, and have put out the word that the Brotherhood has been dismantled."

"But has it, truly?" I asked. "Will the death of their leader destroy the entire movement?"

"There may be a few stragglers, but yes, Nuanda's death has been broadcast through the network. Pictures of his severed head have been released to the news media. There will be no doubt of his fate. He was the lifeblood of the movement. And thanks to Yutani and the members' list, the police have been moving in and over half of them are already in custody. I don't think there should be much trouble finding the remainder. There was no one to take Nuanda's place. He was an excellent orator and it's hard to find someone as compelling as he was."

I was staring into the flames, thinking about the morning. Morgana had been correct—letting my Leannan Sidhe side free had been the only thing that saved me. I couldn't have fought against Nuanda much longer, not with his skill.

"What are you thinking?" Herne asked.

"I'm thinking that I'm learning to understand both sides of my heritage, and appreciate them. I've been so afraid of what I could become, ever since before the Cruharach, when I learned what my heritage is. Now, I'm beginning to understand myself. It's almost like I have three people inside of me. The Leannan Sidhe, the Autumn's Bane, and then—*me*—a combination of both and yet more."

"You almost sound like you have multiple personality disorder," Angel said.

I shrugged. "It doesn't seem far off. It really is like possessing several personalities. I can summon either my mother's or father's blood, and they take over, but then they give me control once I no longer need them. Yet I'm not separate from either one. That's the best way I can explain it," I said. I knew it sounded crazy, but it made sense. There were three sides to me, and I had to accept them all if I was to be comfortable living in my skin.

"I think we understand," Talia said.

Angel nodded. "Ember, you're the primary personality. But there's a definite difference when the other two aspects of yourself come out. I wouldn't call them separate per se. It's almost like you take off one coat and put on another, and that coat shrouds you in a different energy. I could feel it when we were watching you today, when you started running for the lake. Even from where we were, I could feel something shift in you." She didn't seem nearly as concerned as I thought she would be.

"The important thing is that the Tuathan Brotherhood is gone," Morgana said. "I've notified both Saílle and Névé, so you should see things back to normal within a week or two. You know the truce won't last. The Fae had been fighting since the beginning of time. Granted, over on Earth, they don't fight nearly as badly as they do here."

"For which I am grateful," Herne said. "So we should go home tonight."

"Wait for the morning," Cernunnos said. "Tonight, let us break bread together, and celebrate a victory. Remember, there are dark times ahead, so we have to acknowledge our triumphs when we can. The battle with Typhon will be long and insidious and it won't be easily won. I don't think we're on the front lines in terms of fighting against the father of dragons, but we're certainly going to be taking care of collateral damage."

The energy in the room seemed to shift, the shadows growing more ominous. I crossed to the window to stand by Herne. He wrapped his arm around my waist and I leaned my head on his shoulder.

"Thank you," I whispered. "Without your training I wouldn't have made it through. I don't think I could have survived even one round in that circle if you hadn't shown me how to use Brighid's Flame."

"You were brilliant. You did everything you needed to do, and you trusted your instincts. You didn't second-guess yourself. I'm so proud of you." He leaned in, pressing his lips against my forehead.

I closed my eyes, basking in the warmth.

All I could think about was how lucky I was to have him, and how lucky I was to have my friends. If we had to live in a world filled with monsters like Nuanda and dragons like Typhon, at least we had each other. In times of great trouble, friends and family were all we had to rely on. Love and trust and commitment were the foundations that allowed us to go out and fight great evil. Standing up to hate took loyalty and honesty and courage.

And wasn't that what life was about? Fighting the good fight, protecting those we loved, standing up for what was right in this world—that was the core of life. Without belief in the greater good, without putting ourselves on the line for what mattered, life didn't mean much.

"What are you thinking?" Herne asked softly, nuzzling my ear.

"That I'm one of the luckiest women on Earth. That being a tralaeth is something to be proud of. And I'm thinking that my anger against the Fae Courts for the way they've treated me is something I need to let go of. I don't want to become another Nuanda, out for revenge because I feel rejected. They may reject me, but that doesn't matter. Here, with you and my friends, I have found more acceptance than I've ever known. I'm tired of being angry.

I may never walk down the streets of TirNaNog or Navane and be accepted into their society, but I don't need to. And I don't want to carry that anger anymore. From now on, I can make my parents proud of me by fighting against evil, and fighting against hate. I'm going to let go of the grudges because really, all it does is drain energy."

Then Herne pressed his lips against mine again and kissed me. Outside the snow was falling in Annwn, as the moon shone through a sliver in the clouds. Tomorrow we would go home and resume our lives there, but for tonight Cernunnos was right. It was time to celebrate our victories and rejoice that we had made a difference in the world. Because soon, the greater darkness would come, and we needed all our reserves to fight against it.

IF YOU ENJOYED THIS BOOK AND HAVEN'T READ THE FIRST eight of The Wild Hunt, check out THE SILVER STAG, OAK & THORNS, IRON BONES, A SHADOW OF CROWS, THE HALLOWED HUNT, THE SILVER MIST, WITCHING HOUR, and WITCHING BONES. Book 10 —THE ETERNAL RETURN—is available for preorder now. There will be more to come after that.

Return with me to Whisper Hollow, where spirits walk among the living, and the lake never gives up her dead. AUTUMN THORNS and SHADOW SILENCE return in January, along with a new book—THE PHANTOM QUEEN! Come join the darkly seductive world of Kerris Fellwater, spirit shaman for the small lakeside community of Whisper Hollow.

Meanwhile, I invite you to visit Fury's world. Bound to Hecate, Fury is a minor goddess, taking care of the Abominations who come off the World Tree. Books 1-5 are available now in the Fury Unbound Series : FURY RISING, FURY'S MAGIC, FURY AWAKENED, FURY CALLING, and FURY'S MANTLE.

If you prefer a lighter-hearted but still steamy paranormal romance, meet the wild and magical residents of Bedlam in my Bewitching Bedlam Series. Fun-loving witch Maddy Gallowglass, her smoking-hot vampire lover Aegis, and their crazed cjinn Bubba (part djinn, all cat) rock it out in Bedlam, a magical town on a mystical island. BEWITCHING BEDLAM, MAUDLIN'S MAYHEM, SIREN'S SONG, WITCHES WILD, CASTING CURSES, and BEDLAM CALLING: A BEWITCHING BEDLAM ANTHOLOGY are all available. Book six—DEMON'S DELIGHT—is coming in November!

For a dark, gritty, steamy series, try my world of The Indigo Court , where the long winter has come, and the Vampiric Fae are on the rise. The series is complete with NIGHT MYST, NIGHT VEIL, NIGHT SEEKER, NIGHT VISION, NIGHT'S END, and NIGHT SHIVERS.

If you like cozies with teeth, try my Chintz 'n China paranormal mysteries. The series is complete with: GHOST OF A CHANCE, LEGEND OF THE JADE DRAGON, MURDER UNDER A MYSTIC MOON, A HARVEST OF BONES, ONE HEX OF A WEDDING, and a wrap-up novella: HOLIDAY SPIRITS.

The last Otherworld book—BLOOD BONDS—is available now.

For all of my work, both published and upcoming

releases, see the Biography at the end of this book, or check out my website at Galenorn.com and be sure and sign up for my newsletter to receive news about all my new releases.

CAST OF CHARACTERS

THE WILD HUNT & FAMILY

- **Angel Jackson:** Ember's best friend, a human empath, Angel is the newest member of the Wild Hunt. A whiz in both the office and the kitchen, and loyal to the core, Angel is an integral part of Ember's life, and a vital member of the team.
- **Charlie Darren:** A vampire who was turned at 19. Math major, baker, and all-around gofer.
- **Ember Kearney:** Caught between the world of Light and Dark Fae, and pledged to Morgana, goddess of the Fae and the Sea, Ember Kearney was born with the mark of the Silver Stag. Rejected by both her bloodlines, she now works for the Wild Hunt as an investigator.
- **Herne the Hunter:** Herne is the son of the Lord of the Hunt, Cernunnos, and Morgana, goddess of the Fae and the Sea. A demigod—given his

mother's mortal beginnings—he's a lusty, protective god and one hell of a good boss. Owner of the Wild Hunt Agency, he helps keep the squabbles between the world of Light and Dark Fae from spilling over into the mortal realms.

- **Talia:** A harpy who long ago lost her powers, Talia is a top-notch researcher for the agency, and a longtime friend of Herne's.
- **Viktor:** Viktor is half-ogre, half-human. Rejected by his father's people (the ogres), he came to work for Herne some decades back.
- **Yutani:** A coyote shifter who is dogged by the Great Coyote, Yutani was driven out of his village over two hundred years before. He walks in the shadow of the trickster, and is the IT specialist for the company.

EMBER'S FRIENDS, FAMILY, & ENEMIES

- **Aoife:** A priestess of Morgana who guards the Seattle portal to the goddess's realm.
- **Celia:** Yutani's aunt.
- **Danielle:** Herne's daughter, born to an Amazon named Myrna.
- **DJ Jackson:** Angel's little half-brother, DJ is half Wulfine—wolf shifter. He now lives with a foster family for his own protection.
- **Erica:** A Dark Fae police officer, friend of Viktor's.
- **Elatha:** Fomorian King; enemy of the Fae race.

- **Ginty McClintlock:** a dwarf. Owner of Ginty's Waystation Bar & Grill
- **Marilee:** A priestess of Morgana, Ember's mentor. Possibly human—unknown.
- **Myrna:** An Amazon who had a fling with Herne many years back, which resulted in their daughter Danielle.
- **Rafé Forrester:** Brother to Ulstair, Raven's late fiancé; Angel's boyfriend. Actor/fast-food worker. Dark Fae.
- **Sheila:** Viktor's girlfriend. A kitchen witch; one of the magic-born. Geology teacher who volunteers at the Chapel Hill Homeless Shelter.

RAVEN & THE ANTE-FAE

The Ante-Fae are creatures predating the Fae. They are the wellspring from which all Fae descended, unique beings who rule their own realms. All Ante-Fae are dangerous, but some are more deadly than others.

- **Apollo:** The Golden Boy. Vixen's boytoy. Weaver of Wings. Dancer.
- **Arachana:** The Spider Queen. She has almost transformed into one of the Luo'henkah.
- **Blackthorn, the King of Thorns:** Ruler of the blackthorn trees and all thorn-bearing plants. Cunning and wily, he feeds on pain and desire.
- **Curikan, the Black Dog of Hanging Hills:** Raven's father, one of the infamous black dogs. The first time someone meets him, they find good fortune. If they should ever see him again, they meet tragedy.

- **Phasmoria:** Queen of the Bean Sidhe. Raven's mother.
- **Raven, the Daughter of Bones:** (also: Raven BoneTalker) A bone witch, Raven is young, as far as the Ante-Fae go, and she works with the dead. She's also a fortune-teller, and a necromancer.
- **Straff:** Blackthorn's son, who suffers from a wasting disease requiring him to feed off others' life energies and blood.
- **Vixen:** The Mistress/Master of Mayhem. Gender-fluid Ante-Fae who owns the Burlesque A Go-Go nightclub.
- **The Vulture Sisters:** Triplet sisters, predatory.

RAVEN'S FRIENDS

- **Elise, Gordon, and Templeton:** Raven's ferret-bound spirit friends she rescued years ago and now protects until she can find out the secret to breaking the curse on them.
- **Gunnar:** One of Kipa's SuVahta Elitvartijat—elite guards.
- **Jordan Roberts:** Tiger shifter. Llewellyn's husband. Owns *A Taste of Latte* coffee shop.
- **Llewellyn Roberts:** one of the magic-born, owns the *Sun & Moon Apothecary*.
- **Moira Ness:** Human. One of Raven's regular clients for readings.
- **Neil Johansson:** One of the magic-born. A priest of Thor.
- **Raj:** Gargoyle companion of Raven. Wing-

clipped, he's been with Raven for a number of years.

- **Wager Chance:** Half-Dark Fae, half-human PI. Owns a PI firm found in the Catacombs. Has connections with the vampires.
- **Wendy Fierce-Womyn:** An Amazon who works at Ginty's Waystation Bar & Grill.

THE GODS, THE LUO'HENKAH, THE ELEMENTAL SPIRITS, & THEIR COURTS

- **Arawn:** Lord of the Dead. Lord of the Underworld.
- **Brighid:** Goddess of Healing, Inspiration, and Smithery. The Lady of the Fiery Arrows, "Exalted One."
- **The Cailleach:** One of the Luo'henkah, the heart and spirit of winter.
- **Cerridwen:** Goddess of the Cauldron of Rebirth. Dark harvest mother goddess.
- **Cernunnos:** Lord of the Hunt, god of the Forest and King Stag of the Woods. Together with Morgana, Cernunnos originated the Wild Hunt and negotiated the covenant treaty with both the Light and the Dark Fae. Herne's father.
- **Corra:** Ancient Scottish serpent goddess. Oracle to the gods.
- **Coyote, also: Great Coyote:** Native American trickster spirit/god.
- **Danu:** Mother of the Pantheon. Leader of the Tuatha de Dannan.
- **Ferosyn:** Chief healer in Cernunnos's Court.

- **Herne:** (see The Wild Hunt)
- **Isella:** One of the Luo'henkah. The Daughter of Ice (daughter of the Cailleach).
- **Kuippana (also: Kipa):** Lord of the Wolves. Elemental forest spirit; Herne's distant cousin. Trickster. Leader of the SuVahta, a group of divine elemental wolf shifters.
- **Lugh the Long Handed:** Celtic Lord of the Sun.
- **Morgana:** Goddess of the Fae and the Sea, she was originally human but Cernunnos lifted her to deityhood. She agreed to watch over the Fae who did not return across the Great Sea. Torn by her loyalty to her people and her loyalty to Cernunnos, she at times finds herself conflicted about the Wild Hunt. Herne's mother.
- **The Morrígan:** Goddess of Death and Phantoms. Goddess of the battlefield.

THE FAE COURTS

- **Navane:** The court of the Light Fae, both across the Great Sea and on the eastside of Seattle, the latter ruled by **Névé**.
- **TirNaNog:** The court of the Dark Fae, both across the Great Sea and on the eastside of Seattle, the latter ruled by **Saílle**.

THE FORCE MAJEURE

A group of legendary magicians, sorcerers, and witches. They are not human, but magic-born. There are twenty-one at any given time and the only way into the group is to be hand chosen, and the only exit from the group is death.

- **Merlin, The:** Morgana's father. Magician of ancient Celtic fame.
- **Taliesin:** The first Celtic bard. Son of Cerridwen, originally a servant who underwent magical transformation and finally was reborn through Cerridwen as the first bard.
- **Ranna:** Powerful sorceress. Elatha's mistress.
- **Rasputin:** The Russian sorcerer and mystic.
- **Väinämöinen:** The most famous Finnish bard.

TIMELINE OF SERIES

Year 1:

- May/Beltane: **The Silver Stag** (Ember)
- June/Litha: **Oak & Thorns** (Ember)
- August/Lughnasadh: **Iron Bones** (Ember)
- September/Mabon: **A Shadow of Crows** (Ember)
- Mid-October: **Witching Hour** (Raven)
- Late October/Samhain: **The Hallowed Hunt** (Ember)
- December/Yule: **The Silver Mist** (Ember)

Year 2:

- January: **Witching Bones** (Raven)
- Late January–February/Imbolc: **A Sacred Magic** (Ember)

PLAYLIST

I often write to music, and A SACRED MAGIC was no exception. Here's the playlist I used for this book.

- **A.J. Roach:** Devil May Dance
- **Air:** Napalm Love
- **Alice Cooper:** Go to Hell; I'm the Coolest; Didn't We Meet; Some Folks; Poison; Welcome to My Nightmare
- **Alice In Chains:** Man in the Box; I Can't Remember; Sunshine
- **Android Lust:** Here and Now; Saint Over; Dragonfly
- **Arch Leaves:** Nowhere to Go
- **AWOLNATION:** Sail
- **Band of Skulls:** I Know What I Am
- **The Black Angels:** Currency; Don't Play With Guns; Love Me Forever; Young Men Dead; Always Maybe; Death March; Comanche Moon; Manipulation

- **Black Mountain:** Queens Will Play
- **Broken Bells:** The Ghost Inside
- **Buffalo Springfield:** For What It's Worth
- **Camouflage Nights:** (It Could Be) Love
- **Celtic Woman:** The Butterfly; The Voice; Scarborough Fair
- **Crazy Town:** Butterfly
- **Damh the Bard:** The Cauldron Born; Tomb of the King; Obsession; Cloak of Feathers; Taliesin's Song; The Wheel
- **Death Cab For Cutie:** I Will Possess Your Heart
- **Dizzi:** Dizzi Jig; Dance of the Unicorns
- **Dragon Ritual Drummers:** Black Queen; The Fall; Dance of the Roma
- **Eastern Sun:** Beautiful Being (Original Edit)
- **Eivør:** Trøllbundin
- **Everlast:** Black Jesus; I Can't Move; Ends; What It's Like; One, Two
- **Faun:** Hymn to Pan; Iduna; Oyneng Yar; The Market Song; Punagra; Cernunnos; Rad; Sieben
- **Garbage:** Queer; #1 Crush; Push It; I Think I'm Paranoid
- **Gary Numan:** Cars (Remix); Ghost Nation; My Name is Ruin; Hybrid; Petals; I Am Dust; Here in the Black; When the Sky Bleeds, He Will Follow; Angel Wars; My Name Is Ruin; The Sleeproom
- **Godsmack:** Voodoo
- **Gorillaz:** Last Living Souls; Kids With Guns; Hongkongaton; Rockit; Clint Eastwood; Stylo
- **The Gospel Whisky Runners:** Muddy Waters

- **Hedningarna:** Ukkonen; Fulvalsen; Juolle Joutunut
- **The Hu:** Wolf Totem; Yuve Yuve Yu
- **Jessica Bates:** The Hanging Tree
- **John Fogerty:** The Old Man Down the Road
- **The Kills:** Nail in My Coffin; You Don't Own the Road; Sour Cherry; Dead Road 7
- **LadyTron:** Paco!; Ghosts; I'm Not Scared
- **Lorde:** Yellow Flicker Beat; Royals
- **Low and tomandandy:** Half Light
- **Marilyn Manson:** Personal Jesus; Tainted Love
- **Matt Corby:** Breathe
- **Nirvana:** Heart Shaped Box; Come As You Are; Something in the Way; Plateau; Lake of Fire
- **No Doubt:** Hella Good; Hey Baby; Trapped in a Box
- **Opeth:** Windowpane; Death Whispered A Lullaby; To Rid the Disease
- **Orgy:** Social Enemies; Blue Monday
- **A Pale Horse Named Death:** Devil in the Closet; Meet the Wolf
- **Pati Yang:** All That Is Thirst
- **Pearl Jam:** Even Flow; Black; Jeremy; Garden
- **Ringo Starr:** It Don't Come Easy
- **Rob Zombie:** Living Dead Girl; American Witch; Never Gonna Stop; Feel So Numb; Mars Needs Women; Dragula
- **Robin Schulz:** Sugar
- **S.J. Tucker:** Hymn to Herne
- **Saliva:** Ladies and Gentlemen
- **Scorpions:** The Zoo
- **Screaming Trees:** Where the Twain Shall Meet;

Uncle Anesthesia; Dime Western; Shadow of the Season; Alice Said; Gospel Plow
- **Seether:** Never Leave; Remedy; The Gift
- **Sharon Knight:** Ravaged Ruins; Mother of the World; Bewitched; Berrywood Grove; 13 Knots; Let the Waters Rise; Siren Moon
- **Shriekback:** The Shining Path; Underwaterboys; Dust and a Shadow; This Big Hush; Now These Days Are Gone; The King in the Tree; And The Rain; Church of the Louder Light; Wriggle and Drone
- **Simple Minds:** Don't You
- **Steeleye Span:** The Fox; Blackleg Miner; Cam Ye O'er Frae France
- **Stone Temple Pilots:** Sour Girl; Atlanta
- **Sweet Talk Radio:** We All Fall Down
- **Tom Petty:** Mary Jane's Last Dance
- **Transplants:** Down in Oakland; Diamonds and Guns
- **Tuatha Dea:** Tuatha De Danaan; The Hum and the Shiver; Wisp of a Thing (Part 1); Long Black Curl
- **Warchild:** Ash
- **Wendy Rule:** Let the Wind Blow; The Circle Song; Elemental Chant; The Wolf Sky
- **Wumpscut:** The March of the Dead
- **Zero 7:** In the Waiting Line

BIOGRAPHY

New York Times, Publishers Weekly, and USA Today bestselling author Yasmine Galenorn writes urban fantasy and paranormal romance, and is the author of over sixty books, including the Wild Hunt Series, the Fury Unbound Series, the Bewitching Bedlam Series, the Indigo Court Series, and the Otherworld Series, among others. She's also written nonfiction metaphysical books. She is the 2011 Career Achievement Award Winner in Urban Fantasy, given by RT Magazine.

Yasmine has been in the Craft since 1980, is a shamanic witch and High Priestess. She describes her life as a blend of teacups and tattoos. She lives in Kirkland, WA, with her husband Samwise and their cats. Yasmine can be reached via her website at Galenorn.com.

Indie Releases Currently Available:

The Wild Hunt Series:
The Silver Stag

Oak & Thorns
Iron Bones
A Shadow of Crows
The Hallowed Hunt
The Silver Mist
Witching Hour
Witching Bones
A Sacred Magic
The Eternal Return

Whisper Hollow Series:
Autumn Thorns
Shadow Silence
The Phantom Queen

Bewitching Bedlam Series:
Bewitching Bedlam
Maudlin's Mayhem
Siren's Song
Witches Wild
Casting Curses
Demon's Delight
Bedlam Calling: A Bewitching Bedlam Anthology

Fury Unbound Series:
Fury Rising
Fury's Magic
Fury Awakened
Fury Calling
Fury's Mantle

Indigo Court Series:

Night Myst

Night Veil

Night Seeker

Night Vision

Night's End

Night Shivers

Indigo Court Books, 1-3: Night Myst, Night Veil, Night Seeker (Boxed Set)

Indigo Court Books, 4-6: Night Vision, Night's End, Night Shivers (Boxed Set)

Otherworld Series:

Moon Shimmers

Harvest Song

Blood Bonds

Otherworld Tales: Volume 1

Otherworld Tales: Volume 2

For the rest of the Otherworld Series, see website at Galenorn.com.

Chintz 'n China Series:

Ghost of a Chance

Legend of the Jade Dragon

Murder Under a Mystic Moon

A Harvest of Bones

One Hex of a Wedding

Holiday Spirits

Chintz 'n China Books, 1 – 3: Ghost of a Chance, Legend of the Jade Dragon, Murder Under A Mystic Moon

Chintz 'n China Books, 4-6: A Harvest of Bones, One Hex of a Wedding, Holiday Spirits

Bath and Body Series (originally under the name India Ink):

    Scent to Her Grave

    A Blush With Death

    Glossed and Found

Misc. Short Stories/Anthologies:

    Once Upon a Kiss (short story: Princess Charming)

    Once Upon a Curse (short story: Bones)

Magickal Nonfiction:

    Embracing the Moon

    Tarot Journeys